THE ELEMENTIA CHRONICLES

BOOK THREE: PART ONE
THE DUSK OF HOPE

by SEAN FAY WOLFE

To South Kingstown High School Drama Club, Class of 2014-15
for helping me get through school with my sanity intact.

First published in the USA by HarperCollins *Publishers* Inc in 2016 as part of
The Elementia Chronicles: Book Three: Herobrine's Message
First published in Great Britain by HarperCollins *Children's Books* 2016
HarperCollins Children's Books is a division of HarperCollins*Publishers* Ltd
HarperCollins *Publishers*,
1 London Bridge Street,
London SE1 9GF
The HarperCollins *Children's Books* website address is
www.harpercollins.co.uk

3

ISBN 978-0-00-815280-2

Printed and bound in England by
Clays Ltd, St Ives plc

MIX
Paper from
responsible sources
FSC® C007454

Find out more about HarperCollins and the environment at
www.harpercollins.co.uk/green

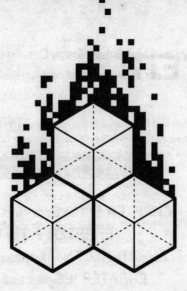

"War does not determine who is right...
only who is left."
—Bertrand Russell

CONTENTS

PART II: THE DUSK OF HOPE

A faint breeze blew through the Great Wood, rustling the leaves of the blocky trees that ringed a small, unassuming knoll. It had been months since Stan2012, so new to the world of Minecraft, had stood at the precipice of Spawnpoint Hill, in awe of the cubic world around him. By all accounts, very little had changed since then. The trees still stood tall, dark and ominous. The hill was still dotted with patches of overgrown grass, and the occasional patch of red and yellow flowers. The squared-off brook still trickled lazily down the hill, passing by the opening to a bottomless ravine.

However, the server was now drastically different from when Stan had first entered it. On this day, the sky was a dull grey, and the air was charged with the onset of a storm. A roll of thunder crashed in the distance. A light drizzle of rain began to fall as the gentle gusts of wind shook the boughs of the leaf blocks in the trees. The midday sun was unable to shine through the clouds above, and the sky cast barely enough light to see.

Then, all at once, a figure appeared on top of the hill.

A streak of lightning crackled in the distance, illuminating the figure for a split second. The figure held nothing in his pale, blocky hands. He wore navy-blue trousers and dark-brown shoes, while the upper half of his body was covered by a black cloak. The covering extended upwards over his head, obscuring his face from view.

This figure was known by many names. One of them was the Black Hood.

The Black Hood took a deep breath, then slowly let it out. He held out his blocky hand and opened it, allowing the rain to cascade over his outstretched palm. He relished the feeling as all his senses slowly came to life and he, once again, felt the sheer wonder of existing in the realm of Minecraft.

Oh, yes, the Black Hood thought, euphoria spreading throughout his entire body. *It has been far too long since I have been in this game. I had forgotten just how it feels. It is so good to be back.*

The Black Hood looked around. Spawnpoint Hill was completely deserted. The Black Hood was relieved as he hastily jogged down the hill and into the forest, taking refuge from the light rain. After all, he was *not* supposed to be here. If anybody found out about him, the Black Hood's life could be compromised.

The Black Hood sighed again, this time with determination. There was a reason that he had come to this server called Elementia. Though he had vowed to never again return to Minecraft after his last experience, the Black Hood knew that this particular server was in a state of horrible unbalance. A great evil had risen here, manifested in a power of untold strength. If this power should win the war now being fought, far more than the server would be destroyed. It might very well pose a danger to the game of Minecraft itself.

The Black Hood knew what he must do. Although this unspeakable evil had spread throughout Elementia, a glimmer of hope still shone. Element City, the stronghold of justice and the spirit of rebellion in the world, was still alive, however weakened it may be. *And as long as Element City remains standing,* the Black Hood mused to himself, *so too was there a chance that the people within may be reunited with the one single player who had the ability to lead them to victory over the great evil once and for all.*

I must move quickly, the Black Hood thought urgently. *Although Element City will never stop fighting the invading forces of the Noctem Alliance, there will inevitably come a time when fighting is futile. And if that time comes before I can reach him . . .* The Black Hood glanced down at his pale, blocky hand. It was imperative that he achieve his goals unseen, which may necessitate that he kill any witnesses he encountered. He would need a weapon to swiftly and inconspicuously dispose of anyone unfortunate enough to cross his path. With all his willpower, the Black Hood concentrated on his hand. He imagined the feeling of a diamond sword clutched tightly in his grasp, equipped with the highest of Sharpness enchant-ments. In a few seconds, the Black Hood could feel the hilt of a sword clutched in his hands, although it was not yet visible. He continued to concentrate.

Just a bit more . . . he thought. *Almost done . . .*

Then, just as the turquoise sword was materializing, there was a crash of thunder and a bolt of lightning lit up the sky, striking near the Black Hood. The explosion on the ground launched the Black Hood backwards, through the air, and he came crashing to the dirt-block ground.

Wincing, the Black Hood opened his eyes. He had lost all concentration, and the diamond sword was nowhere to be seen.

Suddenly, another boom of thunder, louder than the last, screamed above him as the sky broke and rain came pouring down. The Black Hood whipped his head upwards.

This can't just be a coincidence, the Black Hood realized frantically. *He must know that I am here.*

This thought was followed by an ear-splitting boom of thunder that reverberated through the forest. And in the midst of the sound, the Black Hood heard a very distinct voice ring out, not from anywhere in this world, but from within his own mind.

REMEMBER MY LAST.

The Black Hood lay sprawled on his back on the ground,

petrified. He remained that way for a full minute, heart racing and breathing rapidly. However, when no more thunderclaps sounded throughout the sky, the Black Hood finally allowed himself to take a deep breath. Baffled, he looked up at the sky yet again.

What are you trying to tell me? he thought as hard as he could, deeply troubled and puzzled.

There was no reply, from either within or beyond the Black Hood's mind. The only sound that resonated throughout the area was the constant patter of the downpour.

Hmmm . . . This is most interesting . . . the Black Hood thought, intrigued. *Could it possibly be . . . that I cannot use my true power? Is that what you want?*

The Black Hood waited anxiously for a full minute, hoping for a reply that never came. The Black Hood sighed.

Well, he knows that I am here now. This thought unnerved him quite a bit, as he realized the implications that came with this fact. He was now under the constant surveillance and scrutiny of something that had the ability to destroy him at a moment's notice. The Black Hood was surprised that his presence had even been detected, yet he was even more surprised that he had not been destroyed because of it.

I suppose, the Black Hood thought, *that I am safe . . . for now at least. If he knows that I am here, but hasn't yet destroyed me . . . I wonder what else I can get away with. I shall have to experiment with this more as I continue on my mission. As of now, however . . . it's probably for the best to play it safe.*

The Black Hood glanced longingly at his hand. It would have been so simple if he could create his own diamond sword. However, it appeared that was one of the things he was not allowed to do; he supposed he would have to return to the basics.

The Black Hood pulled himself up off the ground, and walked over to the nearest tree. He drew back his fist and sunk it as hard as he could into the wood-block trunk of the tree. Through the dim light of the rainstorm, the Black Hood noticed a small crack appear in the center of the block, and he continued to throw punch after punch into the block of wood.

Look at me, the Black Hood thought to himself with an amused chuckle. *Gathering wood by hand, just like a new player!*

It wasn't long before the Black Hood had punched enough wood blocks to gather what he needed. It didn't take him long to convert the wooden blocks into planks, and the planks into a crafting table. Minutes later, he pulled a wooden pick-axe off the table.

The Black Hood smiled. This tool would suffice until he found time to invest in the creation of better materials. Now, however, time was short. The longer he waited, the further the Noctem Alliance crept towards victory. And if he failed to act, all would be lost.

And so, pickaxe grasped in hand and a resolve of steel in his mind, the Black Hood turned to the west and began to walk, disappearing into the fog.

THE MISSIONS BEGIN

I t was high noon in the Far Western Desert. The sun shone bright overhead in the crisp blue sky, beating down on the heat-baked sand blocks. Two- or three-block-high cacti sprouted up from the tan earth and speckled the dusty landscape with green, while a few odd Creepers and Spiders wandered aimlessly across the barren wasteland. The endless dune sea was nearly as vast as the Ender Desert, and was far less travelled in this day and age. At any given time, the Far Western Desert contained just a few players, and they rarely stayed there for long.

The average player on the Minecraft server Elementia would find it foolish to venture into the Far Western Desert at all. There was hardly anything to be gained from it and everything to lose in the hot desert sun. However, if a player were to make the long trek across thousands of blocks of sand, into the very epicentre of the desert, he or she would find a small cluster of buildings. The houses were centred around a gravel network of roads and constructed of wood planks, clearly indicating that, at one point in the distant past, this town with no name had been filled with NPC villagers.

No villagers were left now.

Instead, this hollow shell of a village had been

populated by players, though they were not the type that anyone would want to run into. These players bore various scars across their skins, and would snarl and crack their knuckles menacingly should you be so unfortunate as to catch their eye. This was the type of town where an accusation over stolen iron or diamonds would start a fight that only one would walk away from.

And there were a lot of diamonds and iron to fight over. Countless valuable items passed through this trading post of the desert in exchange for services of the underhand sort, which the residents of the town were happy to provide. Just like the materials, though, the residents of this town never stayed there for long. This was the place to go if you needed a job done discreetly, so it was not a place where you wanted to be caught.

This particular day started off typically. The sun shined hot, and there had already been various fits of bare-knuckle brawling among the players who were in the town.

When the sun was at its zenith in the sky, a figure appeared on the horizon. As the others went about their daily business, the player slowly approached the town. And as he walked down the dusty gravel road, more and more of the ruffian inhabitants of the village seemed to be giving him a steely glance out of the corner of their eyes. He hardly noticed; he was sure that this desert wasteland had never seen a player as important as he before.

The player was dressed in black trousers and a black shirt, with a golden cloak draped over his head, flowing like a shimmering waterfall onto his upper body. His striking skin was hard to ignore as he briskly turned and headed into a large building on the main road.

This building, which had once been the village library, had been gutted, the inside library furnishings replaced by tables and chairs. These were occupied by players laughing and shouting in raucous fashion, gulping bottles of QPO and SloPo as they did so. A long stretch of wood blocks created a counter that ran the length of the building. From behind this wooden strip, the bartender shouted out, asking if the golden-hooded figure would care for a drink. The figure gave no reply, simply waving his hand in rejection. After all, he was about to attend a meeting of the utmost importance to the cause of the Noctem Alliance. His mind could not be clouded by potion.

As the figure looked around for his contact, he was momentarily distracted by the taunts, jeers, and general cacophony of a fight breaking out in the corner of the bar. The figure allowed himself a moment to watch as two thuggish brutes in tattered clothes locked their pickaxes. Soon an explosion of cheers erupted from the corner as one of the players slumped to the ground beside his pickaxe, and the crowd scrambled to collect his dropped items for themselves. The figure was slightly irritated by the noise, but he knew that it was by no means a bad thing—quite the contrary, actually. This was the perfect place to go if you didn't wish to be overheard.

As the rumble of the fight died down, the figure once again looked around the bar for his contact. It took a few passes before he finally locked eyes with a lone player, sitting across from an empty seat at a table amid the ruckus. This player was dressed in a relatively common skin, bearing the same body colouring as a spider. However, of the many eyes on the player's face, only the two largest ones had a distinctly human trait to them.

The golden-hooded figure walked over and sat down across from the player. He wasted no time in speaking.

"I've heard a lot about you. They say you're good at what you do."

The spider-player smiled. "And I heard that you might show your face around here again. Count Drake, I presume?"

The gold-hooded figure faltered for a moment, but only slightly. He was nearly positive that this was the player he was looking for, but he had to be sure without a doubt.

"I go by General Drake now, actually," Drake responded evenly.

The spider-player held her poker face; Drake couldn't

read her in the slightest. He knew that the time had come, and he reached into the folds of his shawl. From there, he produced an item, the head of a Creeper. He only showed it to the spider-player for a moment before immediately returning it to his inventory. Drake then glanced at the spider-player expectantly.

With her face still locked into a steely gaze, the spider-player reached under the table. Drake focused intently on her hand, and watched as she produced her own Creeper head for a moment before returning it to her inventory.

Instantly, the aura of tension at the table relaxed, and both players smiled. The two old friends had each revealed the unique items they had given each other the last time they had met, and both now knew they could talk freely.

"It's good to see you again, Arachnia," Drake said. Then he smirked. "From what I heard, you've been pretty busy since I left."

"You might say that," the spider-player replied, amused. "I have to say, Drake, it's good to see you too. It's been a long time. So, you're a general now, huh?"

"Sure am," Drake said.

"And am I to assume that this is a position you obtained somewhere other than under the command of President Stan?" Arachnia asked with a smirk.

Drake chuckled. "Oh, don't patronize me. You know perfectly well what I think of the *illustrious* Stan2012." His voice was dripping with oily cynicism. "No, I'm now a general of the Noctem Alliance."

"Really," said Arachnia, raising an eyebrow slightly. "You don't mean that little protesters' group that somehow managed to take over the entire server?"

"That's the one," Drake replied, nodding. "I assume that you know what has happened in the Elementia mainland over the past month."

"Of course I do, Drake. You of all people should know just how much information passes through this settlement," Arachnia murmured darkly. "Although I have to admit, it never did come to my attention that *you* were the one in charge of leading the Noctem Alliance to victory."

Drake looked humble. "Well, I helped, but to be honest, I was just following orders. All the people who truly led the takeover are dead now, and Lord Tenebris appointed me and a few of my colleagues in their places."

"Lord Tenebris . . . I assume that he's the leader of the Noctem Alliance?" Arachnia asked.

A ray of zealous awe crossed Drake's face at this question, causing Arachnia to raise an eyebrow again as Drake replied.

"Oh, he is *far* more than that, my friend. I would say more, but trust me, you'll know soon enough."

Arachnia laughed. "I'll take your word for it. So, what

brings you out here, Drake? Surely an all-powerful general of the ruling organization of Elementia must have a good reason for trekking out into the middle of nowhere."

"As a matter of fact, I do," replied Drake seriously. The pleasantries were over, and it was time to get down to business. "First, let me ask you this . . . do you still have the other members of ELM together?"

"Yes," Arachnia said with a grin. "And we're still the best bounty hunters in all of Minecraft. Why? Do you need us for something?"

"That I do. Actually, it has to do with the Alliance," whispered Drake. He glanced around, making sure that nobody in the rambunctious bar was listening before he leaned in closer to Arachnia and continued.

"In the midst of our campaign to conquer Elementia, the Noctem Alliance managed to capture President Stan2012, and a few of his councilmen as well . . ."

"NO!" Arachnia burst out, unable to contain herself.

"*Shut up!*" hissed Drake, glancing around at several nearby patrons who had given them a sideways glance. "If you don't keep quiet, then the deal is off!"

"Sorry," replied Arachnia hastily. She knew from Drake's tone that this mission of his, whatever it was, was important. And, in her experience, importance equated to quite a large payment.

"Anyway," continued Drake when he was sure it was safe, "it was my job to oversee their prison. Unfortunately, one of Stan's friends sacrificed himself so that Stan could escape. The Noctem Alliance is well on its way to breaking through the walls of Element City and destroying the last of the republic's armies. However, Lord Tenebris is convinced that if President Stan somehow manages to return to the city, he will rally his citizens and turn the tide of the war back in his favour."

"So . . . what you're saying is . . ." Arachnia replied slowly, heart racing as she pieced together what Drake was saying, " . . . you want me to hunt down and assassinate the president of Elementia?"

"Not exactly," replied Drake evenly. "For some reason, Lord Tenebris is dead set on killing Stan himself. To be honest, I'm not sure why, but I do trust Lord Tenebris, and I'm sure that he has a perfectly valid reason. Therefore, I'm asking you, Arachnia, to capture President Stan and return him to Lord Tenebris alive."

"Well . . ." replied Arachnia after a moment, trying to appear uninterested despite the fact that she was in utter awe of what Drake was requesting. "This sounds like it's going to be quite a difficult mission, Drake. If you have no idea where Stan is and no way of finding him, that is . . . and I think that you know as well as I do that no team would be capable of it other than mine."

"That *is* why I came to you," Drake said rather impatiently. He had been expecting her to accept without question.

"And . . . because of that . . . I think you'll understand where I'm coming from when I say that the price of pulling this off will not be small," Arachnia said in a rather sleazy fashion.

Drake didn't hesitate. He reached into the folds of his cloak and pulled out something from his inventory. He revealed it only for a moment before returning it, but it was enough time for Arachnia to see the full stack of sixty-four diamond blocks in Drake's hand.

"I assure you that payment is no problem," Drake said simply.

Arachnia was breathing heavily with excitement now. This was it. She and her team were about to pull off the biggest job in the history of Minecraft, and become rich beyond their wildest dreams.

"General Drake," said Arachnia with a smile, "I'm happy to announce that you now have a team."

Drake grinned deviously. "I knew I could count on you, Arachnia. Now, assemble your team, and head to the mainland as soon as possible. President Stan is likely trekking back towards Element City as we speak, so you must make haste. Take the train line to the western wall of Element City. There, you will find one of the legions of the Noctem Army, which has laid siege to the city. They will give you all the information we have gathered regarding where President Stan may be, and then you may begin your search."

"Whatever you say, Drake," replied Arachnia.

"And remember, Arachnia . . . President Stan is not to be underestimated. Keep in mind that this is the player who bested King Kev in combat. He's an exceptional fighter, very smart and very crafty. The last thing that we need is for him to return and lead his city once again. The fate of the Noctem Alliance may very well rest in the hands of your team, Arachnia."

"Don't worry, Drake," answered Arachnia, her face showing exhilaration and a hint of bloodlust. "Stan is as good as yours."

Drake nodded one final time, and stood up from his chair. Without giving Arachnia one more glance, he pulled his golden hood up over his head, made his way through the rabble of drunken players, and left the bar.

All five players sitting around the dimly lit council table in the stone-brick castle were silent except for the Mechanist, who was in the process of the ceremonial roll call and other formalities. Although Element Castle was a good distance away from the outer walls of Element City, the cacophony of the bombardment of the outer wall could be heard throughout the city, day and night. This council meeting was no exception, as the muffled booms of detonating TNT blocks could be heard even through the stone walls.

These sounds of the Noctem Alliance's barrage of artillery only heightened the tension in the room. Out of the nine council members, three of them—Stan, Charlie and DZ—had been taken hostage in their raid of the Noctem Alliance's Specialty Base. Another one, Blackraven, had been revealed as a traitor who had been working for the Noctem Alliance the entire time. And yet only four players sat around the council room table now.

They had lost someone else.

As the Mechanist finished with the formalities, he put down his papers and glanced around the table with exhausted eyes. In the faces of Kat, Jayden and G, there was no sign of sadness or grief, but rather of unkempt and wild hatred, driven by a passion that can only be wrought by the deepest sort of betrayal. Giving a soft and brief sigh, the Mechanist began his speech.

"As you know," the Mechanist said tiredly, his Texas accent slightly slurred with fatigue, "a most tragic and unfortunate event has befallen us in the past twenty-four hours. . . ."

"Huh, unfortunate . . . yeah, *right*."

"Please, Kat," replied the Mechanist, far too spent to deal with her sarcasm at the moment. "Protocol dictates that I, as interim leader of the council in President Stan's absence, recount what happened so that it goes on record."

Nobody protested. They were so furious that they were happy to hear it again to have another opportunity to relish in the cowardice and detestability of what had happened.

"Yesterday afternoon," started the Mechanist, "all members of this council were called by myself, Mecha11, to this council room to report on how the defence of our outer walls was going. Kat, G, Jayden and I all returned as planned. However, we soon realized that Gobbleguy was missing."

There was a shudder of contempt around the room as the Mechanist spoke that name.

"With the help of the police chiefs, we searched the city, and we weren't able to find him. However, in Gobbleguy's bedroom, Ben discovered a book that he had written. In it,

Gobbleguy said that he was leaving Elementia forever, and going to play Minecraft on other servers. He then proceeded to explain, in probably the most passive and nonconfrontational way I've ever heard, that he couldn't take the pressures of being on the council anymore. He said that it was, and I quote, 'far too much stress and effort to put into a lousy Minecraft server.' Because of his desertion, the police chiefs have charged Gobbleguy with treason, and have a warrant out for his arrest should he ever return to Elementia."

As the Mechanist finished his recap, nobody had anything to say. All they could do was stew in their misery and despise the deserter. It was bad enough that Blackraven had turned out to be a traitor to the council and had been working as a double agent for the Alliance the entire time. It was even worse that his treachery had caused Stan, Charlie and DZ to be captured, leaving the five of them left on the council to wonder if their three friends were even still alive. And now, as one last kick to the emotional stomach of the council, one of their own members had up and left them for no reason other than his own weakness.

"Good riddance, I say," spat Kat in disgust.

"I agree," replied Jayden, his brow knit in scorn. "If Gobbleguy wants to be a selfish little jerk, then it's for the best that he's gone."

"Yeah. I mean, what did he even do?" said G in a nasty

voice. "He just sat at the meetings, looking like a timid little bunny rabbit, never saying anything, and not even having the guts to speak up for himself. Honestly, what did we lose when he left?"

"Nothing at all!" exclaimed Kat fervently.

"True!" Jayden said in an unusually deep voice. "I say we just forget he ever existed and move on."

There were nods and mumbles of assent around the table. Everybody was privately doing the same thing, and trying to project the feeling that they were happy Gobbleguy was gone. In actuality, however, all four of them were scared senseless by the ramifications of his departure.

Although they would rather die than admit it, the remaining members of the council realized that, when Gobbleguy logged out of Elementia, the Noctem Alliance had claimed him as their victim. Even if Gobbleguy had been useless in the grand scheme of things, the fact remained that he had been driven out by the fear and pressure that the Noctem Alliance was spreading throughout Element City so effectively.

The most frightening fact of all, though, was that the council had reached a startling landmark: of the nine of them who had started the war against the Noctem Alliance, more than half of them were now gone.

"I think that it is fairly safe to say," the Mechanist spoke after a moment of scared silence, "that our city is, as of now, incredibly well protected. Due to various innovations in defensive technology—"

"All of which you created," Kat cut in with a smirk. There was a grim chuckle of agreement around the table. In fact, Kat was right; the Mechanist had been the one who had designed the city's superb outer defences.

"Well, yes, that's true," replied the Mechanist humbly, "but it is also beside the point. As I was saying, because of the resources that we have put into the defences of our walls, I think that the Noctem Alliance will have a difficult time getting into our city. We are well equipped to fight off any approach of theirs as of right now, whether it be through stealth or by brute force. However, I think that it is also time that we acknowledge that the Noctem Alliance is, at the very least, equal to us in power."

There were sounds of repugnance around the table. The council still found it difficult to accept that what had started off as a small protesters' group had grown into an organization that had pushed them to the brink of annihilation in just a single month. Although they could not bring themselves to disagree with the Mechanist, saying it aloud would mean accepting it, something that Jayden, G and Kat were not prepared to do.

"Therefore," the Mechanist continued, reaching under

the table and pressing a button as he did so, "I am forced to assume that our current stalemate is temporary. The Noctem Alliance will manage to break through our walls if we are not able to weaken them somehow. For that reason, I've asked Bob to come in here and brief us on what we, as high-ranking members of the city, should do to actively fight the Noctem Alliance."

"Wait a sec," said Kat as she realized what he was saying. "Are you saying that you want us to actually go out into the server and fight the Alliance? Like, in combat?"

The Mechanist nodded. Kat's face lit up, and she looked psyched at the prospect of finally going out into the field and actively doing something to take down the Noctem Alliance.

"Hold on," asked Jayden, a puzzled look crossing his face. "If we're out in the server doing the fighting, then who's going to run the council?"

"That's actually the one thing we need to discuss before Bob gets here," the Mechanist said tiredly. "In my talks with Bob, he suggested that while the rest of the council goes out and undertakes several highly important objectives through-out Elementia, I myself remain here as the sole governor of Element City.

"I was the first to point out," the Mechanist continued quickly, as all three of the other council members looked alarmed, "that this idea would give me sole power over the entirety of Element City, which is something that our constitution was designed specifically to avoid. After all, if handled improperly, the idea of a single person leading the city sounds dangerously similar to the doctrine of King Kev.

"However," the Mechanist said as the others nodded in agreement, "it does say in the constitution that one person is allowed to control Elementia by him- or herself in time of emergency. This can be done if the other council members are required to take action to resolve the emergency, and only if the police keep a sharp eye on the single ruler to make sure that he or she does not turn into a selfish dictator, and keeps the well-being of the city in mind until such time as a council may be re-established. I don't think anybody will disagree with me when I say that we most assuredly have an emergency on our hands at the moment."

Nobody at the table even felt the need to say that they agreed; they all knew that it was true.

"Let us be honest with ourselves, my friends," the Mechanist explained, sounding exhausted. "The four of us, along with the police chiefs, are the most powerful players in Element City. There are various tasks that need to be done for the sake of protecting our people and ending this war, and I believe that we, the council members, should carry them out. Of the four of us, I think we can all agree . . . and forgive me if I sound arrogant . . . that I am the best leader."

There was a moment of silence. All the other members gave slow, consensual nods.

"So are we all in agreement?" the Mechanist asked with a definite air of finality about him. "I will stay here and lead Elementia while the three of you complete the missions that Bob has put together for you?"

"Sounds like a plan to me," said Kat with a grin, and G and Jayden both nodded in agreement.

"Well, good. That's settled then," the Mechanist sighed, clearly relieved that none of them had been opposed to this admittedly radical idea. As a matter of fact, the three of them seemed hyped and incredibly excited to finally take action against the Noctem Alliance instead of endlessly plotting out troop movements over the stone brick–block table of the council room .

There was a knock at the door, and all turned to face it.

"Enter," ordered the Mechanist authoritatively.

The wooden door swung open, and in marched Bob. He looked somber, and judging by his appearance, he had clearly just come from the front lines. His scarlet jumpsuit was ripped and torn in various places, and his pale face and blond hair were tarnished with soot from being at the back end of a TNT cannon. He was seated on Ivanhoe, who looked equally war hardened; his once-shiny saddle was now worn down, the colour faded, and the pig himself bore the marks of various wounds that had been healed by potions.

"Ah, good to see you, Bob," the Mechanist said quietly. "How are the defences holding up?"

"We're doing pretty good as of right now," Bob answered wearily. "The Noctems didn't launch any major attacks today, and we were able to repel the usual bombardments. That being said, it was pretty obvious that the Noctems weren't fighting full force either. They didn't even seem to have that many guys there. I have a feeling that they're planning something . . . some sort of stealth mission, maybe."

"You're probably right," the Mechanist said. "I trust that you and your brothers will have all the alarms online soon, should they try to use the Invisibility Potions."

"Of course," Bob replied.

"Good. Now, you've arrived just in time, Bob. The council has just agreed to our plan. I will stay here and run Element City under your supervision while Kat, Jayden and G head out into the server and carry out your missions. Are you ready to brief them?"

"Yes, sir," Bob responded, nodding and looking over to the enthused council members. As soon as they realized that he was speaking to them, Kat, Jayden and G sat straight up in their seats, their ears perked as Bob began to speak.

"As of right now, all available forces in our army are being used to defend the outer walls of Element City from penetration by the armies of the Noctem Alliance. However, there is a pressing situation that must be dealt with as soon as possible: the hostages. As of right now, Stan, Charlie, DZ and Commander Crunch of the navy are being held prisoner on the Greater Mushroom Island. We don't know anything about their status, but we must assume for now that they are all still alive, and the Noctem Alliance will be using them to demand a ransom very soon.

"Also, you'll remember that when the offensive on Nocturia failed and our armies were pushed back to the city, the Noctem Alliance captured around two dozen residents of the Adorian Village. My brothers and I have sent some scouts out, and we've determined that these players are being held hostage in Nocturia. If the Noctem Alliance demands anything in exchange for the safety of those players, then we will have to comply. Even ignoring the fact that it's the right thing to do, if we have the opportunity to help those lower-level players and we don't take advantage of it, the citizens of this city will turn on us like a pack of wolves.

"This is why I need you three," said Bob, sounding official. "One of you is going to have to go with a volunteer to sneak into the prison in the Mushroom Islands and free Stan and the others. The other two are going to have to infiltrate Nocturia and liberate those lower-level players."

The three players around the table were quiet as they

thought about what they had just been asked. The idea of sneaking into Nocturia and the Specialty Base, the Noctem Alliance's two most heavily fortified strongholds . . . it wasn't going to be easy.

Kat in particular found herself quite surprised. She had been expecting Bob to ask them to lead a crazy head-on assault with the Elementia Army to drive the Noctem forces back into the Ender Desert. She wasn't anticipating the request to partake in a stealth mission. Nonetheless, she was eager to participate.

"Sounds like a good plan to me," she said, a wicked grin crossing her face.

"Yeah," agreed Jayden, nodding with a subdued smile.

"I agree with you guys," said G proudly. "That's definitely a job for experienced players like us."

The Mechanist gave a tired yet genuine smile at the enthusiasm of these young, spirited players. "All right then," he said. "Let's start planning. First of all, let's determine who's doing what. Who wants to get Stan and the others out of Nocturia?"

"I do!" came two shouts as both Kat's and G's hands shot up into the air. The two turned to look each other in the eye, and instantly they both looked away awkwardly. There was a moment of uncomfortable silence before Bob spoke.

"So . . . um . . . do you two really want to . . . ?"

"No," Kat said firmly, looking back up at G, this time with a hint of contempt.

"Aw, come on, Kat," said G, sounding mildly irritated. "You don't think that just this once—"

"G, I am not working with you," Kat repeated. The Mechanist gave a sigh, while both Jayden and Bob threw their heads back in exasperation.

"Kat, come on, we have to think about the well-being of Elementia. . . ."

"I *am* thinking of the well-being of Elementia," Kat replied coolly. "If I'm going to sneak into a secret base to try to break Stan, Charlie and DZ out of jail, I need to be in top form. And I guarantee that if you're with me, it'll be that much harder for both of us."

"Oh, *grow up*, Kat," cried G in irritation. "Can't we please just be mature about this, bury the hatchet, and . . ."

"I said, *No, G!*" Kat bellowed through gritted teeth. She glared across the table, staring daggers at G, who was recoiling in intimidation.

"*Enough*, you two!" bellowed Jayden. He grabbed G by the shoulders and spun him around so the two were facing each other. G looked shocked.

"G, you know as well as she does, and as well as the rest of us do, that it's a bad idea for you two to team up. How about you team up with me, and the two of us go and free the hostages in Nocturia?"

G opened his mouth, then closed it again. His expression was outraged as he looked at Kat, then Jayden, then Kat again, then the Mechanist, and then back at Kat one more time before finally turning to Jayden and sighing.

"Fine," he mumbled. "We can do that."

"Well, that's settled then," said Bob. *Crisis averted,* he thought to himself in relief.

"In that case," the Mechanist said, "Kat, are you willing to team up with a volunteer to go and free the officials trapped in the Mushroom Islands?"

"Definitely," Kat said almost robotically, deliberately staring directly at the Mechanist and avoiding any eye contact with G.

"OK," Bob said, sighing, glad that was over. "We have to get going. The sooner that these hostages are out, the better. Jayden and G, you come with me. We'll go down to the police station, and you'll get your briefing. After that, you're off. Kat, you just wait until we've found a volunteer to go with you, and then you'll do the same thing."

"So," the Mechanist said as the three council members nodded respectfully to Bob. "If that's all, then I officially adjourn this council meeting. Everybody, go do what you need to do."

And with that, Kat, G and Jayden stood up. Bob walked

out of the council room towards the corridor, tailed closely by Jayden and G, while Kat took the passage that led to her room. On the way out, G and Kat nearly bumped into each other, but as G was about to open his mouth to say something, Kat turned her back to him and continued walking. G looked crestfallen as he followed Jayden out of the room.

The Mechanist now sat alone in the room. The occasional boom, chatter and whizz of warfare still droned on outside. The barrage was constant; although the wall was holding up well, the Noctem Armies never relented in their assault on the walls. The Noctem Alliance was definitely planning something. The Mechanist knew it. Although the constant assault on the outside walls was easily repelled, it certainly did keep the Elementia Army busy. And perhaps that distraction was all the Noctem Alliance needed to set their grand plan into motion.

The Mechanist knew that, whoever Lord Tenebris was, he was incredibly cunning. Because of this, the Mechanist was well aware that nothing the Noctem Alliance did was arbitrary. Everything was planned, everything was deliberate, and everything had a point. Element City's defences may have been holding up splendidly, but the Mechanist knew that it was only a matter of time before the Alliance managed to find some way around them. And until that time inevitably came, the population of Element City was desperate and furious, no longer able to obtain any resources from the outside. They were simply left to try to survive while trapped within the walls.

And now he bore the entire weight of the situation on his own shoulders, and his shoulders alone.

The Mechanist was already feeling overwhelmed, leading the council in these dark times. He had had to put up with G and Kat's bickering, as well as the constant news that all their efforts had barely put a scratch in the Noctem Alliance's offensive. He was well aware of how important it was that the hostages be rescued, but the Mechanist was at the point of having a nervous breakdown when he realized that the fate of this country, which was already teetering on the brink of destruction, was now in his own hands.

He felt so stressed, so anxious, and so panicked. The world was crumbling around him, and he alone was responsible for holding it together. He was doing all he could, yet it was hardly helping in the least. As the gravity of the situation spiralled around the Mechanist, he wished with all his might that somehow, somewhere, there was some way that he might be able to escape from it, just for a little while. . . .

Kat sat in the waiting room of the police station. In front of her, a window stretched from floor to ceiling, revealing a landscape view of the lower-level district of Element City. In the far distance, the grey stone-brick wall of the city stood proud and tall. About twice a minute, there would be a flash of white light at some point along the wall, accompanied a second later by a muffled boom.

Kat gritted her teeth and tried to keep herself together. It tore her apart inside that her people were being forced to suffer within the city, with food and supplies being rationed during the siege. It killed her even more that, because of the persistence of the Noctem Alliance, the Elementia Army was being forced to work day and night to combat the attackers, with more and more innocent civilians being drafted from their homes every day to keep up with the demanding costs of fighting this war. Life in Element City was miserable, and there was nothing she could do about it!

Kat forced herself to take a deep breath, and then let it go. *No, there* is *something you can do about it,* Kat thought to herself, trying to keep a calm mind. *Just focus on getting Stan and the others back here. That's all you can do right now.*

As she thought this, Kat began to grow more and more irritated. The minutes ticked by, and still nobody had arrived to tell her that the volunteer was ready to join her. Kat began to get angry.

If they weren't ready, then why did they call me down here? she thought bitterly, just as the wooden door swung open. Kat looked up expectantly, and was surprised to see Ben looking extremely uncomfortable.

"*Finally!*" Kat cried, jumping to her feet. "Do you have my partner ready yet?"

"Kat," said Ben, and she was alarmed by how nervous his voice sounded. "Before you find out who your partner is, I need you to realize something. We tried as hard as we could to find somebody else . . . but there was nobody else qualified who wasn't already occupied with something else in the war."

Kat was befuddled. "What are you talking about?"

Ben took a deep breath and let it out in a hefty sigh.

"Come on in," he announced miserably.

Ben stepped out of the doorframe, and another player walked up behind him. Kat's jaw hung open, and her eyes boggled in disbelief. She would recognize that pale skin, those giant red lips, that snow-white leather armour, and that smug expression anywhere.

"Oh, no," Kat breathed in horror.

"Oh . . . yes, I'm afraid," simpered Cassandrix in her patronizing, upper-class accent. "It's good to see you again, Kat, darling."

Stan opened his eyes. He took a deep breath of air and let it out slowly. He tried to move his arm but was only able to move it a few inches before wincing in pain. Reluctant to move again, Stan allowed himself a few more minutes of peace lying in bed.

Stan heard faint voices coming from down the wooden stairwell, and he turned his head to glance around the room. The torchlight gave the wooden attic a faint glow, and he noticed that the closet door was slightly ajar. Stan shrugged it off, figuring that it was nothing, and he closed his eyes once again.

As he lay in bed, nearly incapacitated by wounds and fatigue, Stan reflected on just how extraordinarily lucky he was to still be alive. His body ached all over from his leap into the ocean from the Noctem Alliance's prison at the peak of Mount Fungarus on the Greater Mushroom Island. Filled with anguish over the death of DZ and reckless panic at the Noctem forces quickly closing in on him, Stan hadn't been thinking clearly. Rather, he had simply grabbed DZ's sword and taken a leap of faith—a leap, it turned out, that had hurt quite a lot.

After landing in the ocean and plummeting fast and hard to the ocean floor, Stan had swum as fast as his screaming limbs could carry him away from the island, the sirens wailing from the prison and troops shouting as they mobilized to pursue him. At one point Stan glanced back at the island and saw Mount Fungarus, silhouetted tall and proud against the setting sun, with half its top blown off, and troops scurrying around the various outer levels like ants around an anthill. Desperate to find cover from the incoming troops, Stan dived underwater to the seabed (which was thankfully quite shallow around the islands) and, by a stroke of incredible luck, he had found a bubble of air sitting on the ocean floor, a two-blocks-square cube. Far too relieved to question what the glitch was doing there, Stan had instead dived straight into it, lying on the ground and taking a huge breath of fresh air.

Inside that air bubble, Stan lay still for hours, exhausted from his desperate and narrow escape. Throughout that day, he broke down on and off over the death of DZ and the thought that Charlie and Commander Crunch were being tortured mercilessly as he lay there, unable to do a thing about it.

When he wasn't crying or sleeping, Stan spent the rest of that day looking outside the air bubble. Squids would jet by Stan in schools, their rectangular black bodies propelled forward by a set of eight tentacles, with a rather frightening spiked mouth at the center. The surface of the ocean was illuminated with sunlight, and he could see the bottoms of dozens of wooden boats drifting to and fro across the water, undoubtedly searching for him.

Eventually, the day slowly darkened into night, and the watery world around Stan had become black. His stomach was growling, demanding that food be supplied soon, lest his health start to fade like the setting sun. After scouting out the surface to ensure no boats were directly above him, Stan had jumped out of the top of the air bubble and, kicking as hard as he could, propelled his way back to the surface.

As Stan looked around, he saw no ships anywhere near him, but he did notice the bright lights and strident sound that the Lesser Mushroom Island was emitting. Slowly but surely, Stan paddled his way towards the island, which held the promise of food and a temporary shelter. He had to duck underwater hastily, sometimes for minutes at a time, when a Noctem patrol boat had passed by, but in the end, Stan was able to make it onto the island undetected.

Footsteps echoing up the stairwell startled Stan out of his train of thought. He glanced over at the opening in the floor, and slowly the head, torso, and then legs of a player emerged. She wore black leather trousers, silver metallic gloves and a zipped-up navy-blue hoodie, out of which emerged a streak of magenta hair that fell over her deep brown eyes.

"How you doin'?" she asked in a quiet, rather harsh

voice. Stan shook her tone off; he had realized that her tone was not to be taken personally.

"A bit better," Stan replied, propping himself up on his elbows, despite the aches flaring up again.

"Well, that's good," the player replied, pulling a piece of bread from her inventory and tossing it in Stan's direction, followed immediately by a Potion of Healing. Stan caught the two items, and stared at the bottle of red liquid in disbelief.

"Olea!" he breathed in disbelief. "Where did you . . ."

"It don't matter where I got it," Olea replied brusquely as she started to head back down the stairs. "A Noctem soldier just came and told me that we gotta meet in the central plaza in five minutes. I don't know what they're planning, but I gotta hunch it'll destroy whatever safety you have here, President Stan."

"I understand," Stan replied, nodding grimly. "I'll get out of here as soon as possible."

Olea nodded, and walked down the stairs again. As he poured the red potion down his throat and watched her go, he thought about how fortunate he had been to encounter her. When Stan had pulled himself out of the water and onto the shore of the Lesser Mushroom Island less than twenty-four hours ago, he had been shocked to find that it was overrun with Noctem troops. He had ducked from alley to alley, moving with great agility despite his wounds, careful to avoid detection.

It was only when he had passed by the back door of a shop called GoddessOlea's Boat Rentals that he had been pulled into a building from behind by an unseen pair of hands. When he came to his senses, Stan found himself being interrogated by a player who he later found out was called GoddessOlea, or just Olea for short. When she discovered who he was, she wasted no time in bringing him up to her attic and beginning to heal him. The process of healing had been slow, as resources had been incredibly scarce on the Lesser Mushroom Island since it had been invaded by the Noctem armies. The troops had pillaged all stores that sold potions, golden apples and other healing supplies, meaning that Stan's recovery, which should have taken just a few minutes, had been ongoing for a full day now.

Somehow, though, Olea had managed to get her hands on a Potion of Healing. Now that the red miracle liquid was in Stan's body, he felt all his aches disappear. Stan was sure that this particular potion had been brewed with glowstone; it was particularly strong. Stan leaped out of the bed and onto the wood-plank floor.

He knew that now that he was healed, he had to get off the island as soon as possible. The innocent people of the Lesser Mushroom Island were already suffering enough just because the Noctem Alliance was present there. He knew it was only a matter of time before the Alliance realized that he must be on the island, and when they did, Stan could only imagine what would happen. And if the Noctems found out that Olea had been harbouring him . . .

As soon as Stan had finished cramming the last of the bread into his mouth, he jogged over to the chest in the corner of the room and flung it open. It was totally empty, save one item: a diamond sword, clearly old and well worn, with a violent enchantment glimmering dangerously on the blade. Stan reached into the container and clutched the handle of the sword. He had asked Olea if there was a place that he might be able to acquire an axe, but she had told him that, as long as the Noctem troops remained on the island, it would be impossible. So as of now, DZ's diamond sword, endowed with a Knockback enchantment, was his only means of defence against the world.

Stan made his way over to the stairs but halted at the top. He realized that it might be wise to glance out the window and check the conditions on the street before going downstairs. Stan walked over to the wood-plank wall and ducked down beneath the open window before peeking his head up to look outside. He cursed under his breath but was quite glad that he had looked outside first, since the entire street was lined with Noctem troops. Stan sighed, accepting that he would have to wait until this big announcement was over to make his escape.

Then Stan did a double take out the window and realized that he could see the entire congregation of citizens in the central plaza of the city. Stan realized it was risky to stay near the open window, but his curiosity got the better of him and he watched the meeting commence.

The players of the city were gathered in a gravel plaza around a giant brown mushroom, which had been decorated with red mushroom blocks and turned into a water fountain. The crowd seemed confused, and unsure of why they were there. Then, suddenly, there was a collective gasp as two dark forms emerged onto the top of the brown mushroom.

The player further towards the back looked identical to Stan, though slightly darker in overall tone and covered head to toe in dark spores. Stan clenched his fist in hatred as he realized that he was looking at the chief of the Greater Mushroom Tribe, who had betrayed him and his friends to the Noctem Alliance in their raid of the Specialty Base. Slightly in front of him stood another form that Stan did not recognize. He was wearing the black leather armour of the Noctem Alliance over a camo-coloured army uniform and an assault vest.

"Greetings, people of the Lesser Mushroom Island." The camo figure spoke in a voice that Stan was shocked to find that he recognized. "My name is Spyro, general of the Noctem Alliance."

Stan's fist clenched even tighter as he heard that name.

The last time he had seen Spyro, the Noctem soldier had turned Oob and his family into Zombies and recruited them into the Noctem Alliance. Stan shook with rage as he realized that this was probably why Spyro had been promoted to general. Although he knew that he couldn't be reckless, Stan still found himself longing for the day when he could sink a blade into both players standing up on the fountain.

"As you all know," Spyro continued, "tonight marks the start of the third day since the Noctem Alliance established its presence on this island. Therefore, I, the commander of this legion of the Noctem Alliance, believe the time has come to make certain announcements. Firstly, it is my pleasure to announce that the Greater Mushroom Island will, from this day forth, no longer be an independent nation, but rather a province of the Nation of the Noctem Alliance."

Horrified gasps and screams erupted throughout the crowd at this announcement, and intensified as troops began to pour in from the streets leading into the plaza. These soldiers were not clad in black like the Noctem troops, but rather in a light grey.

"The people of the Greater Mushroom Tribe," said Spyro affectionately, gesturing to the troops now encircling the population of the city, "have been instrumental in the agenda of the Noctem Alliance, and we are now amiably considered mutual allies. In repayment for their help, the Chief of the

Greater Mushroom Tribe has requested just one favour for his people. Therefore, in fulfillment of this favour, the Lesser Mushroom Island is now, and forever shall be, under the rule of the Greater Mushroom Tribe."

Although Stan could not see the expressions on the faces of the crowd, he could imagine that they looked absolutely terrified at the implications of this turn of events. Stan felt his heart clench. A conversation came flooding back to him . . . a secret talk between Blackraven and the Chief of the Greater Tribesmen while he himself had been feigning sleep in his jail cell on Mount Fungarus. He had to let the people of the island know of the incredible danger they were in. His mind immediately went into scheming mode as he tried desperately to think of how to warn the Lesser Tribesmen in time.

"The people of the Greater Mushroom Tribe," continued Spyro in an almost casual manner, "feel that you, the people of the Lesser Mushroom Tribe, have betrayed the sacred ideals of the Mushroom Tribe by living in the way that you have for the past six months. Therefore, under the new mandate, the Greater Tribesmen will see that you are put firmly back into your place."

Spyro gave a smug little chuckle, which caused another collective outburst of terrified cries as Stan's stomach flooded with acid. Spyro merely continued, "The second announcement regards a matter of national security. It has come to the attention of the Noctem Alliance that Stan2012, President of the Grand Republic of Elementia and Public Enemy Number One, has escaped Fungarus and is now in hiding on this island."

The crowd was silent. Stan knew they must have been shocked but were far too terrified to speak out.

"As I am sure you are aware," Spyro continued, malice dripping from his voice, "the Noctem Alliance does not take kindly to any who work against us. This island is, as we speak, being surrounded by a heavy blockade by sea. Escape from the island will be impossible. Therefore, if anybody has any information regarding the whereabouts of Stan2012, you are to deliver it to a member of the Noctem Army immediately. Should you carry information regarding the president's location and fail to report it, you will receive a punishment that fits your crime.

"And now I am instating a curfew. All citizens are to return to their dwellings and are not to leave until sunrise."

Immediately, the citizens filed out of the plaza with surprising speed. As a wave of people filed back towards Olea's store and towards their own houses, Stan could practically feel the cloud of dread wafting off them. Stan saw Olea break from the rabble and re-enter the front door to her store. Stan turned around as she clambered up the stairs, looking disgruntled.

"How much did you hear?" she demanded.

"All of it," Stan replied. "Olea, I . . ."

"Don't say nothin'," Olea said, speaking quickly and with an urgent look on her face. "You gotta wait for an opening, and then get off this island. It's a hazard to you as well as the people living here the longer you stay."

Stan nodded, his breathing shallow, as he walked back over to the window, looking out the corner. Olea walked over beside him to view the scene on the streets as well, and Stan could almost hear her racing heartbeat, which matched his nearly perfectly.

The roads were now cleared. Not one person could be seen in the streets, illuminated by the redstone lamps even as the sun was vanishing behind the skyline. The only forms of life remaining outdoors came in the form of the mass of grey-armoured troops standing in rows in front of the fountain and staring up at the Chief of the Greater Tribesmen.

"The time has come, my brothers and sisters," the voice of the chief rang out over the plaza. "Our evil brethren have desecrated these sacred islands with their heathen ways for the last time. It is time for us to finally rid this server of the barbaric savages once and for all. We have long prepared for this day. You know what to do."

The Greater Tribesmen cheered and pumped their fists into the air, some empty and some clutching bows. Then they dashed out of the plaza, flooding the streets. What happened next made Stan's stomach drop in horror.

Half the Greater Tribesmen were sprinting down the streets, throwing small black objects into the windows of some of the street-side stores. The objects shattered the windows and were immediately followed by a burst of fire and light from within the store. As the blaze from the fire charges intensified, players burst out of the doors of their burning houses and into the streets. There they instantly fell dead to the ground, with arrows sticking out of them courtesy of the Greater Tribesmen, who were armed with bows.

Stan whipped around to face Olea. "What in the . . . what the . . . ," he sputtered, his mind unable to grasp what he was seeing.

"It's the Great Purge," Olea breathed, glancing in awe at the fires now erupting all around them, and the countless civilians being shot to death in the streets. "They talked about it for months . . . but I never thought it'd actually happen. . . ."

"What are you talking about?" Stan demanded.

"The Greater Tribesmen are killing all the Lesser Tribesmen," Olea said, her voice quavering with fury. "They talked about it before, called it the 'Great Purge.' We've always known that the Greater Tribesmen hated the Lesser Tribesmen, but we never figured that they'd go through with something like this. . . ."

"We have to stop them!" cried Stan, looking around frantically at the carnage in the streets and drawing his sword.

"Put that away," growled Olea, grabbing Stan's sword out of his hand and tossing it to the floor. "There's nothin' you can do to stop this, and you know it."

"But . . . I have to . . . ," Stan stammered, unable to accept the truth of what she was saying.

"Whatcha gonna do?" spat Olea cynically. "March out there by yourself and fight the entire Noctem Army? Listen, Stan. I hate what's going on out there just as much as you do, but I know there's nothin' I can do to stop it."

"Well . . . well, what about you?" Stan shouted, trying to get her to see reason. "Won't they come after you, too?"

"No," Olea replied bitterly. "They only attack the places where the Lesser Tribesmen live. They're ignorin' the citizens of the mainland and lettin' 'em be. Though if they want to destroy this city in the first place, I'm not sure what the point of that is. . . ."

"I know why," answered Stan as the conversation in the jail cell rushed back to his head. "The Greater Tribesmen made an agreement with the Noctem Alliance. They're going to take the republic citizens as hostages and then destroy all the buildings on the island."

Olea's eyes widened and then glazed over for a moment, and Stan could see the gears whirring behind them. Then she pulled herself together and looked at Stan.

"Stan, you gotta get out, undetected and fast," Olea said quickly, glancing nervously out the window. "You gotta get back to Elementia if we're gonna win this war, and save not only your people but us here on the Mushroom Islands, too."

Stan nodded, trying to ignore the boiling feeling in his stomach. He knew that, as abhorrent as the massacre outside his window was, he would have to ignore it for the time being, however painful it may be for him. He was about to thank Olea for all that she had done for him when suddenly a sharp knock came from below.

Stan and Olea held each other's glance for an instant. Then Olea, an unnerved look on her face, hissed *"Hide!"* under her breath as she walked over to the stairwell, clearly trying to remain calm. Stan, meanwhile, felt his heart skip a beat as he clutched DZ's sword and ducked into the closet, closing the door quickly yet silently behind him.

The closet was tiny, with barely enough room for Stan to stand in. He was surrounded by chests, stacked wall-to-ceiling, on all sides. Stan spun around to face the door, feeling incredibly claustrophobic in addition to his terror of whatever had come knocking at the door. Stan tried to calm his frantic breathing so that he could hear the voices arguing downstairs.

"Whaddaya want?" Olea's brutal voice demanded.

"We're looking for President Stan," a second voice replied aggressively. "We got a tip that he might be hiding out in here."

Stan nearly gave a squeal of panic, but managed to suppress it. How did anybody know that he was here? He had made sure he wasn't followed!

"Well, whoever told you that was a no-good liar!" retorted Olea, her voice confident and bearing no hint that she was misleading them. "I know better than to risk my life by protectin' that fugitive, even against you cretins."

"Well, then how do you explain the fact that your neighbour saw two heads looking out your window? We know that you live alone."

"Who told you somethin' as ridiculous as that?" Olea inquired, sounding outraged, as a fist of ice clenched Stan's heart. "And how do *you* know that I live alone?"

"Well, let's just say that if your best friend's house is engulfed in flames, and you're talking to a man with a fire charge in his hand, you're willing to hand over information a bit easier."

"You are the *lowest* of the low . . ." seethed Olea. Stan could envision the almost inhuman snarl of disgust on her face.

"Oh, how wrong you are, little girl." The guard snickered. "If you want to see the lowest of the low, just take a look at who your good friend President Stan has pledged his life to defending. Come on, search the house."

"Whaddaya think you're doing?" shouted Olea, and Stan could hear the scuffle downstairs as the soldiers ransacked her shop. "If you don't stop right now, I will *kill* you!"

"He's not here," the second voice grunted. "Search upstairs."

"Stop that right now!" bellowed Olea, as Stan heard the clomping of footsteps growing rapidly louder. "This is breakin' and enterin'! What are you . . . this is my bedroom! I demand that you leave right now! What the . . . ? Oh, no, don't you dare open that . . ."

Stan was prepared. Just as the wooden door in front of him was flung open, flooding his eyes with light, Stan surged forward with a battle cry, thrusting DZ's sword forwards and directly into the stomach of the soldier. The Greater Tribesman gave a yell of anguish as the diamond sword tore through his grey leather armour and came out his back.

Olea whipped out a diamond sword of her own and slashed into the soldier nearest her as the Knockback enchantment on DZ's sword took effect, sending Stan's soldier flying across the room and into the wood-plank wall, his items bursting into a ring around him as he landed. Olea quickly gained the upper hand on the second soldier as the third and final soldier in the room rushed into Stan.

Stan was able to repel the soldier reasonably well, countering the blows and jabs of his opponent, but Stan's skill with a sword was only rudimentary, and he found himself unable to connect a blow of his own. One well-placed hit later, and Stan found DZ's diamond sword spiralling across the attic and landing in a corner with a clattering sound. Stan frantically dived to avoid the following strike from the soldier's iron sword and landed flat on his face. He rolled onto his back and tried to scuttle over and retrieve his sword.

Right as he reached the weapon, the soldier was upon him, leaving no time to arm himself. The soldier's sword didn't hit, however. Before the soldier could deliver a blow, two diamond swords poked point-first out of his stomach, and the soldier collapsed at Stan's feet, a ring of items bursting from around him. Stan looked up and saw Olea, pulling her two swords out of the soldier's back and latching them onto her hips.

"You OK?" Olea asked, not breathing heavily in the slightest as she reached a hand down to pull Stan to his feet.

"Yeah, I'm fine," Stan panted in response. He was too shell-shocked to think and just grasped Olea's hand and let her pull him to his feet.

"I swear . . . when I find out which of those disgustin' vermin ratted us out . . . ," hissed Olea under her breath, but she stopped when she noticed Stan. He was staring at the floor, where the items of one of the three dead players lay—namely, the player who had died at Stan's hand. He stared, almost uncomprehendingly, at those items.

Stan found himself unable to speak. For the first time in his life, Stan2012 had killed another player.

"Hey, don't dwell on it," Olea said, walking up beside Stan and turning her blocky head to face him. "You didn't have a choice. It was either him or you."

Stan sighed. "Yeah, I know," he replied, his voice sounding almost meek. "It's just . . ."

"Just nothin'," Olea replied firmly. "It had to be done, and you know it, so it's not worth thinkin' about no more. You can't waste no more time, Stan."

"Yeah, you're right," Stan said, looking at Olea and a bit disturbed with himself as he found that, despite the fact that he had just ended another life for the first time since he had joined Elementia, he was able to put the conflict within him aside relatively easily. "OK, I'll head out now."

"Good," Olea replied, "You can slip out the back door."

Stan grabbed his sword, took a deep breath, and marched downstairs. Stan was totally floored to see the complete devastation of the shop that the soldiers had managed in just a few seconds. It looked like they had checked around the few pieces of furniture in the most destructive way possible.

Various picture frames sat on the floor, which was

sprinkled with shattered glass from the busted-out windows. The glass dust was twinkling with radiant red light, and Stan looked out at the blaze now engulfing the city. The fire was spreading to the houses of the other citizens as well, and the streets were flooded with people desperately trying to extinguish the fires and protect their livelihoods from being lost in the inferno.

Stan could hardly take in what he was seeing. He remembered, just days ago, when he had stood in the centre of this great city, on tour with a guide named Danny, and was blown away by the brilliant displays of lights and lively players bustling through the streets like blood through the veins of a magnificent living being. At the rate the flames were spreading, the city would all be gone by morning.

What Stan did next was without thinking. It was without logic. It was without any form of common sense whatsoever. Stan burst out of the front door of Olea's shop and into the streets. He was acting on raw, unbridled emotion, wanting to do everything he could to draw the Noctem Alliance, these harbingers of destruction and pain, as far away from this city as possible. Stan raised his arms, still clutching DZ's sword and, with a vein pulsing in his forehead, he opened his mouth and gave a mighty roar.

"HEY! SPYRO! COME AND GET ME!"

Immediately, hundreds of heads, civilian and military,

whipped towards him. There was a moment when time seemed to freeze as the entire populace of the burning metropolis locked their eyes simultaneously on to Stan. Then chaos reigned.

From all across the streets, dozens of soldiers, clad in black and grey, started charging toward him, some releasing a battle cry and some firing off arrows. Stan spun around and sprinted as fast as he could through the alleyway of the city and onto the mycelium shoreline, barely noticing the shower of arrows falling just short of him. He only glanced over his shoulder once, and his eyes locked not on the wave of troops pouring after him, but on Olea poking her head out the back door of her shop. The look on her face was a mix of surprise, fury, gratitude and trying to comprehend what in the world he was thinking.

Stan didn't look for long, though. He sprinted down the mycelium-covered hill that led to the water's edge, where he noticed a patrol boat quite close to the shore. The black-suited pilot of the dinghy barely had time to turn his head when Stan sent him careening into the ocean via a shock-wave of Knockback energy from DZ's sword. Stan landed haphazardly in the boat, and by the time he had seated him-self properly, the Noctem soldiers were already splashing into the bay, just blocks away from him. Before the troops could destroy his boat with their weapons, however, Stan had desperately willed the boat to fly forwards like a rocket, leaving the Noctem soldiers in a trail of bubbles behind him.

Stan quickly glanced up at the white rectangle that was the nearly full moon and aligned himself to face east, towards Element City. As he turned the boat, Stan noticed something black poking out from under the boat's seat. He investigated further, and found a black leather tunic and cap, presumably one that the piloting Noctem soldier had had as a backup. Stan gratefully pulled them on; a little extra protection never hurt.

Finally, Stan gave one last glance behind him. He saw no other boats following him, and he noticed a swarm of dark forms scuffling around the shoreline, preparing to follow him. Though he knew that he ought to be thankful that the Noctem troops hadn't been fully organized and ready to pursue him yet, Stan hardly noticed this in comparison to the city. From this distance, the tallest skyscrapers of the Lesser Mushroom Island still stood proud and tall, even amid the scarlet blaze that illuminated the night from beneath them.

As Stan stared in awe at the downfall of this great city, a single tear rolled down his cheek. Stan's mind began to flood with the memory of all the death, slaughter and betrayal that he had witnessed in the city, but he forced himself to tune it out. All he had to remember, he told himself, was that it was all because of the Noctem Alliance. And the only way that he stood even the slightest chance of taking them down, once and for all, was to return to Element City.

So, with new resolve and a heavy heart, President Stan2012 turned his back to the Lesser Mushroom Island and willed his boat to accelerate at top speed towards Element City.

I still can't believe just how immature she's being," G muttered under his breath to Jayden. Jayden took a deep breath, counting to ten in his head. He could barely comprehend that, even though the two of them were sitting in a military camp and preparing to sneak into the camps of the Noctem Alliance, G was still ranting about Kat.

"G, for the last time," said Jayden slowly, trying to keep his composure despite his frustration, "we kind of have other things to be focussing on. Like . . . you know . . . *a war*?"

"I just really expected more from Kat," G said, throwing back his head in exasperation. "She's a smart, reasonable person, so why can't she just let bygones be bygones like I have? We could have worked together fine. We still make a great team! Yet she continues to harp on it and hate me for it, totally refusing to let it go. . . ."

"Do you even realize what you're saying?" spat Jayden, his tolerance finally snapping. "G, *you're* the one who's refusing to let it go! You haven't shut up about Kat this entire time. *You're* the one who's turning this entire situation into a giant thing, and, frankly, none of us want or have time to hear it."

"Oh . . . that's just great," grunted G, glaring at

Jayden. "Now my best friend won't even take my side."

"I'm not taking anybody's side!" yelled Jayden, his eyebrow twitching in irritation. "I don't know everything that happened, so it's not my place to judge. But what I *do* know is that now is the worst possible time to talk about it! You want to work out your issues with Kat? Fine, go ahead and give it a shot. But wait until after we've destroyed the people who have been trying to kill us nonstop for the past month, please!"

G opened his mouth, then closed it again, glancing at the floor. Although he knew that Jayden was right, he didn't really care, and was so infuriated by the whole situation with Kat that he wanted to rant and rave about it for as long as possible. However, an explosion directly outside the wall they were next to snapped him out of his thoughts. Realizing that they would be entering combat soon, G pushed his anger with Kat to the back of his mind, and made himself promise it would stay dormant until his mission was over.

G noticed Jayden glancing upwards, and he followed suit. The army encampment where the two of them were gearing up was located right at the base of the outer wall of Element City, on the east side. The explosion from above had been fired from the outside, and a considerable chunk of the upper wall had been blown apart by the blast. The two councilmen watched in fascination as, through the power of the soldiers standing at the ready, the mighty stone wall seemed to repair itself, like some great animal regenerating its tissue. Meanwhile, other soldiers could be heard yelling from atop the massive wall, accompanied by the high-pitched whistling of fireballs streaking down and into the outside woods, surely targeting the Noctem Troops waging war below them.

"These people," Jayden muttered, more to himself than anyone else. "They're putting so much on the line to defend our city . . . to keep freedom alive on this server . . . I wonder . . ." And Jayden's voiced trailed off into nothing. There was a moment of silence, punctuated only by the yells and other sounds of the ongoing war.

"What?" G finally asked.

"It's just . . ." Jayden said, clearly in a quite pensive state. "Well . . . it's the Mechanist. I know that he's a fantastic leader and all, and if anybody should take over the city while we're gone, it's him. But . . . all these people are fighting for justice and equality, and now that the council is spread out all over the server, the entire city is under the control of just one person. And I know that we have the police watching the Mechanist and all, and I trust him. But . . . what do you think the citizens will think?"

G was about to respond when suddenly a door opened in the wall, and a soldier dressed in a full Elementia Army uniform appeared.

"Councilman Jayden, Councilman Goldman," the soldier said, addressing them respectfully but with a tone of urgency. "The target group of Noctem soldiers is massed in the woods directly outside the wall. Our intelligence suggests that they won't be there for long. If we are to make our move, we must do it now."

"OK," Jayden replied, leaping to his feet alongside G. The two of them drew their diamond weapons, all thoughts of the previous conversations wiped clear from their minds. It was time to take action.

"Follow me," the soldier replied, and he marched through the iron door and into the wall, with Jayden and G close in tow.

Neither of them had seen the inside of Element City's outer walls before, but they were totally blown away by just how much was going on. What from the outside appeared to be a ten-block-thick wall of solid stone bricks was actually hollow, filled with various staircases and ladders that led to stone-brick platforms at various levels of the massive height. Soldiers scurried to and fro inside the wall, manning various battlements on the outside, and preparing fireball launchers and TNT cannons. G heard a rush of noise directly above his head, and looked up to see a mine cart rushing across a powered rail above, surely delivering vital materials to a point even further down the wall.

The two players hardly had time to marvel at the pinnacle

of Minecraft defensive technology that was the Element City outer wall. The soldier led them over to a battalion of players, bearing weapons and dressed in an amalgamation of diamond, iron and leather armour. They all stood in front of a series of pistons that were set up against the outermost side of the inner wall.

"OK, men," the soldier announced in a booming voice, walking to the front of the group of players. "You know the drill. When the blast doors open, make a charge across no-man's-land into the woods, and engage the Noctem soldiers. They outnumber us by a reasonable degree, so we will only engage them briefly . . . just enough to buy time for Councilmen Jayden and Goldman to execute their mission."

There was a shuffling in the crowd as all heads turned to face Jayden and G. The looks on the faces of the soldiers unnerved them a bit. These were players who had been entrenched in the rage of war for longer than they had ever expected, and their expressions seemed to demand that the two councilmen not blow their one chance to take a huge step in ending the conflict.

"Corporal!" came a shout from somewhere within the highest reaches of the wall, where Jayden and G couldn't see. The soldier leading the charge glanced upward.

"You have to go now!" the voice rang out again. "They're preparing to move out!"

"OK," the soldier said to his troops, turning to face the wall. "It's time to go. *Open the blast doors!*"

At the soldier's command, Jayden and G heard a series of clicks and whirs as the pistons retracted, pulling the stone bricks with them and opening the wall to the world outside Elementia.

There were no words to describe the white shock that overtook Jayden's and G's minds as they saw what lay beyond the outer walls. The last time they had been there, just weeks ago, the area surrounding Element City had been lush and green, with forest growing right up to the wall.

Now there wasn't a tree in sight. The ground had been reduced to a field of dirt piles on a stone field pockmarked with craters. Everywhere their horrified eyes looked, Jayden and G could see fires blazing and the inventories of dead players scattered across the hilly ground. The remaining forest couldn't even be seen from their position directly outside the wall, as the smoke from the fires was too thick, obscuring the world around the outer wall like render fog.

All this ran through the heads of Jayden and G in an instant. Then they found themselves barrelling forwards, into the valleys and craters created by the TNT cannons, following the command of the captain who had yelled *"CHARGE!"*

The group of around thirty soldiers, with Jayden and G in the middle, was sprinting as fast as they could, but it was difficult to progress. The uneven terrain underfoot made for a lot of stumbling as they pressed onwards, staying together as a group. Then, as the edge of the forest finally came into view, the arrows started to fly.

It was a desperate struggle as the squad of soldiers fought their way out of the craters and towards the forest while dozens of black-clad soldiers rained arrows down on them. Jayden heard the clinking sounds of arrows bouncing off the solid armour of the warriors, along with the occasional cry of anguish indicating that a hit had been scored.

As the soldiers finally managed to reach the top of the hill, a rain of fireballs started flying in from behind them. G glanced over his shoulder and saw lit blocks of TNT, flying far over their heads and landing in the forest with a massive blast. The turrets and battlements on the walls, he knew, were backing them up from afar.

As the soldiers poured forwards into the forest, it seemed that the majority of the Noctem soldiers were still scrambling for their gear and weapons. It had been fairly obvious that they hadn't been expecting the attack. Jayden and G hardly noticed this, though. They were sprinting to the side, ducking into a small copse of trees, out of the Noctems' line of sight.

As soon as they were safely hidden within the vegetation, the two councilmen stripped off their armour as fast as possible. They then proceeded to yank black leather caps and tunics out of their inventories and pulled them on. As soon as they had both adorned themselves in the enemy's uniform, Jayden and G made a roundabout back into the trees and emerged behind the Noctem fighters.

It was mayhem on the battlefield. Arrows whizzed through the air, some lit on fire via enchantments, while a steady rain of fire and explosions fell from the smoky skies of the Elementia side. The soldiers were engaged in full-on combat, swinging swords, axes and pickaxes at a rapid pace, while the vapours of dozens of potions drifted up and into the air.

Jayden rushed forward into the combat right as a Noctem soldier faded into Invisibility right beside him. He whipped out his diamond axe, ignoring all combatants on either side until he found who he was looking for. The corporal leading the attack was fighting a Noctem soldier with a diamond sword that glowed with a red lustre. Jayden rushed in to meet the corporal just as he finished off the Noctem soldier. The corporal was about to strike Jayden when the two locked eyes. The corporal realized who it was, and a flash of relief crossed his face. The plan had succeeded. Jayden and G were now in the enemy camp.

"Retreat!" the corporal bellowed, giving Jayden a nod before turning and sprinting back down into the valley. "All forces retreat!"

Within the next few seconds, the Elementia troops were

disengaged from the combat and heading back down into the valley of haze as the rain of fireballs and mortars stopped falling. Although a few Noctem soldiers continued to fire arrows into the crowd of fleeing Elementia troops, the majority just looked confused, wondering what had happened.

"Where did that come from, General?" Jayden heard a voice ask from somewhere in the crowd.

"I'm not sure," a female voice responded slowly. "That attack came out of nowhere . . . and it was over awfully fast. . . ."

"Maybe they just underestimated our numbers," the first voice replied.

"You're right," responded the general, who Jayden still couldn't see. "That's probably what happened."

"So, back with the mobilization?"

"Yep," the general said, before yelling at the top of her lungs, "All right, everybody! It's time to move out! We have to hurry. That attack set us back, and they need us back in Nocturia as soon as possible!"

As the mass of black leather started to march, Jayden glanced around wildly, trying to find G. Before long, his eye caught the eye of a player with green eyes and bronze-textured skin under the leather armour. Jayden nearly began to panic, wondering why this random soldier was keeping eye contact with him, before he remembered that this was G's new skin.

Jayden sighed in relief. He was so used to seeing G in his old skin that he had forgotten the change, which was necessary so that no Noctem troops would recognize his extremely distinct appearance.

The two friends and councilmen gave each other a quick nod and returned to marching. Jayden shivered in excitement. This was it. The plan had worked, and now the two of them were marching their way toward Nocturia, with the Noctem Alliance none the wiser.

"Do you *honestly* need to be so loud?"

Kat halted in her tracks, her foot falling to the ground with a loud squishing noise. She clenched her teeth even tighter than they had been, to the point where she imagined that they were near shattering.

"Cassandrix," she said, trying to keep her head on straight, "this is a *swamp*. Because we are in a *swamp*, the ground is very *soggy*. Therefore, it is difficult for me to walk on it *quietly*. Do you understand?"

"Well, *I* seem to be managing just fine," Cassandrix trilled in reply. "And, of course, considering that we are attempting a *sneak attack* here, well, *I* think that we should practice being as quiet as possible. But if you're not capable of handling that, Kat, I understand . . . I'm not surprised, but I understand."

Kat clenched her fists. She wanted to kill the arrogant,

stuck-up player who trudged through the swamp in front of her. However, she held herself back. As annoying as Cassandrix was, Kat knew that she had to be the bigger person and deal with it. They were on a mission that might decide the fate of her best friends, and Kat knew that she had to stay focussed.

Nonetheless, she resented the fact that the two of them were being forced to bushwhack their way through miles and miles of swampland instead of simply sneaking a pair of boats out of Diamond Bay Naval Harbour. That was how Stan and the others had gotten to the Mushroom Islands in the first place, and, despite the fact that the Noctem Alliance now had control over the Northwestern Ocean, Kat saw no reason that she and Cassandrix couldn't do the same thing. However, the police chiefs had overridden them and demanded that the rescue mission stay a secret. Therefore, Kat and Cassandrix had been forced to take a different route, which involved trekking down a long peninsula of uncharted swampland and then sailing to the Mushroom Islands from the north.

Honestly, it wasn't the prospect of the uncomfortable trek through the swampland that bothered Kat, though. Quite the contrary, she was thrilled at the potential for danger and excitement that the swamp held—it was a far cry from the boring council meetings and debates that had consumed the last few months of her life. Rather, Kat had been turned off to the adventure because of the prospect of dealing with the constant stream of whininess and unbelievable snootiness that would surely be pouring out of Cassandrix's mouth the entire way.

And sure enough, the trip thus far had lived up to her expectations. The night before, Kat had gotten the opportunity to fight off skeletons, spiders, Creepers and an endless horde of Zombies (she suspected that the Zombies in particular had gotten smarter and stronger during the recent update to Minecraft) with Rex the dog by her side, defending Cassandrix as they set up their shelter for the night. It was great fun, and Kat relished the adrenaline rush of the fight; it felt just like old times again. On the other hand, the entire rest of that night had been nothing but Cassandrix yelling at Kat for letting a Zombie or two reach her and complaining about how gross it was to be spending the night in the soggy and putrid swamp, while Kat had been demanding that she just shut her mouth.

Still fuming, neither one of them had had anything to say to the other all day. Occasionally, Cassandrix had made a snide remark to Kat, which Kat answered with stoic silence, but beyond that they had kept largely quiet. The two simply walked single file, stopping occasionally for a silent meal of bread, as the hours slowly ticked by.

Now the sun was finally beginning to set. The two play-ers continued to trek onwards through the saturated grass and occasional pools of water, but it was becoming more and more difficult to see. Kat was about to suggest that they make camp when she heard a voice from not too far away.

"Ey, guys! Dat spot looks kinda dry! We should camp dere!"

"Shut up!" a second voice hissed, barely audible over the natural ambiance of the swamp.

Cassandrix whipped around and looked at Kat. They locked eyes, saw the panic in each other's face, and glanced around the swamp, trying to locate a place to hide. As the arguing voices grew closer and closer, Kat's gaze fell on a stone hole in the moist ground. She drew an Ender Pearl from her inventory and pitched it towards the mine. Kat reached over and grabbed Cassandrix's arm, and before she could question what was happening, the two girls warped to the inside of the cave.

Cassandrix glanced around wildly, trying to piece together what was going on as Kat waited desperately for Rex. By the time he magically warped beside her, Cassandrix had realized what Kat had done. The two of them scurried downwards into the cave, tailed by Rex, and halted where they were no longer visible from the cave entrance. Hearts pounding, the two girls listened as hard as they could, trying to catch the conversation that was going on above them.

"Why do you *always* have to talk so loud?" an enraged male voice sounded out from above. "Are you familiar with the term 'stealth'?"

"Ey, don't you yell at me!" a stupid-sounding male voice continued loudly on. "I don't have da control ober how loud by boise is!"

"Shut up!" the angry voice hissed again. Kat was taken aback by the sheer level of harshness in the voice. "Good Lord, you're useless. . . ."

"Cut it out," a third voice ordered, this one female, sounding slightly annoyed, yet still deadly serious. "Lay into him all you want later, but right now we have to find a place to stay for tonight."

"Omigosh, Arachnia, I am, like, *so* not sleeping in this disgusting suh-*wamp*!" a fourth, ditzy-sounding female voice replied. "It's all, like, soggy and stuff, and the Slimes out here leave these, like, icky puddles of goo all over the place! Ew! It's, like, totally guh-*ross*."

"Oh, get over yourself," spat the third voice, apparently named Arachnia. "Hmm . . . you're right about one thing, though . . . we shouldn't camp up here—it's way too out in the open. Come on, guys, let's head down into that mine over there. . . . That should keep us hidden."

And, to her horror, Kat heard a symphony of footsteps

slogging their way through the grass above and getting louder and louder. Kat realized that Cassandrix had already taken off, running deeper into the mine, and Kat turned on her heel and sprinted in pursuit, Rex hot on her tail. Kat barrelled down the natural stone steps of the mine like a cart on powered rails, sending a few bats flying out of her way in surprise. As the footsteps above suddenly turned into the sharp echoes of feet against stone, Kat dashed faster, finally catching up to Cassandrix, who was standing directly in front of a pool of lava. The cave had led them to a dead end.

Immediately, Kat whipped out her sword and sank into a fighting stance, praying that, whoever these people were, they were peaceful, or at the very least bad fighters. As the footsteps grew louder, another sound registered in Kat's ears—a rhythmic tapping directly behind her. She glanced over her shoulder and realized that Cassandrix was swinging an iron pickaxe and digging a hole in the wall, just tall and wide enough for them to escape through. Feeling a combination of stupidity for forgetting this option and hope that their escape would go without a hitch, Kat glanced forwards again.

"This spot looks good." Arachnia's voice echoed down into the cavern as the footsteps came to a halt. "Creeper Khan, would you mind making the area a bit more . . . spacious?"

"It would be my pleasure," the enraged voice, apparently

named Creeper Khan, growled back in return. Even now, when he sounded thrilled at whatever it was he was about to do, he sounded remarkably angry.

Suddenly, without warning, the booming blast of an explosion sounded throughout the cavern, deafening Kat's unprepared ears. Another blast followed, followed by a series of rapid-fire detonations that shook the mine. Kat sprinted backwards into the tiny hole that Cassandrix had created, terrified by what could be causing this horrific effect. Were these players detonating TNT? Had they run into a horde of Creepers? Or . . . and Kat shuddered as she imagined the implications . . . was it something else the player was doing?

Then, suddenly, the explosions stopped. There was no damage to any part of the cavern that Kat could see, but she wasn't planning to stick around to find out what was really going on. She just wished that Cassandrix would dig faster.

"Omigosh, Arachnia, this is, like, *so* much better," the unfocused, flighty female voice said again. "I mean, it's still, like, totally dark and underground-y and stuff, but at least it's not, like, the suh-*wamp*, or anything. . . ."

"You're welcome," spat out Creeper Khan in disgust.

"OK, team," Arachnia announced, "Let's set up, and try to get some sleep. Tomorrow, the real hunt for President Stan begins!"

Kat, who was walking through the tunnel and nearly out

of earshot of these players, spun around. Did she really just hear that? Intrigued, Kat dashed down to the end of the tunnel, poked her head out, and continued to listen.

"Hey, Arachnia, I hab a question!" the stupid-sounding voice rang out again, sounding particularly loud as it echoed around the chamber. "Ow do you know dat da President hasn'd already godden dis far?"

"Zomboy," seethed Creeper Khan, *"just SHUUUT UP!"*

A small explosion rang out not too far from Kat, but she didn't care. She was suddenly far too desperate to hear what these people had to say. Were they saying that . . . somehow . . . Stan had escaped?

"Khan, calm down!" exclaimed Arachnia in irritation. "We can't have you lose control in here, not in such close quarters! And besides, it was a decent question. Zomboy, President Stan escaped just a few days ago. He's probably still out in the Northwestern Ocean, hopping from island to island."

"Oh," Zomboy replied. "Dat bakes sense."

"I swear," Creeper Khan growled, glaring at Arachnia, "if you don't find some way to make him less annoying, then I am going to use my Final Nova on all of you!"

"Don't even joke about that!" Arachnia gasped. "I don't want you to use it by accident. . . ."

"Oh, relax." Creeper Khan laughed darkly. "You do realize

that my Final Nova is powerful enough to level an entire city, right? Trust me, I'm not gonna use that attack unless I really, *really* have to."

Suddenly, Kat felt a hand grab her shoulder and whip her around. Kat was totally caught off guard, and her hand immediately went for her sword. However, she saw that it was simply Cassandrix, staring her in the face with an incredulous expression.

"What do you think you're doing?" Cassandrix hissed, as quietly yet incredibly urgently as possible. "We have to get out of here!"

"Shut up, I'm listening," Kat hissed back, pushing Cassandrix to the side and trying to hear what they were saying again. However, before anything could register, Kat found herself being dragged back into the tunnel.

"Are you really that stupid?" Cassandrix whispered, her face showing pure disbelief. "They're distracted. We have to leave now!"

Kat didn't have time to deal with her. These players, whoever they were, were discussing vital information about Stan, and Kat had to hear it. Hoping it would buy her a few seconds, Kat gave Cassandrix a full-on shove, sending her tumbling back into the hole. Kat stuck her head back out to hear Creeper Khan's voice.

" . . . still can't believe that Stan managed to get out of

that prison. It was so well guarded . . . or at least, that's what I heard. What was it, didn't some friend of his blow himself up in order to get Stan out?"

"Yeah," Arachnia replied. "I think his name was DieZombie97 or something, one of the council members . . . killed himself by setting off the bomb that let Stan escape."

After that, the two players continued to talk, but Kat didn't care. She couldn't hear them any more. All she could hear was that one phrase, resonating in her mind over and over again . . . *DieZombie97 killed himself, DieZombie97 killed himself, DieZombie97 killed himself. . . .*

Stan had broken out of the prison. And DZ was dead.

Kat was having trouble processing, trouble comprehending what was being said . . . DZ, her friend who had been with them for months, for as long as they had been in Elementia . . . could he really be . . .

A hand struck Kat hard across the face, and she felt a flash of pain; her vision went white for a moment before refocussing to see Cassandrix, her face almost inhuman with fury.

"You *dare* to shove me, you obnoxious little brat!" Cassandrix seethed, her nostrils flaring. "I swear, if you *ever* do that again, I will not hesitate to . . . Oh, stop crying, you deserved it and you know it!"

"He's dead . . . he's dead . . . ," Kat managed to get out between shallow, raspy breaths, tears running silently down her face. "Cassandrix . . . he's dead. . . ."

"What are you talking about?" Cassandrix demanded, looking up into the cave in horror; Kat may have been having her breakdown quietly, but they were still in the presence of these hooligans.

"They said . . ." Kat managed to get out between forcing her snorts of sorrow and fury to stay in her chest, "that DZ . . . is dead. . . ."

"Kat, that doesn't matter!" Cassandrix hissed, her eyes bulging. "We have to get out of here now."

Kat looked up to face Cassandrix. She could not believe what she had just heard. Her eyebrows knitted, and her eyes blazed with fire as she snarled in outrage. Had Cassandrix *really* just had the *audacity* to claim that DZ's death *didn't matter*?

Cassandrix had crossed the line. Kat drew out her diamond sword and prepared to let out a bellow of rage. She knew nothing but an all-consuming desire to destroy Cassandrix. Kat raised her sword and was about to bear down on Cassandrix with all her fury when, all of a sudden, she felt a dull blow to the side of her neck.

Kat fell to the ground, suddenly no longer angry at Cassandrix, or sad about DZ for that matter. In fact, she wasn't able to feel anything aside from a strange feeling of calmness spreading from her neck across her entire body. She was vaguely aware of Cassandrix falling to the ground beside her. As the world around her started to blur, Kat's fading eyes caught the image of a player dressed as a Spider drawing back a glowing hand right before she finally passed out.

The white rectangle that was the moon shone bright in the sky, casting a cool glow down onto the ocean below. The vast expanse of water stretched out as far as the eye could see, only being dotted by a few lonely islands far off in the distance. At the surface, the ocean was totally flat, except for one living being swimming forwards, creating a slight rippling around him.

Leonidas was totally exhausted. He had been swimming for days on end, through the seemingly endless brine. The few islands that he had found to rest on throughout his journey had been barren. They held no trees with which he could construct a boat, and only one of them had any food on it, a single cow that Leonidas had killed with his bare hands, desperate and starving for food (he had been so delirious with hunger that he had forgotten that he still had an iron sword on hand). The little bit of rations that he'd had when he'd left Fungarus had nearly depleted, and Leonidas had no idea when his next meal would come.

There was one particular food item, though, that Leonidas had held on to since he had left Nocturia more than a week ago. Although he knew that the golden apple would fill him, and make him feel much better as well, he refused to eat it. He was saving it for . . . a very particular occasion. It was so important that Leonidas's mind had stopped classifying it as food, and rather as a tool. As food swam to the forefront of his mind now, he didn't pay the golden apple in his inventory a lick of thought.

Leonidas was so exhausted, and so miserable, that he had half a mind to simply stop, to allow himself to sink underwater, and wait until his oxygen ran out and he drowned. However, Leonidas knew that he couldn't do that. He had been working for the forces of evil for far too long in Elementia to leave now. He had to redeem himself before he could leave Elementia with any degree of integrity. And so, Leonidas forced himself to paddle onwards, closer and closer to the Elementia mainland, praying that it would come into sight soon.

Leonidas wondered what was happening within the Noctem Alliance right now. He knew that, with Caesar dead and he himself deserting, the Noctem Alliance was short a chancellor and a general. If Leonidas had to guess, he would say that since Blackraven had officially revealed himself as a traitor to Elementia, he would take over Caesar's role as chancellor. As for the general . . . Leonidas clenched his teeth as he realized that Drake had almost certainly taken over his position. He couldn't wait for the day when he would finally get to face that self-righteous little brat again.

Leonidas paused for a moment to catch his breath,

treading water and focussing as hard as he could on conserving energy. There was still no island in sight, and he would likely be swimming through the night until he found one. After he had caught his breath, Leonidas was about to continue swimming when he heard a faint noise behind him. He soon realized with a start that it was the sound of a wooden boat cutting through water, and it was growing louder and louder.

Leonidas glanced behind him and saw, far off in the distance, a lone boat sailing straight towards him. As he squinted at it, Leonidas could barely make out a figure, unidentifiable at this distance, clad entirely in black leather armour.

A grin crossed Leonidas's face. It was a Noctem Alliance boat, surely out in the ocean to try to find him. Leonidas hastily took a deep breath and ducked his head underwater. He hoped that the Noctem soldier hadn't seen him or, if they had, they would assume that he was just a squid, poking up above the water as they occasionally do.

Leonidas allowed himself to sink down to the seabed. Thankfully, it was shallow here, a mere ten blocks or so below the surface. Leonidas crouched down on the clay basin of the ocean, ready to launch himself upward. Leonidas reached into his inventory and drew out his iron sword. In this situation, he figured that it would be a better choice than his bow.

Leonidas stood absolutely silent, watching the boat,

silhouetted against the moonlit surface, come closer and closer to where he was. Then, just as the boat was above him, Leonidas kicked off the clay blocks, rocketing upward toward the surface, sword outstretched in his hand. Leonidas broke the surface of the ocean and felt himself launched into the air. The player in the boat had hardly comprehended what was happening before Leonidas's sword had struck him across the black leather chestplate, cutting it open and sending the player tumbling out of the boat and into the water.

Leonidas fell back down into the ocean with a splash and saw the player haphazardly trying to gain his bearings and figure out what was going on. Leonidas let out a breath that turned into a swarm of bubbles, realizing that he should probably kill this player. As much as he wanted to abstain from killing, he knew that leaving this Noctem soldier alive was far more dangerous than it was worth.

Leonidas returned his sword to his inventory and drew out his bow and an arrow along with it, taking aim at the player. By now, the player had gained his bearings and was staring back at Leonidas, glowing diamond sword in hand. Leonidas saw that underneath the ripped tunic, a turquoise shirt was visible, and the player's face was pale and shocked. However, only when Leonidas looked the player in the eyes did he come to the realization of who he had just attacked. The eyes, which held the same type of gleam that was unique to every player, were horribly familiar. . . . They were the eyes of Stan2012.

Leonidas couldn't comprehend what had just happened. This Noctem soldier he had just attacked . . . was President Stan? How was that possible? Stan had escaped? He was on his way home? And Leonidas had just attacked him?

Oh, no, thought Leonidas, his mind refusing to accept what had just happened. *What did I just do?*

Leonidas didn't have too much time to think about it though. He instinctively raised his bow in a feeble block as Stan sent an axe blow directly at Leonidas's head, sending them both careening away from each other. Leonidas was totally stuck. He knew that he couldn't fight back against Stan, and he also knew that Stan wouldn't be particularly keen on listening to his explanations, not that they could even speak in this underwater environment.

Leonidas felt a dull blow to his stomach as Stan's sword connected with his black leather chestplate. Leonidas had been thinking so hard about how to avoid fighting Stan that he had forgotten that, eventually, Stan was going to counter-attack. As Leonidas sunk down to the ocean floor, he noticed a trench right beside him. Desperately, he swam downwards into it, well aware that Stan was following him in hot pursuit.

As Leonidas plunged deeper and deeper into the trench, he found it near impossible to see. That was the least of his worries, however; his oxygen supply had nearly run out. Leonidas aimed a punch forwards, and, by some miracle, his hand struck dirt. As fast as he could, Leonidas threw punch after punch at the wall, hoping to create a tiny safe haven to utilize. Just as his breath was about to give out, Leonidas punched away the second dirt block, creating a small compartment just large enough to stand in, which Leonidas quickly dived into.

Leonidas took a deep breath and felt the air rush back into his head, his bearings quickly returning to his body. Thanking Notch for Minecraft's broken water physics, Leonidas continued to punch into the dirt wall, eventually creating a room large enough for two people to stand and walk around in. Hopefully, if Stan was planning on making his way down to the trench to finish him off, Leonidas would be able to explain what was going on.

However, Stan didn't come down. After a while, Leonidas gave a deep breath and a sigh. He was furious with himself for making such a crucial mistake; he would have a much harder time convincing Stan that he was planning to join the Elementia Army now. Leonidas gave the wall a lurid punch of frustration before slipping out of his air pocket and rising back toward the surface, planning how he could fix the damage caused by this monumental error.

Stan was barely managing to keep himself afloat. The cut across his chest by Leonidas's sword had torn through his armour, leaving a light cut in the centre of his chest. This wouldn't have been so bad if it weren't for the fact that he had then tumbled directly into the ocean, ramping up his pain to excruciating levels as the salt water seeped into the open wound. Add that to the fact that Stan had accidentally swallowed a mouthful of seawater during his plunge, and he had become so weak that it had been a struggle to pull himself back into the boat.

And that was back when he still had the boat. The struggle against Leonidas had done substantial damage to the craft, to the point where it barely floated anymore, and he couldn't control it. He had half a mind to just leave it there in the middle of the ocean, but he knew that there was a chance Leonidas might find it and somehow use the wrecked dinghy to his advantage, so he had destroyed it. Stan now held three wood-plank blocks and two sticks in his inventory, the only remnants of the boat.

Stan quivered with fury. He couldn't believe that Leonidas had followed him all the way out here just to ambush him. Actually, now that Stan thought about it, he realized that he shouldn't be surprised at all. He knew that out of all the Noctem Alliance's forces, Leonidas was the most savage, alongside Minotaurus. Leonidas had probably volunteered to hunt him down, Stan thought in disgust.

The one thing that Stan was slightly confused by was how he had managed to escape Leonidas. But, the more Stan thought, the more he realized that it was probably because Leonidas had let his blind bloodlust take over his common sense. He probably hadn't meant to knock Stan into the water. Leonidas most likely was a terrible underwater fighter, and had fled to avoid fighting Stan while he had that disadvantage.

That being said, Stan knew that Leonidas couldn't be far behind him. He was probably just trying to heal up from his underwater mêlée with Stan, and would be in hot pursuit in no time. Stan was in no condition to repel the Noctem archer now, and he had no place to rest up. *If only,* thought Stan as he gritted his teeth, *somewhere, in this entire ocean, there was . . .*

Stan's heart leaped for joy as finally, on the far horizon, he could see a dark mass of blocks expanding up from the surface of the ocean. *Finally,* Stan thought as he gave a sigh of relief.

As Stan paddled closer and closer to the island, his enthusiasm grew less and less. This island had barely anything on it. There were no trees, no animals, and not much of anything else. It was just a small mound of dirt expanding out from the ocean. At the very least, though, there didn't appear to be any Noctem forces anywhere near it.

Stan finally reached the shoreline and dragged himself up onto the dirt-block shore. Stan collapsed face-down on the ground. He didn't care that he was completely exposed and out in the open. He didn't care about the potential monsters roaming this dark island. All Stan cared about was finally being back on dry land. At that moment, fatigued beyond comprehension from the ordeals of the last few days, all Stan wanted to do was sleep, and escape from his cares in the world.

If Leonidas wants me, thought Stan as he drifted off into sleep, *let him find me.*

"Stan?"

Huh? Stan thought stupidly.

"Stan? Stan, is that you?"

That's funny, thought Stan vaguely, through the cloud of exhaustion in his mind. *I could have sworn I heard a voice. . . .*

"Stan! It is you! Oh, fantastic, I've been trying to contact you for ages . . . come on, wake up, noob!"

"Wait, wha . . . *ow!*" Stan exclaimed, sitting up quick as a bolt and feeling a massive rush of blood from his head because of it. "Ugh . . . Sally, is that you?"

"Yeah, it's me," Sally's voice replied out of the ether, crackling and punctuated by static. "Listen Stan . . . I've got way too much to tell you . . . and not enough time . . . I need you to follow my instructions and fast, OK?"

"Yeah, of course," Stan replied, trying to force himself to

wake up in the midst of his reconnection with Sally.

"OK," Sally continued, her voice fluctuating greatly in volume as she spoke through the terrible audio. "Here's what you *need* to do, Stan . . . I need you to *leave* Elementia and join the server that I am about to invite you into."

"Did . . . did I just hear you right?" Stan asked, bewildered. "You're asking me to leave Elementia?"

"Just for . . . little while . . ." Sally replied, her voice now a consistent volume but barely audible over the outside interference. "You'll . . . able to get back . . . into Elementia . . ." The static was getting worse and worse. "Trust . . . I'll explain . . . when we . . . to meet . . . other in . . . my server . . . called . . . SalAcademy . . . See . . . soon . . ."

And then, with a loud static crackle, Sally's voice disappeared.

Stan was stunned. He had been beginning to doubt that he would ever hear Sally's voice again, and now, here she was asking him to leave Elementia and join her in a different server. Stan didn't even know if it would be possible. He didn't know much about Minecraft servers, but he did know that Elementia still had mods that King Kev had put in place. He didn't know what these mods were—in fact, nobody really did—but Stan knew that they made going in and out of Elementia a risky business.

There were two things that Stan was sure of, however. One

of these things was that Sally knew much more about computers than he did. It took skill to bypass King Kev's leftover defences against hackers, as well as the efforts against her by whatever tech junkies the Noctem Alliance had on their side. The second thing was that he trusted Sally. She had never led him wrong before and, with her superior knowledge in the subject area, Stan was sure that he wouldn't regret listening to her now.

And so, Stan sat down cross-legged on the dirt beach of the island, took a deep breath, and focussed hard on his desire to leave Elementia. For a moment, nothing happened, and Stan began to wonder if he was doing this right. Then all at once, a question appeared in his mind, written out as clearly as if it were actually visible.

DISCONNECT FROM SERVER?

And with a deep breath, and a sense of disbelief that he was actually doing this, Stan answered out loud.

"Yes."

And with that, Stan2012 disappeared.

From his place treading water in the ocean that surrounded the dirt-block island, Leonidas's jaw was slack, his mouth hanging open. What did he just see?

Leonidas was surprised that he had managed to catch up to Stan at all. For starters, Leonidas had given him a pretty good head start. After Leonidas had resurfaced from his underwater hideaway, he had immediately begun to swim towards the Elementia mainland, sure that Stan was headed in that direction.

And now that he finally had Stan, what happened? Stan started talking to himself, pacing around, and then he had left Elementia? Leonidas started to panic . . . He knew that the Noctem Alliance was gaining more strength by the day, and Element City was losing just as much. How could Stan just abandon them like that? Leonidas was almost ready to give a shout of fury at Stan for abandoning his people in the midst of this crisis.

Then Leonidas took a deep breath, and tried to clear his mind. If he himself was to return to Element City, he would have to try to keep as levelheaded as possible. And as Leonidas released his breath, he realized that Stan would never abandon Elementia. He had probably just gone to a different server for a while . . . or maybe he had homework to do . . . or maybe had had to pee or something. In any case, Leonidas assured himself that Stan would be fine, and that he'd probably be returning any moment.

Suddenly, it struck Leonidas what an interesting position he was in. Stan had temporarily left Elementia . . . but he would return eventually. And when he returned, he would be in the exact same spot where he had left. And if he were to return right now, he would see Leonidas standing right in front of him.

Leonidas sat down on the dirt-block mound and squinted his eye, trying to figure out what to do. On the one hand, he had been looking for the perfect time to tell Stan that he had abandoned the Noctem Alliance. Maybe here, on this island, with the two of them and nobody else, was the perfect place for him to do it. In any case, Leonidas didn't imagine that a better time would be coming anytime soon.

On the other hand, though . . . their last meeting had not gone particularly well. After that little fiasco, Leonidas had no idea how he was going to convince Stan that they were on the same side . . .

Suddenly, Leonidas whipped his head up, the debate in his mind instantly vanishing. He could hear something. Ringing out of the dark sea, far beyond sight, was a song that he couldn't quite make out. It sounded like a Minecraft song he had heard on the Internet a long time ago . . . and it was growing louder and louder. Leonidas ducked down behind a pile of dirt blocks. He peeked his head over the top, gazing far into the distance. Out in the sea, emerging from the render fog, Leonidas could see a small fleet of ships. He couldn't make out the exact numbers, he guessed about six . . . but what he could make out quite clearly were the black tunics that each of the players was wearing.

Leonidas glanced around in a panic, looking for a place to hide should soldiers happen to land on the island. His gaze locked on a small cave, not too far away, which led into the centre of the dirt mound. With great grace and agility, Leonidas dive-rolled out from behind the dirt pile and into the mouth of the cavern. He peeked his head out the side, praying that the soldiers didn't see him. Thankfully, they hadn't seemed to notice. While they continued to head toward the island, there was no hint of recognition in their voices, just the continuing ring of the sea shanty.

Leonidas sighed in relief. He could hide deep in the mine, and win through ambush if any of the troops should find him. He was about to turn back and begin his trek down into the cavity of rock when an alarming realization slammed into Leonidas like a train.

Leonidas stuck his head out of the cave again, and glanced at the spot where Stan had despawned. He glanced back out at the ships and realized, with a wrench to his gut, that Spyro was at the head of this fleet of six boats. They had stopped their singing. All of them were on course to land on the island, right at the spot where Stan had sat just a few minutes ago.

Stan would return to Elementia. Leonidas didn't know when, but he didn't imagine Stan would be gone for long. And when Stan did despawn, he would find himself right in the middle of the squadron of Noctem troops, totally caught off guard and unprepared to defend himself.

The Noctem troops had gotten out of their boats. The six of them had all manner of weapons drawn, from bows and arrows to diamond swords and axes. Spyro walked over directly to the spot where Stan had been and turned his back to Leonidas, facing his men.

"OK, men," Spyro said gruffly. Leonidas was floored that he sounded so much older and more weary. "You know the drill. Search every nook, cranny, and crevice of this island. Your target is President Stan. Should you find anybody else, bring them to me."

"Yes, sir, General Spyro!" the other five soldiers yelled in unison.

And with that the troop dashed around the island, starting to inspect every block for a sign of a hidden player. And right as Leonidas ducked his head into the mine to avoid detection, he realized that Spyro was not moving. In fact, he was standing in the same place where he had addressed his men, surveying their progress, and staring directly at where Stan was eventually bound to reappear.

Leonidas ducked back into the cave in a panic. His heart was racing, and the fact that Spyro had somehow jumped up quite a few ranks from corporal to general was barely registering in his mind. All he knew was that these Noctem troops would comb every nook of the island, and eventually they would find him. But even more horrifying was that Stan could reappear in Elementia at any minute. And when he did, he would appear right in the midst of the enemy soldiers.

As Leonidas heard footsteps approaching him, he hastily ducked further down into the cave, his mind racing as he tried to work out what to do next.

Stan opened his eyes. He glanced around, bewildered. All he could see was an expanse of flat, green grass, stretching as far as the eye could see. There were no structures, no landscapes . . . no anything. Nothing but a never-ending expanse of grass.

Stan was puzzled. He was sure that he had picked the right server . . . he had distinctly heard Sally say the words SalAcademy, and when he looked at the list of servers available to join, there it was. He was positive that this had to be the place. But then where was . . .

Suddenly, Stan became aware of a presence behind him. He whipped around, his hand going to his axe, as he had forgotten that his inventory was now empty. Feeling defenceless, Stan glanced around wildly. Then, slowly, his gaze shifted upward.

Levitating in front of him was a player, who slowly started to descend from the sky. As Stan watched in awe, more and more of her features came into view. She was wearing black trousers and a black biker jacket, with a purple X across the front of it. Her jet-black hair was no longer in a braid but now hung down, half covering her face, and a streak of neon orange ran through it. However, as Stan looked into her totally unchanged pale face and single exposed green eye, he knew that, although her skin had changed, he was looking at the same person.

"Welcome to the Academy, noob," Sally smirked as her feet finally touched the ground.

The Mechanist's head snapped upwards, and he grunted in confusion. Slowly, his sense returned as he remembered where he was. The council room was deserted aside from himself, and all was silent except for the omnipresent sounds of the bombardment on the city walls. The Mechanist rubbed his eyes. He realized that he had been sleeping for a while, though he was unsure of exactly how long.

He looked around the empty room. He was puzzled. What was he doing in here? Why did he remember so little about the time before he had passed out? Why had he passed out in the first . . . ?

And then, in a rush, the Mechanist remembered.

He had been sitting in the council room, poring over battle strategies submitted for his approval, when Bill had burst into the room. He had been frantic and had tears in his eyes. The Mechanist had demanded to know what was wrong. And Bill managed to get out between his choked-back sobs that the Noctem Alliance had sent them a message, and their military had managed to confirm it—that DZ had been killed in an accident at the prison.

The news had slammed into the Mechanist like a truck. He had demanded that Bill leave him be, that he had to be alone. And then . . . what? The Mechanist could barely remember what had happened after that. He vaguely remembered a feeling of overwhelming grief, but besides that . . .

A glint of light from the floor caught the Mechanist's eye. He ducked down under the table and examined the empty glass potion bottle lying on the floor. Intrigued, the Mechanist examined the bottle more closely. There, sitting at the bottom of the container, sat a single remaining drop of the blue-grey potion.

The Mechanist gave a sigh of understanding. Now that he thought about it, he did have a faint recollection of when he had been sobbing over the death of his fellow councilman. He had only experienced grief like that once before in his life, when King Kev had banished him into the town of Blackstone as a labourer. To this day, the Mechanist still couldn't hear the words that the King had spoken to him without the psychological scars of that day floating to the surface.

So when the news of DZ's demise had come to light, the Mechanist had tried to remember what he had done to overcome the trauma of his banishment. The answer was quite simple: he had turned to SloPo. And it looked like in the death of one of his closest friends, the Mechanist had turned to SloPo yet again . . . though for the life of him he couldn't remember where he had gotten it.

The Mechanist shook his head in disgust. He remembered

what Gobbleguy used to tell him back in Blackstone, about how he was when he was on SloPo. He never had any recollections of how he acted, but he knew that he definitely wasn't in the mindset to lead a nation when he drank it.

The Mechanist picked up the glass bottle and shoved it firmly into the deepest depths of his inventory. With a knitted brow, he vowed to never drink the potion again, regardless of how stressed out he may be, as he turned his eyes back down to his work.

Jayden and G were both trying very hard to keep their breathing steady, to keep their bodies from shaking in anticipation. They were standing in the middle of a group of twenty upper-level players, standing in a five-by-four player line, in the centre of the Capitol rotunda in the heart of Nocturia.

Both players were relieved that they had managed to merge into the Noctem forces so easily without arousing suspicion. They had spent the last day and a half marching through the forest, jungle and desert until they reached the tundra where the Noctem capital of Nocturia was situated (they had overheard the higher-ups saying that the fast-travel highway through the Nether was still under construction).

As they marched across the countryside, Jayden and G had been horrified to see the evidence of Noctem occupation of the region. Scattered across all the biomes were Noctem bases constructed out of cobblestone, with black figures swarming around them. Once, they had walked by a community of players living at the edge of the jungle, and they had seen the players living there forced to go underground with no armour by Noctem soldiers armed with diamond weapons. G had found it difficult to keep himself from breaking free of the group and liberating the village.

Finally, after the endless trek through the tundra, they had arrived at Nocturia. The two councilmen found the city to be beyond impressive. In the middle of the endless expanse of snow-white hills and frigid blizzard, the Capitol Building of Nocturia stuck out like an ornate, gothic and eerie thumb. Beyond the ornate and intimidating design of the stone-brick structure, what most stuck out about the outside design were the pillars of light. These thin rays of iridescence flashed out of the top of Nocturia and protruded high into the dark sky of the eternal snowstorm. G had later informed Jayden that these were Beacons, blocks that omitted light rays and were constructed of very rare materials added into the game a few updates back.

Surrounding the Capitol Building were dozens of other structures. These small stone-brick enclosures with gravel paths running between them were hardly impressive, but the two councilmen knew that within each of those small buildings were more Noctem troops, more soldiers ready to add to the bombardment of the Element City walls.

It had been late last night when G and Jayden had finally made their way into the Capitol Building with the other troops, amazed that they had managed to make it all the way to Nocturia undetected. As they had entered the building, Jayden and G had split from the group as soon as possible, and had, without much searching, found what they were looking for: a wooden sign on the stone-brick wall that read **TRAINING AREA** with an arrow pointing in their direction.

After following more signs, the duo had reached the training room, and, as their military intelligence had led them to believe, a new group of new recruits to the Noctem Alliance were waiting in the room. The two had waited outside the room until a figure appeared to escort the trainees to their quarters, and when the rabble of new recruits had passed, Jayden and G subtly shed their black armour and mixed into the crowd.

In the large stone-brick quarters lined with two dozen beds, the group of twenty recruits had been loud and raucous, in the process of meeting their new friends. Jayden and G had taken part, trying to look as casual as possible. When the redstone lamps lighting the room finally turned off, signalling curfew, Jayden and G had taken adjacent beds and drifted off to sleep, still not believing how smoothly their plan had run so far.

Now, the next day had come. It was early in the morning, and most of the recruits were groggy, having had to drag themselves out of bed to get their first-ever briefing by one of the generals of the Noctem Alliance. Not G and Jayden, though; the two councilmen were totally awake, well aware that at any point, they might pick up on a tidbit of information that would allow them to locate and rescue the hostages of the Adorian Village.

Suddenly, the entire crowd snapped to full attention, as a player walked onto the elevated platform above the rotunda floor. This player's upper body was covered in black leather armour, but the pink face and white ponytail down her back clearly distinguished this player as female. She had a no-nonsense look in her eye as she stared down the rows of new recruits.

"Greetings, my brothers and sisters," the player spoke in a voice that was neither overly hard nor overly cheery. Immediately, it rang in G's and Jayden's ears as the general who had led them from the battlegrounds of Element City back to Nocturia.

"My name is General Tess," she continued. "I am one of the three leaders of the armies of the Noctem Alliance, subservient only to the illustrious Lord Tenebris."

At the sound of the name, a shudder of excitement rippled through the crowd. They had all heard tales of the great

Lord Tenebris, and were thrilled to finally be serving under him. Jayden and G, meanwhile, gave a shiver of dread as they imagined what the leader of the Noctem Alliance was like.

General Tess smiled. "I can tell that you are all excited at the prospect of meeting the glorious Lord Tenebris. Let me tell you right now that your wish probably won't come true. The exalted supreme commander of the Noctem Alliance will only address his generals, myself included. Furthermore, he is a being shrouded in great mystery. I have never before seen his face, only heard his voice. None but the founders of our great Alliance have ever laid eyes on the magnificent Lord Tenebris . . . and lived to tell the tale."

This time, the wave of fear that passed through the new recruits was not just limited to Jayden and G.

"Nonetheless, in coming here, you have put your fate in the hands of Lord Tenebris and the Noctem Alliance. In doing so, you have already joined the ranks of those who seek truth, and shall therefore be saved. The magnificent Lord Tenebris has already led his armies to nearly conquer the uncivilized, lazy barbarians led by President Stan2012."

At the mention of Stan's name, there were hisses and grunts of disgust throughout the crowd.

"The Noctem Alliance has not yet been able to take back Element City, the greatest bunker of Stan's resistance. This is because those rallying behind Stan won't give up without a fight. They have unwavering faith in their belief that lower-level players of this server deserve to be pampered and babied. They believe that we, the hardworking upper-level players of Elementia, should go out of our way to help the lower-level players rise to equal our strength.

"What they forget," continued Tess, staying calm yet raising her voice to be heard above the angry grunts and roars of outrage from the crowd, "is that we, too, were once lower-level players. And we had nobody holding our hands as we endured the countless hardships, cruelties and struggles that accompanied our rise to where we are now. But in the end, it was worth it, my friends! Elementia has transformed from nothing into the greatest server in the history of Minecraft! And the server has only us, the Golden Age Players, to thank for it!"

A cheer burst forth from the crowd of new recruits.

"King Kev understood this," Tess went on, her voice dripping with earnest passion. "He realized that, as payment for our work, all we desired was the ability to live our lives happily, reaping the rewards of what we had worked so hard to build. So naturally, when the spineless new players whined that the game was too hard and that they wanted their cut of the wealth, King Kev wouldn't hear it. The world is cruel, however, and King Kev was taken from us by the scum known as Stan2012. Just like that, the upper-level players of Elementia lost a great leader, who died with no crimes besides defending his righteous and honest beliefs. My friends, let us take a moment of silence to honour our fallen hero, King Kev."

Tess bowed her pink head to look at the ground, as did all the other recruits, including Jayden and G. While the two councilmen were clenching their fists to keep calm, the other new recruits around them seemed legitimately solemn. They even heard an occasional sob escape from the crowd.

"The Noctem Alliance," Tess continued after a moment, "was founded out of fate. It was by fate that our founding fathers survived the Battle for Elementia. It was by fate that the glorious Lord Tenebris appeared to them, offering them the guidance and wisdom to destroy Stan2012 once and for all. And it was by fate that all our meticulous planning was carried out flawlessly. The Noctem Alliance has managed to take back nearly all of what was stolen from us by President Stan. And yet, the great Element City, which we built, which we were forced to fight for, and which contains our houses, is still occupied by Stan.

"Many of you have left your homes in Element City to join the Noctem Alliance. Perhaps your realization of the vile nature of lower-level players is new, or perhaps you are just now willing to put your faith into the Noctem Alliance. For whatever reason, you have joined the Noctem Alliance quite late in the game, in the final stages of our operations.

Regardless of this, you have done the right thing. Better late than never, as I always say."

There was an awkward pause before the crowd realized that they were supposed to find this funny. They then burst into gales of laughter. G and Jayden rolled their eyes as Tess smiled at the soldiers' indulgence.

"The road ahead of you won't be easy," Tess continued after the strikingly artificial mirth had faded. "It's my job to transform you all from players into something more. The upcoming weeks of your training will not be pleasant. They will not be comfortable. I will treat you like the warriors you are expected to be, and mercy will *not* be tolerated. However, you'll leave this programme as soldiers, ready to storm the battlefields of Elementia and take back what rightfully belongs to you, your brothers, and your sisters!"

Tess pumped her fist into the air. All the recruits followed suit, giving an animalistic roar of power and excitement as they did so.

"And now, my brothers and sisters, the time has come for you to, once and for all, affirm yourself as a true member of the Noctem Alliance! Are you all ready?"

"Yes, ma'am, General Tess," all the soldiers responded in unison. G and Jayden shut their mouths in horror; they had been about to give another shout of agreement, yet that clearly wasn't the right thing to do.

Tess nodded. "Now repeat after me: *I vow to fight for my rightful place in Elementia.*"

"I VOW TO FIGHT FOR MY RIGHTFUL PLACE IN ELEMEN-TIA," the crowd responded almost robotically.

"*I vow to do all in my power to further the cause of the Noctem Alliance.*"

"I VOW TO DO ALL IN MY POWER TO FURTHER THE CAUSE OF THE NOCTEM ALLIANCE."

"*I vow to submit to every command of the illustrious Lord Tenebris.*"

"I VOW TO SUBMIT TO EVERY COMMAND OF THE ILLUS-TRIOUS LORD TENEBRIS."

"*I hereby denounce President Stan2012, all his teachings, and all his followers.*"

As the group of players repeated the last lines back, G shuddered as he spoke the words. Although he himself didn't mean a word of it, he couldn't help but be terrified by the zealous fervour instilled in the crowd of players as they said this one particular line.

"*And I hereby surrender myself to the Noctem Alliance.*"

"AND I HEREBY SURRENDER MYSELF TO THE NOCTEM ALLIANCE."

"*Long live Lord Tenebris!*"

"LONG LIVE LORD TENEBRIS!"

"*Long live the Noctem Alliance!*"

"LONG LIVE THE NOCTEM ALLIANCE!"

"Viva la Noctem!"

G grimaced. He had been wondering when he would be forced to say that hateful phrase, the slogan that he had despised since he had first heard it at the Noctem rally more than a month ago. He took a deep breath, swallowed his pride, and belted out the motto of the Noctem Alliance alongside Jayden and all the Noctem recruits.

"VIVA LA NOCTEM!"

Kat's eyes fluttered. Her head felt heavy and clunky. She recognized this feeling from many months ago, when she had been attacked by a horde of poisonous spiders in an abandoned mine shaft. Luckily, Stan and Charlie had been there to fight off the Spiders and heal her then. . . Now, though, Kat could only guess at how long she'd been knocked out.

She took a deep breath, and realized that she was sitting in a tiny, cramped cobblestone cell with an iron door in front of her. Kat grimaced as she forced herself to sit up straight, and realized what had woken her up. The shrill, irritating, upper-class accented voice of Cassandrix echoed through the space outside her cell. Kat pulled herself to her feet and put her ear to the door, listening to the conversation.

" . . . will have you know that I am a high-ranking member of the hierarchy of Element City!" Cassandrix squealed.

"If you don't release me this instant, Element City will bear down on you with all its might!"

Kat banged her head against the door in frustration. Did Cassandrix honestly think that she was in any position to make demands?

"Ha!" a deep female voice replied from the outside hall, sounding amused. "Do you honestly think you're in any position to make demands?" (Kat slapped her forehead with her blocky hand as she heard this.) "We know exactly who you and your little friend are, and believe me, General Spyro has some business with the two of you."

"I won't tell you *anything* unless you set me free!" bellowed Cassandrix.

The guard gave a chuckle. "Oh, we'll see about that. You'll find that we here at Mount Fungarus can be . . . well . . . rather *convincing*, shall we say."

Kat's ears perked up. *Well,* she thought glumly, *at least they had made it to Mount Fungarus in one piece.*

"What are you talking about?" demanded Cassandrix.

"Well, allow me to put it this way," the guard continued, clearly enjoying hearing Cassandrix sound so desperate. "When the esteemed Councilman Charlie first arrived at this prison, he wasn't willing to talk either. But now . . . well, let's just say that not only have we retrieved some very interesting information from that brilliant mind of his, but he also will probably never be able to walk properly again."

Cassandrix let out an audible gasp of horror as the guard chuckled yet again. Kat shuddered, trying to convince herself that the guard was lying, and that they weren't too late. As Kat heard the footsteps of the guard walking away, she knew that they had to get out of their cells as quickly as possible. If the guard was telling the truth, and Charlie was being tortured to the point of becoming crippled, then they didn't have a single second to spare.

"Hey, Cassandrix," Kat said, trying to be as loud as possible without attracting attention.

"Oh . . . *you're* here . . ." Cassandrix sighed from somewhere down the hall.

Kat gave a grunt of frustration. "It's good to see you, too. How long have you been up?"

"Oh, I awoke as soon as the guard came, darling . . . what, did you just wake up? Well to be frank, I'm not surprised. What with your low intelligence and strength, it only stands to reason that I would be able to shake off the poison first . . ."

Kat gave a roar of anger and punched the stone wall in frustration. "You're infuriating, you know that? We get captured and thrown in jail, and still you can't stop being so stuck-up!"

"Well, pardon me, darling," Cassandrix replied,

sounding offhand yet also angry, "but I seem to recall that it was your impudence that got us into this situation in the first place, so pardon me if I find it difficult to suppress my indignation!"

"Oh, I'm sorry," Kat spat in response, "pardon *me* if I actually tried to listen in to find out valuable information from those bounty hunters, and then didn't take it lying down when you said that DZ's death didn't matter!"

"Oh, stop being such a baby." Cassandrix seethed in exasperation. "Honestly, you young players are all the same . . . thinking that you know what's best, barrelling headfirst into dangerous situations, letting your emotions get the best of your common sense . . ."

"Excuse me," replied Kat, deeply offended and disturbed, "but you're starting to sound like a member of the Noctem Alliance."

"How *dare* you!" screamed Cassandrix. "I resent the implication that I am on the same level as those evil lunatics! I mean, do I resent the fact that since Stan took over, our city has devoted itself to pampering the younger, lower-level players into wealth and fortune with next to no work on their part? Of course I do! But never in a thousand lifetimes would I dream of discriminating against them or attacking them! It would be like attacking a toddler!"

"WHAT?" shouted Kat. "You think that the new players

have it *easy*? I'm sorry, but I seem to recall that my first few weeks in Elementia were spent fighting an evil dictator who was trying to kill me because of my *level*!"

"Oh, but you succeeded, didn't you?" Cassandrix shot back. "In a matter of weeks, you were able to upgrade your skills and materials until you were able to go toe to toe with the leaders of King Kev's army, players who had been training and gathering materials for years! Do you think that *I* had an Adorian Village to teach me when I first joined Elementia? Do you think that Element City or the Adorian Village would exist today if the people of my level hadn't struggled and toiled to raise it from the ground? And don't get me started on the Spleef tournament . . ."

"What does Spleef have to do with anything?" Kat demanded.

"Oh, don't make me laugh, darling," Cassandrix replied with a bitter, forced chuckle. "I'm referring to players like *you*, Kat."

"What are you—"

"I have worked for as long as I've been in Minecraft to become the best Spleef athlete in the world," Cassandrix spat, an almost imperceptible catch in her voice. "And all throughout King Kev's reign, I was never able to achieve any success. I was the best player in the league, but despite my hard work, it never amounted to anything. When Spleef returned after the fall of King Kev, I realized that, finally, I would have my chance in the spotlight and become the undisputed best Spleef player in the world. At long last, my hard work would pay off.

"And yet, all around me, I saw that new players, who had only been in Elementia for weeks, were playing Spleef along-side the best of us. While I was still the best Spleef player in the league, I was still barely ahead of these spoiled newer players, whose lives have been so easy that that they've been able to pick up the art of Spleef almost effortlessly. And right at the forefront was you, Kat . . . fighting alongside Ben and DZ, two older players who had put in just as much effort as I had. And yet, despite all your inexperience, you still equalled them in skill, while surpassing them handily in arrogance.

"So, yes, Kat, I *do* have a few problems with lower-level players. I hope that you can forgive me from up there on your high horse." Cassandrix sighed bitterly.

Ordinarily, Kat would have jumped on the opportunity to scorn Cassandrix for her insults, but now, she felt no such desire. In fact, Kat wasn't sure what she was feeling. Obviously, she knew that many of the things that Cassandrix had just spouted out were wrong and misguided, but . . . there also seemed to be very real elements of truth to them. And furthermore, Kat suddenly found herself in the inexplicable position of feeling sorry for Cassandrix. Kat hadn't realized just how much Cassandrix had been keeping bottled up, nor how unprepared she had been to see it erupt.

Suddenly, Kat heard footsteps coming from down the hall, and she snapped out of it. This wasn't the time to be thinking about such things. Their only priority had to be freeing themselves, and then finding Charlie and Commander Crunch.

Kat glanced out the tiny window of the steel door and saw the guard, totally obscured by a mask and her black armour, stop outside the door to Cassandrix's cell. Her hand went down to a lever outside the door.

"You in there," she grunted in Cassandrix's direction. "Back to the wall. You're coming with me to see General Spyro. If you cooperate, you won't be hurt."

Kat's heart skipped a beat. They were coming for them already? It had been less than five minutes! Kat's mind raced wildly, trying to formulate a plan.

"And don't even think about trying anything funny," continued the soldier, drawing an iron pickaxe from her inventory, "or I'll lodge this pickaxe into your back."

Suddenly, a thought struck Kat. Quickly, she glanced down the hallway. It was narrow but she was pretty sure that he'd be able to make it, wherever he was.

The soldier pulled the lever, and Cassandrix stepped out into the hallway. Kat saw that, although her white and golden flowing clothes were stunning, Cassandrix's white face was downcast and depressed. Kat only hoped that Cassandrix would take advantage of the opportunity that Kat was about to give her.

"Walk forward," the soldier commanded.

Kat took a deep breath, and gave a two-note whistle. Instantly, Rex appeared in the middle of the hallway. The soldier whipped around just as the wolf's eyes locked onto her.

"Sic 'em, boy!" Kat shouted.

Instantly, Rex's eyes glowed red, and he barrelled down the hallway towards the soldier, snarling and barking like mad. She gave a shout of surprise before dropping into a fighting stance, and raising her pickaxe to strike. Rex leaped through the air towards her, and before the soldier could deliver the blow, Cassandrix body-checked her from the back, sending her smashing into the wall and tumbling to the floor.

The pickaxe went flying through the air and landed in Cassandrix's hand as Rex landed on top of the soldier, pinning her to the ground. Cassandrix brought the pickaxe above her head and drove it directly into the center of the soldier's leather armour. Immediately, a ring of items burst out from around her, signifying her demise.

"Good boy, Rex!" Kat shouted out from her cell as Cassandrix picked up the soldier's dropped items. Rex pounced over to the door of Kat's cell and began pawing at the steel barrier, whimpering. Cassandrix walked over to a second lever on the wall and pulled it down, allowing the door to swing open. Rex tackled Kat to the ground, licking her face.

"It's good to see you, too, boy!" Kat laughed, as she scratched the dog under his red collar, causing his tail to wag harder than ever. Cassandrix walked over to them.

"If you two are done," Cassandrix said in a determined voice, "we've still got to find Charlie and Crunch. And I'm sure the guards will be sending some reinforcements up soon. That attack wasn't exactly silent, you know."

Kat opened her mouth, ready to acknowledge in the most sarcastic way possible that Cassandrix hadn't even thanked her for saving her life, but she realized that Cassandrix was right. They had a mission to finish.

"You're right," Kat replied, nodding. "Let's go."

Sally!" cried Stan as the two players ran towards each other, and met in a tight embrace. "Oh, it's so good to see you again! In person, I mean."

Sally chuckled as she let him go. "Haha, yeah, I missed you, too, noob. I mean, being your omnipresent spirit mentor is nice and fun and all, but it's so much more hilarious when I can mess with ya in person."

Stan smiled. "Man, you just don't change, do you? Even after all this craziness, you're still exactly the same person that I met in the Adorian Village all those months ago . . ."

"Oh, don't go getting sentimental on me, noob," Sally scoffed, crossing her arms. "We've got a lot of work to do, and not nearly enough time to do it, so we can't waste any more words."

"Oh . . . OK," said Stan, feeling slightly awkward. *Yep,* he thought to himself. *Nothing's changed at all . . .*

"Anyway, I'm guessing that you want to know why you're here, noob."

"Well," replied Stan, slightly taken aback, "I, uh . . . assumed it was because you just wanted to see me again."

"Oh, Stan, Stan, Stan," Sally chuckled, closing her eyes and shaking her head in amusement. "You know what they say, noob . . . When you *assume,* you make an . . ."

"Hey!" exclaimed Stan, cutting her off. "If assuming things is so bad, then why did you assume that I wanted to know what I'm doing here?"

Sally opened her mouth, then closed it again. She scratched her head for a second, looking confused, and then nodded reasonably.

"Good point, noob," Sally replied agreeably. "Well, regardless, the important thing is that we both ended up looking stupid."

"OK, fair enough," Stan replied. "So, why do you want me here, anyway?"

"Well, there are actually two reasons," Sally said. "The first reason is that I wanted us to be able to establish a place where we can meet up and talk without any problems. As of now, I've been spending only half my time spying on the Noctem Alliance, and the other half has been spent trying to contact you to tell you about it. Now that I have this server up and running, we can meet here if I have anything to tell you. It'll be much easier to find you for a minute and tell you to meet me here rather than to try to tell you the entire report in Elementia."

"OK, fair enough," Stan replied, nodding his head. "So I'll still hear your voice in Elementia, and when I do, it means come onto this server?"

"Yes," Sally answered.

"OK, good thinking," said Stan. "So, do you have any news to report to me?"

"Nothing yet," Sally replied. "I don't know who the Noctems have got doing their tech work, but they're clearly doing their job exceptionally well. I've never seen anything as difficult to hack in my life as Elementia is right now. And the worst part is, even if they're killed in Elementia, they'll still be able to keep working from beyond the server, like I am."

"Well, that's unfortunate," Stan said bitterly. "But I guess that it's a given, and we have to work with it. Anyway, you said you had two reasons for getting me to come over here."

"That I do, noob," Sally said nodding her head, a wild gleam of excitement shining in her eyes. "I'm gonna cut straight to the chase with you, Stan: I'm gonna try to get you operating powers in Elementia."

"Wait, what?" Stan asked, bewildered. He wasn't sure what he was expecting her to say, but it certainly wasn't that.

"You heard me," Sally replied.

"But . . . how . . ."

"Because I think I've figured out how," Sally said. "I was trying to work out how I could rejoin Elementia, but I found out that it wasn't possible. I did figure out that I should be able to give you operating powers, though. And if you had operating powers, then defeating the Noctem Alliance would be cake."

"So . . . hold on . . . questions . . . ," Stan sputtered as he tried to put together what Sally was saying. "Let me ask you this first . . . I've heard a lot about operating powers since I've been in Elementia . . . I know that King Kev and Avery used to have them, but then King Kev gave them up, and now nobody has them . . . but I'm still not entirely sure what operating powers are. I mean, what can you do with them, exactly?"

A devious grin crossed Sally's face. "Weeeellll . . ." she said.

Then, without warning, Sally jumped off the ground, propelling herself into the air . . . and didn't come back down. She rocketed higher and higher into the sky, and then dipped downwards. She bolted around the air like a superhero, performing loops and U-turns, all before returning. She flew suspended in the air directly above Stan, who stood motionless, and entranced.

"Well, you can fly, for one," she shouted from the air, her voice giddy.

Sally closed her eyes for a moment and then, without warning, a diamond sword popped out of midair and landed in her left hand. She stretched out her left hand towards the ground a distance away, took a deep breath and, with a rumbling sound, a tower of brick blocks began to construct itself, reaching high into the sky in a matter of seconds.

"You can also create items and blocks using your mind."

Sally rocketed off directly towards the brick tower, her fist outstretched. Stan watched in awe as she barrelled directly through the centre of the tower, leaving a gaping hole behind her. She circled backwards and cut through the tower at six other points of various heights before finally flying back. Sally punched her fist through the air towards the tower, and immediately, an explosion rang out, taking a chunk of the tower with it. Sally aimed a blitz of quick jabs from the ground to the sky, destroying the tower from the bottom to the top.

"And you can also destroy blocks, either by hitting them with one punch or by creating explosions."

After the explosions had ceased, Sally flew back down to the ground, stopping just above Stan.

"So, yeah, those are a few things you can do with operating powers. There are a bunch more, too, but for now, there's really only one more that I want to show you."

Sally tossed her sword into the air, and stretched out her left hand towards it. The sword stood still in midair. As Sally moved her hand from side to side, the sword moved along with it, slicing through the open space. Sally clenched her fist, and the sword began to spin around in circles, like a midair top. As Sally released her fist and the sword hovered still once more, she directed her right hand down at the ground, towards Stan.

Instantly, Stan found himself unable to move. His arms and legs stiffened, as did his neck, and he began to levitate into the sky. All at once, Stan wasn't feeling blown away by these wonderful powers; quite the contrary, he felt terrified. He wasn't prepared to totally lose control of his body, especially when he was off the ground.

"OK, Sally, you've made your point," Stan said firmly, trying not to hide the fear that was welling up in his body. "You can stop now."

But Sally didn't stop. Rather, at his request, a psychotic grin crossed Sally's face as she jerked her right hand upwards. Stan let out a squeak of terror as he felt himself rocket into the air, jerking to a stop high above the grassy ground below. Sally's left hand moved a little, and the sword spun to face Stan.

"Sally . . . what're you doing?" asked Stan in horror.

"Teaching!" Sally replied, her eyes flashing with madness as she clapped her hands together in front of her. All at once, Stan felt himself fly forwards at breakneck speeds, right toward the flying diamond sword.

Stan barely had time to comprehend what was happening before the sword had pierced him through the stomach and shot out his back. Stan felt an instant of pain, followed by a vacuum of light and sound until everything went black and silent.

Then, all at once, Stan found himself on a field of grass. His heart was racing. He glanced around wildly. He was sitting in the middle of the endless expanse of grass, and Sally was still levitating in the air next to her diamond sword. Immediately, Stan's hand went to his stomach . . . and found no wound. There wasn't even a rip in his shirt. And as Stan realized this, he also found that he wasn't in any pain. Confused out of his mind, he glanced up at Sally as she landed next to him.

"What did . . . how . . . are you insa . . . but I was de . . . *WHAT JUST HAPPENED?*" Stan demanded in fury.

Sally chuckled. "Oh, I just thought I'd kill two Creepers with one arrow. You know, demonstrate what my operating powers can do and show you that you can't die on this server at the same time. You know, you—"

"OK, back up," Stan managed to get out, his head spinning. "First of all . . . why exactly am I not dead?"

"Oh, you poor sap," Sally replied, shaking her head and clicking her tongue in mock sympathy. "You've played on Elementia your whole life, and you're so ignorant to the rest of the Minecraft world."

"Wha . . . ?"

"Elementia isn't like other Minecraft worlds, noob," Sally said wisely. "On most Minecraft servers, after you die, you just appear back in the last bed you slept in . . . or at the spawnpoint, if your bed was destroyed or you haven't slept yet. Elementia is different because King Kev locked the server into Hardcore PVP mode. That means that the difficulty of the monsters is permanently on the hardest setting, players can hurt each other and if you die you're banished from the server forever."

"So . . ." Stan said slowly, trying to put things together in his head. "This server . . . SalAcademy . . . isn't like that?"

"Nope," replied Sally. "It's just a normal PVP server. Which means we can hurt each other, but we can also respawn, and operators like me can change the game mode."

"OK, well, that leads into my other question, actually," said Stan. "How did you manage to get operating powers on this server?"

"You automatically get operating powers if you start a server," Sally answered, as if it were obvious. "Besides that, the only way to get operating powers is if somebody who already has operating powers gives them to you . . . like I'm about to do for you, in fact."

"Wait," exclaimed Stan, jumping to his feet and looking Sally in the eye. "You're gonna give me operating powers? I'm gonna be able to do all that stuff you just did?"

"After I train you," Sally replied, nodding with a smile.

"And once I get my powers," Stan said quickly, becoming more excited by the second as he realized the possibilities this development held, "I'll be able to use them anywhere? Both here and in Elementia?"

"No," Sally replied, shaking her head. "You'll only be able to use operating powers here, in SalAcademy."

"Well, then . . . what's the point?" Stan asked, crestfallen.

"The point is that, here, I'll be able to teach you how to use them," Sally said. "It takes a lot of training and practice to master the use of operating powers. It's not nearly as easy as I just made it look. I'm going to try to illegally hack the powers onto you in Elementia, but before I do, you need to learn how to use them. Once the Noctem Alliance realizes that I'm going to try this, they'll try to stop me, so I'll only have one shot at giving the powers to you without getting blocked. I want to make sure that you know how to use your powers when I take that shot."

"Well then, what're we waiting for?" Stan asked eagerly. "Give me my powers, and let's get training!"

"Haha, OK, noob," Sally replied as Stan bounced around like a puppy about to get a treat. "Stand still and calm down. And close your eyes."

Stan took a deep breath and stood still. He let the breath out and closed his eyes. After a moment, he felt a hand touch his forehead. An instant later, he felt like his entire body was going numb from an electric current. The sensation lasted for an instant . . . and then it stopped. Stan opened his eyes, and saw Sally drawing her right hand back.

"How do you feel?" Sally asked quizzically.

"Well, I felt something for a second . . . I don't feel much different now, though," Stan replied, confused.

"Well, there's only one way to find out for sure if it worked," replied Sally, stepping back and cracking her knuckles. Then she paused.

"Well," she continued, "actually, there are a few other ways we could check—we could check the file systems and such—but this way is a lot more fun!"

Sally stared at the ground in front of Stan. She took a deep breath and pushed her open-palm hand forwards. Instantly, a three-block-high pillar appeared in front of Stan. These weren't blocks that Stan had seen before. They were dark stone blocks, streaked across the surface with the colors grey, black, and white.

"This is bedrock," Sally said, her eyebrows knit into a serious face. "It's the hardest block in Minecraft, it makes up the bottom layer of the world, and it's impossible to mine through. If you are a true operator, noob, you'll be able to destroy it in one punch."

"OK," Stan replied. He stared at the pillar, fists balled up under his chin. He bounced back and forth on the balls of his feet. He started mumbling to himself under his breath.

"All right . . . come on, Mr Block . . . you're going down . . . what, you made outta bedrock? I'll tell you what else is made of bedrock . . . my *fist*! Well actually . . . not really . . . but it's as hard as bedrock . . . well, not really, but metaphorically I mean . . . and metaphorically, it's just as tough, too . . . and I'll tell you what else, metaphorically . . . ."

"Just throw the stupid punch!" Sally shouted in irritation, snapping Stan out of it. He shook his head and focussed in on the block. Then, in one graceful motion, he pulled back his fist and sunk it as hard as he could into the bedrock block.

"Daaaugh!" Stan shouted, clenching his teeth as he grabbed his throbbing fist. He shot an irritated look up at the bedrock block, still sitting there, obnoxiously solid.

"Try again," sighed Sally in a bored voice.

"All right," grunted Stan, "let's *go . . . argh*!"

Once again, he shook his fist in pain. Angry now, he threw punch after punch into the bedrock block, all accompanied by grunts, and all resulting in nothing more than an awful lot of agony in his fists.

"You're doing it all wrong, noob," Sally spoke after a moment. "You're punching the block with all your strength, which is the totally wrong way of going about it. You know that you have the ability to destroy the block . . . but you're still going about it as if you didn't have the powers. You're punching the outside of the block. Don't stop at the surface, Stan . . . I want you to punch straight through!"

And with that, Sally leaped into the air, and threw a punch directly through the highest block in the tower. Stan watched her fist, and saw that she was right: she didn't stop the punch at the surface of the block. Her first plowed directly through the centre, causing the block to disappear in the process.

Stan took a deep breath and focussed on the block directly in front of him. He looked at the grey-streaked surface and drew back his fist. Then, with all his might, Stan drove his fist into the block. His fist shot through the centre of the bedrock block, and it disappeared into thin air. Stan's aching fist didn't feel a thing.

Stan drew back his hand, and looked at his fist in wonder.

"Congratulations, noob," said Sally with a smirk, clapping her hands together. "You're an operator now."

Stan grinned and looked back at Sally, overcome with jubilation.

"And all it took was a little advice from good ol' Sally," she continued with a laugh.

"You know," Stan said, looking at her in an adoringly accusatory way, "perhaps you could've brought up that insignificant little tidbit of advice *before* I nearly broke all my knuckles."

"Yeah, I suppose I could've . . . but that wouldn't have been *nearly* as funny, would it?" Sally responded with a chuckle. "Now come on, noob!" she continued as Stan glared at her in exasperation. "You've got to get back to Elementia soon, but there are a few things I want to show you first!"

Leonidas was beginning to worry. The search had been going on forever now, and every second that he sat holed up in the cave, the chances increased that Stan would return and find himself in the midst of a quintet of heavily armed Noctem fighters. Leonidas had managed to silently take out one of the soldiers who had wandered down the cave to search. He was able to replenish his supply of arrows from the archer. All the others were still scuttling around the tiny dirt island like ants on an anthill. Leonidas was just pondering how much more there was to search when he heard a shout from above.

"All troops, fall in!" Spyro's voice rang out.

Leonidas heard footfalls on the ground above his head, and he crept his way up the cave to spy on them, careful not to alert any bats in the process. He poked his head out of the side of the cave and saw the four black-clad players circled around Spyro, whose face was illuminated by the moonlight.

"OK, first and foremost," said Spyro, glancing around his men, "where's ShadowNinja?"

"I'm not sure," one of the players replied. Leonidas

recognized the distinct, high-pitched squeaky voice as Commander Squid, an old private of his. "He must still be out searching."

"Hmm . . . he can't be far . . . this is a pretty small island . . . ," Spyro said to himself. "Anyway, not important, we'll find him in a minute. For now, let's set up camp."

Leonidas's heart dropped out of his stomach. They were staying the night? He watched in horror as the Noctem soldiers pulled beds, furnaces and anvils from their inventories, setting them up all around the spot where Stan would no doubt be re-entering Elementia soon.

I have to kill them all, Leonidas thought desperately, *or at least severely weaken them. There's no way that Stan'll be able to handle that many guys if he comes back . . . he'll be totally blindsided! What should I do . . .*

Leonidas knew that he had no time whatsoever to think his plan out further; he would simply have to go for broke. Leonidas poked his head out from around the wall of the cave and drew his bow. He notched an arrow in the string, pulled it back, took aim, and, after he had a clear shot, he let it fly, ducking back into the cave immediately after he did so.

Leonidas heard the cry of anguish that accompanied his arrow and knew that he had hit the mark. He heard the shouts of surprise and terror from the ring of Noctem troops, and Spyro's voice bellowed out, "WHO'S THERE? SHOW YOURSELF!"

Heart pounding out of his chest, Leonidas readied another arrow, and took another shot at the circle, this time aiming for the closest soldier. Again, the shout of pain, and the renewed round of terrified confusion.

"What's going on here?"

"Who's shooting at us?"

"Look, over there! I saw someone in the mine!"

"Argh," Leonidas grunted to himself as he sprinted out into the open. He saw the three remaining soldiers glare at him, but he sprinted away before they could catch his eye.

"It's ShadowNinja! He betrayed us!" bellowed Spyro in fury.

For a moment, Leonidas was confused, but then he realized what had happened. The player he had killed in the mine—ShadowNinja, apparently—had also been an archer. They must have assumed that, with his black leather armour, he was their comrade gone renegade. In any case, thought Leonidas to himself, none of them would live to realize the truth.

Leonidas sprinted his way up to the top of the dirt mound that was the island, and when he was at the peak, he glanced down. Commander Squid was making his way up the island, eyes blazing in fury and iron axe in hand. Another figure who Leonidas didn't recognize was taking aim at him with a bow from the beach below. Leonidas had no idea where Spyro was, but he had more pressing matters to deal with at the moment.

Leonidas sidestepped the arrow fired his way from the beach, and stood back up to find that Commander Squid was upon him. He launched a powerful axe strike at Leonidas's head, which he simply ducked under, sending Squid tumbling back down the slope with a body check.

Having dealt with that problem for the time being, Leonidas then focused his attention on the archer on the beach. He had to duck two back-to-back arrows before he finally managed to get a clear shot on the archer. As fast as possible, Leonidas fired an arrow to the left of the archer, then directly at him, and then to the right. The plan worked; the archer hopped right to avoid the first two arrows, directly into the path of the third. Leonidas sent another well-placed arrow down to finish him, and the ring of items bursting from the beached archer indicated Leonidas's victory.

Leonidas hardly had time to celebrate, however, as Commander Squid was nearly back upon him. Almost effortlessly, Leonidas managed to stay out of the range of Squid's frantic axe swipes, and sunk three arrows into him in a matter of seconds. Leonidas took a deep breath and glanced around the island below him, hoping to locate where Spyro went.

Then, without warning, Leonidas sensed something behind him. He lunged as hard as he could out of the way of the diamond sword that had stabbed at him from behind. Leonidas fell off the top of the hill and landed on the ground with a crash, tumbling painfully down the hill until he landed with a thud on the beach below.

Aching but not badly hurt, Leonidas kicked up onto his feet, loading his bow and standing perfectly still, trying to control his breathing, in the hopes that he might feel the invisible player moving around him.

Before long, Leonidas sensed a presence coming directly towards him. He shot his arrow forwards to no avail, and was about to fire another when an invisible fist sunk hard into Leonidas's stomach, knocking the wind out of him. This was quickly followed by an uppercut under his chin that sent him flying backwards, leaving him sprawled out on the ground. Dazed, Leonidas focussed hard on staying conscious. When a sword appeared from nowhere above him, Leonidas suddenly felt wide awake as he rolled to the side. The sword drove deep into the ground, and Leonidas sent another arrow flying towards the weapon.

There was a grunt of agony as the arrow found its mark, and Leonidas saw the pained body of General Spyro flash into view for a moment before it disappeared again. However, the arrow in his arm remained, revealing where he was. Then,

Leonidas watched in horror as a Potion of Healing poured onto the wound. The arrow popped out of the invisible arm and onto the sand.

"Well, well, well," the invisible Spyro laughed to himself as he picked up the arrow from the ground and snapped it in half. "If it isn't Leonidas . . . the once-great general of the Noctem Alliance."

Leonidas was too exhausted to answer. He chose to devote his energy to coming up with an attack plan during this moment of rest rather than responding.

"I'm gonna get another promotion for this kill," Spyro laughed to himself. "They'll have to invent a rank above general!" And with that, the levitating diamond sword barrelled forwards, straight towards Leonidas.

Having not established a surefire plan yet, Leonidas raised his bow to fire again, but Spyro's sword cleaved it in half, the tension of the weapon sending the two halves flying into the distance. In the following instant, Leonidas considered drawing the bow he had gotten from ShadowNinja, but instead chose to draw his iron sword and engage Spyro in combat.

The effort, however, was futile. Spyro outclassed Leonidas in sword fighting by a remarkable degree, and it wasn't long before Leonidas's sword spiralled high in the air, landing with a splash in the nearby ocean. Leonidas took off sprinting, though from what, he did not know. He now realized that his efforts were futile and, eventually, Spyro was going to catch him.

Suddenly, Leonidas came across a block-high drop on the sand beach and, not expecting it, he tripped and tumbled across the sand. He landed face-up, and he became aware that Spyro's diamond sword was just blocks away from him.

This is it, thought Leonidas as the diamond sword rose above him. He closed his eyes.

Then, Leonidas heard a clash of two blades, and a grunt of pain. A moment later, he heard the sound of a player landing on the dirt, and Spyro's voice yelling out, "What the . . ."

Leonidas opened his eyes, and painfully propped himself up on his arm before glancing up. Standing there, his back to Leonidas, was a player. In the faint moonlight, Leonidas could just make out dark-coloured trousers and shoes. A black cloak obscured the top half of his body, blowing faintly in the ocean breeze. In his pale left hand he held a diamond sword, pointed at the ground.

Leonidas saw Spyro a distance away. He was sitting on the sand and flashing in and out of sight as his Potion of Invisibility began to wear off. Spyro glanced up at the mysterious hooded figure standing between him and Leonidas and looked shocked, infuriated and scared.

"Who are you? Where did you come from?" Spyro demanded.

The figure didn't answer. He simply stood there, not moving a muscle.

"That player is a wanted criminal. In the name of the Noctem Alliance and Lord Tenebris, I order you to stand down!" bellowed Spyro, raising his diamond sword into an attack stance.

Again, the figure didn't respond. But he did raise his right arm, crossing his sword over the front of his body in what was clearly a defensive stance.

"All right, if that's the way it is!" hissed Spyro as he charged the hooded figure. The Noctem general launched countless high-power sword strikes at the figure. The speed and technique was very impressive, yet the figure was able to block every attack without moving a muscle except for his right hand.

After a minute of fighting, the figure executed a twist-block manoeuvre, sending Spyro's sword flying, and he sunk his left fist hard into Spyro's stomach. Spyro fell to the ground with a thud, cringing in pain. The figure didn't continue the attack; rather, he simply moved his sword back into a defensive stance.

Grimacing, Spyro looked back up at the figure, tears in his eyes.

"Who . . . what . . . are you?" he managed to get out, fear manifested in his voice.

The figure, once again, said nothing. Spyro gazed into the face of the figure for a full minute. And then . . .

"You're gonna get it," Spyro spat, and he whipped a boat out of his inventory and hopped in the water, moving as fast as possible back in the general direction of the Mushroom Islands.

Leonidas looked up at the figure, wondering what to say. He had no idea who this player was, or where he came from, but he had just saved Leonidas's life.

The robed figure turned to face Leonidas. As Leonidas glanced up, he realized that he could not see the figure's face. The black cloak covered the upper body, and the hood obscured the upper half of the player's face, revealing only a pale mouth. And although the figure still said nothing, Leonidas somehow knew the figure's name, despite having no idea who he was.

"Thank you, Black Hood," Leonidas whispered.

The Black Hood turned to face the ocean. Then, in an instant, he dived into the water and disappeared into the murky depths. Leonidas forced his aching body to stand up and glance down, hoping to catch any indication of where the player had gone. And yet there was nothing. When the ripples of the splash finally disappeared, it was as if nobody had ever been there.

Leonidas was perplexed, and was about to start pondering

what had just happened when he heard a noise across the island. Quietly, Leonidas crept back to the top of the island and glanced over the peak. The view of the ocean expanded forever up here, and Leonidas could see Spyro's ship going further and further into the distance. And on the bottom beach of the island, Leonidas could see Stan, pulling a bed from his inventory and walking over to the cave.

Leonidas realized just how tired he was. Stan had the right idea; it was late. Leonidas was far too exhausted to think about Spyro, now delivering his whereabouts to Lord Tenebris, or to figure out just who it was who had just saved his life. All Leonidas wanted to do was find the softest pile of dirt he could and go to sleep.

As G and Jayden walked down the hallway towards the Training Centre Gymnasium, neither of them spoke. They both knew that, to keep their cover, they should have been chatting like the other trainees around them, eager to partake in the sparring tournament that was only moments away. However, they had given themselves a pass, as they had both been plagued with nightmares last night after yesterday's tour.

Not that the tour hadn't been extremely helpful, because it had. The walk around the Capitol Building had been crucial to figuring out where the Adorian hostages might be held. There had been areas where the tour wasn't allowed to go, and they had pegged those as various places where the hostages might be. The tour of the training facility had been equally helpful, as the layout would have to be memorized if they wanted to be able to make an impromptu escape.

However, towards the end of the tour, the two boys had seen a sight that would haunt them forever. From a glass room overlooking a dark, stone pen, they had finally gotten a glimpse of Stull and Mella. The two Zombie villagers were disgusting, letting out moaning noises and occasionally garbled rambles that resembled speech. Jayden and G had watched in horror as unconscious Elementia soldiers had been dropped into the pen, immobile prey to the Zombie villagers.

It was all that the boys could do to stop from getting sick, and they weren't the only ones. While a few of the recruits either watched in amazement or cheered for the Zombies, the majority of the players just looked really uncomfortable. None could feel the effects more profoundly than Jayden and G, though. Those villagers had visited them in Elementia a good few times, and the sight of them eating Elementia soldiers haunted them even the next day as they went into the area.

"Welcome," said Tess as the recruits filed into rows, the early-morning sunlight blinding them from the glass roof above. "Today is your Aptitude Tournament. You will be called up by me, and two players will fight each other until one is unable to continue. Killing and permanent crippling is not allowed, but all else is. The winner will advance to the next round, and so on. Based on your performance during your fights, I will determine your base rankings during your training. Now, everyone stand at the sidelines. The first fight will be between MasterBronze and LemonKipper."

G took a deep breath and stood up; MasterBronze was his cover name. He stood in the centre of the ring, and another player stepped into the arena across from him. Although he was now covered in black leather armour, G recognized this player. He had the skin of a merman, and was cocky to a fault.

A black foot soldier stepped forwards from behind Tess and walked over to the two of them. "What is your weapon of choice?" he asked G.

"Pickaxe," G grunted in response, and the soldier reached into his inventory, pulled out a stone pickaxe, and handed it to G. *Well,* he thought, turning it over in his hand, *it's not diamond, but it'll have to do.*

"What is your weapon of choice?" the soldier asked, turning to face Kipper.

"Sword," Kipper replied in a Welsh accent, snatching the stone sword that the soldier had pulled from his inventory.

"OK," Tess announced as the soldier backed away. "Ready? And . . . Fight!"

G raised his pickaxe in a defensive stance, allowing Kipper to make the first move. He gladly obliged, holding his sword in an attack stance and bouncing on the balls of his feet.

"You're going down, kid," Kipper hissed as he tried for an overhand strike at G's head. In one motion, G sidestepped the attack, caught the sword in his pickaxe, and twisted the weapon out of Kipper's grip. Then G dropped to the floor and swept Kipper's leg, sending him tumbling to the ground. While his foe was dazed, G grabbed the stone point of his pickaxe and clubbed Kipper over the head with the wooden end, knocking him out.

"We have a winner!" Tess announced, and all the recruits clapped. G didn't feel like it was much of an accomplishment. Kipper obviously wasn't a very skilled fighter. He took his place back in line, and received an encouraging nod from Jayden.

A series of fights followed the first one, ranging from two totally equally matched fighters, to two cowards running away from each other, to one player totally dominating the other. G found the fights to be rather tedious, and only really paid attention when it was Jayden's turn.

Jayden's fight was against an archer, and he initially played defensive, blocking every arrow shot with his stone axe. Eventually, though, he found an opening, and managed to use a carefully placed axe throw to deliver a leg wound, causing him to win so the wound could be healed with potion.

The next round of the top eight fighters wasn't very interesting either. Both Jayden and G outmatched their opponents by a considerable degree, and managed to take them out without much effort. The other matches were slightly more interesting to watch at least, ranging from an intense sword fight to two archers sniping at each other.

After the top eight were narrowed to the top four, a series of matches ensued that were a bit more interesting.

Jayden locked swords with an impressive pickaxe fighter, who used the weapon more as a projectile than a mêlée weapon, dodging Jayden's axe swipes while trying to hit him from afar. Eventually, though, Jayden was able to land a solid blow on her, and he won.

G went into combat with one of the archers, who actually gave him a rough time. The pickaxe was much harder to block arrows with than the axe, and the archer actually managed to land a couple of shots. It wasn't long, though, before G managed to force an approach, and he won his battle with a blow to the stomach not long afterwards.

"OK," announced Tess as the last cringing recruit pulled himself off the field. "We're down to the final round. It's MasterBronze versus Drayden!"

Taking a deep breath, G walked back into the ring. As he looked Jayden in the eye, it occurred to him that he really didn't know who would win this match. Although he and Jayden were both easily better than the rest of the recruits, mostly upper-level players who had lived their whole lives in luxury, he and Jayden were both a bit out of practice. They hadn't sparred at all since before King Kev had fallen, when they were still working in the Adorian Village together. And even back then, they were very evenly matched.

"Ready . . . and . . . FIGHT!" announced Tess.

G caught Jayden's eye, and he knew they were both

thinking the same thing. The two of them had the same fighting style, where they played defensive until they found an opening, and then broke into a ruthless, all-out attack. But if both of them played off counterattacking, then how were either of them going to win?

G sunk into an offensive stance. *It doesn't really matter who wins,* he thought to himself, a*s long as we both get high scores so we can work our way into the higher ranks of the army faster. So I guess I'll give Jayden an opening.*

G rushed in, pickaxe blazing, as Jayden sunk back, ready to counter. Just as he was about to strike, though, he cut left, dodging Jayden's axe jab and knocking the axe out of his hand with a stray strike. G lunged in to follow up with a pickaxe blow, but Jayden rolled out of the way, landing by his axe. Jayden snatched his weapon off the ground and sent it spiralling through the air towards his opponent. G feinted out of the way, but the handle of the flying axe caught his hand, sending his pickaxe into the air. Jayden and G watched as their weapons clattered to the ground beside each other.

The two friends caught each other's eyes for a moment, and then rushed as quickly as possible to retrieve their weapons. G had the head start, but Jayden was faster, and they grabbed them at the exact same time. The two players pressed into each other's blades as hard as they could, struggling for an advantage. Then, right as G was thinking that he couldn't keep up the fight much longer, the two stone blades shattered into a thousand pieces, sending the two players reeling back away from each other.

G turned around to glance at Tess, unsure of whether or not he was in trouble. She just looked at him expectantly, waiting for him to finish. A lightbulb going on in his head, G sprinted towards the recovering Jayden. As the two locked eyes, G, with his back to the others, winked at Jayden and made a face as if he were knocked out before drawing back a punch.

Jayden got the message. G threw the punch at Jayden's head, missing him by a millimetre, but Jayden still went tumbling backwards through the air. He landed on the ground with a thud, seemingly unconscious.

"Well done, MasterBronze," Tess said with a smile as a soldier went over to Jayden and poured a Potion of Healing in his mouth. Jayden's eyes fluttered, then opened as he pulled himself to his feet. Though he was rubbing his face where he got punched, he still walked over to G and shook his hand. As the other recruits cheered for them, Jayden shot G a smile and a wink, which he happily returned.

Kat took a deep breath as she caught sight of a Noctem soldier walking down the hallway. She forced herself not to look, and instead to focus on the unarmoured back of Cassandrix, and the pickaxe she was holding up to it.

As the duo passed the soldier, he gave a polite nod in Kat's direction. She returned the gesture, and continued walking down the hallway, until he was out of sight.

Kat released the breath she had been holding in. It was a relief to know that the armour that Cassandrix had looted from the Noctem guard disguised her so well. She told herself that it was all fine, and that even if she was captured, she could always just call Rex back out of hiding to help her.

"Seen anything yet?" Kat hissed to Cassandrix as they turned left down a hallway, past a new row of jail cells.

"If I had seen either of them, darling," Cassandrix whispered back in irritation, "don't you think I would have said something?"

Kat bit her tongue to hold back her retort, and forced herself to keep walking. It hurt her to see that, while most of the jail cells were empty, some of them housed players who were clearly not even soldiers. She could only assume they were civilians from the Mushroom Islands. As much as she wanted to, Kat knew that she couldn't break those players out. They just had to find Charlie and Commander Crunch as quickly as possible and be on their way.

The two rounded another corner and checked another row of jail cells, lining both sides of a hallway that led to an iron door. None of these cells held Charlie or Crunch either;

in fact, they were all vacant. Kat snorted in irritation, and was just about to make a left turn at the iron door when a soldier stepped around the corner and into her way.

"What do you think you're doing here, soldier?" the player demanded. He had the skin of an extremely muscular Mexican wrestler.

"I'm just moving this prisoner to a holding block for interrogation," replied Kat sombrely, hoping that her prison jargon was believable.

"Do you have clearance to come this way?" the guard interrogated further.

"No," replied Kat, gears whirring in her head. "I wasn't aware that this area was blocked off."

"Lord Tenebris is operating dangerous procedures behind that door, kid," the soldier grunted.

Kat's eyebrows shot up. "He is?"

The guard eyed Kat suspiciously. "Of course . . . and you should know that. Weren't you at the meeting this morning, soldier?"

"Well, I . . . uh . . ."

"You're an imposter!" the guard exclaimed. "*Secu—* ugh . . ."

The guard's shout was cut off as Cassandrix launched forwards and wrapped her arms around the guard's neck in a chokehold. Before he could shake her off, Kat slammed the pickaxe into the guard's forehead, knocking him out, and finished him off with a powerful blow to the stomach. A ring of items, mainly food, burst from the player and onto the ground.

"Hey! What's going on over there?" a voice rang out from down the hall, and Kat heard the stomping of footsteps running towards them. Kat raised her pickaxe and dropped into a defensive stance, and was just about to panic when a pair of hands whipped her around. Cassandrix was looking back at her, clad head to toe in the dead soldier's black armour.

"Stay calm," Cassandrix murmured, "and follow my lead."

And with that, Cassandrix bent down and began to pick through the items lying on the ground as the soldier's body disappeared. Kat did the same, praying that Cassandrix did indeed have a plan.

Moments later, a group of six players, armed with bows and fire charges, burst around the corner and aimed directly at the two girls.

"What happened here, soldiers?" the player at the front of the group demanded.

"It was an escape attempt," Cassandrix replied solemnly. "We were transporting a prisoner to interrogation, and she tried to overwhelm us. We were forced to kill her . . . and judging by the inventory she dropped, she's been planning this escape for a while, hoarding her food and everything."

"Which prisoner was it?" the head guard asked. "And what cell did she come from?"

"Well, I know that the prisoner's name was Cassandrix," Cassandrix continued, giving Kat a glare of steel when her eyes widened, "but I'm not sure what cell she was from. The two of us received her a few hallways back from another pair of soldiers whom I didn't recognize."

"Well, if that's the case, I'm going to have to ask the two of you to come with me," the head guard ordered as his soldiers lowered their bows. "General Spyro will be returning from the island raids soon, and you'll present all your findings to him."

"I'm sorry, but that's not possible at the moment," Cassandrix replied, not missing a beat. "The two of us were meant to escort the prisoner to this point, and then hand her off to yet another pair of guards. You see, we were ordered to stop here to guard this door . . . as I'm sure you know, the illustrious Lord Tenebris is operating dangerous procedures in there."

"Very well then," the guard replied. "Who was supposed to pick up the prisoner from the two of you?"

"Again, I'm not sure," Cassandrix replied. "My apologies, but my partner and I are new transfers to Mount Fungarus. We still don't know everybody yet. . . But as soon as we're done standing guard for the glorious Lord Tenebris, I promise you that we'll be able to show you who the players are if you line up the guards in front of us."

The head guard nodded. "All right, soldier. I trust that you and your partner will report back to the common area as soon as your duties here are completed."

"Please," Cassandrix replied with a snide chuckle. "We stopped an escape on our second day here! Don't think for a moment that we won't want to personally take credit for that."

"Right," the guard said with an amused smile. "At ease, soldiers." And with that, he turned and marched away, followed by the rest of his archers.

Kat looked at Cassandrix in admiration. "That was amazing!" she exclaimed.

"Well, you know, I'm quite good on my feet, darling," Cassandrix simpered. "One would think that after all your experience against me in the Spleef arena, you would realize that."

Always has to kill the moment, doesn't she, thought Kat bitterly. Then again, with the way Cassandrix had managed to save them just then, Kat was willing to let it slide.

The two players turned to face the iron door. Kat reached for the stone button on the wall, but Cassandrix slapped her hand down.

"What do you think you're doing?" Cassandrix demanded.

"Lord Tenebris is behind that door!" Kat whispered urgently. "This might be our only chance to see him . . . or maybe even to take a shot at him."

"Are you insane?" Cassandrix hissed. "Now is neither the time nor place to pull a vigilante stunt. We have a mission, Kat, and even with your abnormally lacking attention span, I'd think you'd be able to remember that."

"I didn't forget," Kat growled, "but this might be our only chance."

"You already said that, Kat," Cassandrix cut in, "and frankly, it's not worth it. You're willing to risk what might be your one chance to save your friends just so you *might* have a *tiny chance* to take down Lord Tenebris?"

"Well . . ."

"Kat, we might never be in this situation again! The guards think that we're with them, and we have plenty of time before they realize that we've escaped! And furthermore . . . GET BACK HERE RIGHT NOW!"

Cassandrix sprinted forwards to grab Kat, who had jammed the button on the wall and was already through the iron door. Cassandrix pulled on Kat's tunic as hard as she could, but Kat was too strong, and Cassandrix tumbled forwards through the passage just as the iron door slammed shut behind them.

The two girls were now standing in a room made entirely of stone. Redstone lamps kept the areas light enough to keep mobs from spawning, but even then it was quite dark. The room had a very high ceiling, with stone pillars that stretched from the floor to the top. Across from them, standing against the other wall, was a Nether Portal, glowing purple with luminescence and spewing purple particles into the room. Between the two pillars furthest away sat a throne made entirely of obsidian.

Cassandrix looked around wildly, trying to find another button on this side of the wall. She was shocked, however, to find none. Except for the indentation of the door, the wall on this side was totally flat.

"Oh, for heaven's sake," whined Cassandrix, "who designs a door that automatically locks from the outside?"

"Uh, I don't know," replied Kat, shrugging her shoulders. "Admittedly, that doesn't seem like a very practical design choice . . ."

Cassandrix wheeled around to face her partner. Her face was alight with fury.

"Look what you did, you little brat!" she hissed. "We're trapped in here with no way to get back . . . wait a second!" Cassandrix's eyes drifted slowly to the pickaxe Kat was holding. Before she could respond, Cassandrix had snatched the iron tool from her hand.

"What are you doing?" Kat demanded as Cassandrix fervently rushed her way back over to the stone wall.

"I'm getting us back to the safe side of the wall!" she said, her eyes almost glowing with lunatic fervour as she drove the iron pickaxe as hard as she could into the stone wall.

The effect was immediate. The iron pickaxe snapped off its handle, and landed on the floor with a clang.

For a moment, Cassandrix stared blankly at the wooden handle of the tool. Then, without warning, she sunk to her knees, clutching her head in exasperation, and bemoaning the fact that not only were they now trapped, but they had lost one of the only weapons that they had. As Cassandrix lay crippled on the floor, mumbling to herself, Kat picked up the two parts of the weapon and examined them, fascinated.

"This pickaxe . . ." she said slowly, glancing at the two halves. "It looks like . . . it looks as if this thing has never been used before. The blade is shiny, and there aren't any dents on it. . . If I didn't know better, I'd say that this pickaxe has never seen mining or combat before. I mean, it certainly wasn't close to being used up when you tried to use it . . ."

Kat glanced incredulously up at the stone wall. "What kind of stone is this?" she asked quizzically.

As Cassandrix glanced up at the wall, she suddenly forgot to act distraught. She was intrigued, and also a bit unnerved, by this wall. The stone that made up the wall wasn't cobblestone, nor any variety of it. These were dark stone blocks, streaked across the surface with the colours grey, black and white.

"Kat, I recognize this," Cassandrix said slowly. "This room . . . it's made out of bedrock."

"I'm not familiar," Kat said, glancing at the wall. "It must be pretty hard, though. Is this . . . bedrock . . . harder to mine through than obsidian?"

"It's not just hard to mine through. It's *impossible* to mine through," Cassandrix whispered. "Nothing in all of Minecraft can put a dent in this stuff, not even a charged Creeper blast. Usually it makes up the bottom of the world, and indicates the absolute lowest point that you can mine."

"So . . . if it can't be mined . . . what's it doing up here?" Kat asked.

"There's only one explanation," Cassandrix replied, and she turned to look Kat directly in the eye. "This bedrock must have been put here by someone . . . or something . . . incredibly powerful."

Just at that moment, the two girls heard a whooshing sound and saw a flash of purple light. Somebody was entering through the Nether Portal. Thinking fast, the two of them ducked behind the nearest pillar.

Peeking round the sides, Kat and Cassandrix watched with racing hearts as a player walked into the centre of the area, right before the obsidian throne. The player was dressed in black trousers and a black shirt, and a golden cloak was draped over his shoulders, the hood pulled back. He turned his head, and Kat recognized the face of Count Drake.

A twinge of resentment struck Kat. She had vivid memories of her past encounters with Drake, from his escape from Brimstone up to his attack on the Spleef World Finals. She pulled a bow and arrow that she had looted from the dead guard and drew it back. She was starting to take aim when suddenly, Drake knelt down before the obsidian throne and spoke.

"Oh great and powerful Lord Tenebris," Drake chanted, "I have returned!"

There was a sound, the same sound an Enderman made upon teleporting. And then, all at once, a player appeared on the throne.

This player had dark brown hair and shoes, a turquoise shirt, and navy-blue trousers. His eyes were closed, and his fingers were pressed together in front of him in a business-like manner.

Kat felt the need to slap herself, because she couldn't believe that what she was seeing was real. Could that . . . could it really be . . .

"Oh, exalted one," Drake replied from his position on

his knees, "I have acquired the materials that you have requested."

"You have done well, General Drake," the figure replied in a deep, booming voice as he opened his eyes.

Kat sighed in relief. Now she knew for sure that it wasn't Stan. She knew for a fact that Stan didn't have that deep, booming voice, nor did he have white eyes.

Kat was a little bit surprised. She didn't know exactly what she was expecting of Lord Tenebris, the founder and supreme commander of the Noctem Alliance, but it certainly wasn't this. This player didn't look at all like he would be the most evil person in Elementia since King Kev. In fact, except for his eyes, he looked exactly identical to Stan.

Those eyes, though . . . there was something incredibly disturbing about those eyes. As Kat looked at them, she tried to see if there were any traces of familiarity. However, she could only look into them for a few seconds before she had to look away in discomfort.

Kat turned to Cassandrix to see what she thought, expecting her to be equally confused. What she didn't expect to see was Cassandrix staring slack-jawed at Lord Tenebris, eyes bulging, expression as terrified as if she had laid eyes on a ghost. Kat assumed that she was just petrified that she was staring face to face with the leader of the Noctem Alliance, but she still couldn't help but feel as if Cassandrix had just realized something about Lord Tenebris that she herself hadn't.

"Thank you, sir, your praise means the world to me," Drake spoke on. "And I assure you, the collection of these materials was not easy."

"And why is that?" Lord Tenebris asked, raising an eyebrow. "You had all you needed to obtain the materials in a timely manner."

"Oh, no, sir," Drake replied quickly, his voice shaky. "I found the patch of Soul Sand without difficulty. However, in terms of the Wither Skeletons, they required . . . how should I put this . . . a bit more thought to handle."

"Go on," inquired Lord Tenebris, tapping his fingers together.

"Well," continued Drake, "as of now, I thought that it might be . . . shall we say . . . prudent to not anger the Wither Skeletons. Our forces have nearly broken through the walls of Element City, and when they do, I have a feeling that we'll need all the security in Brimstone that we can get our hands on."

"I suppose," Lord Tenebris replied, sounding bored, while chills went down Kat's spine. She couldn't help but worry about just how truthful Drake was being, and just how close the walls of Element City really were to cracking.

"In any case, I peacefully requested that they supply their Skulls to me, for the sake of appeasing you, Your Benevolence. They were able to give me two skulls of their fallen brethren after long negotiations, and then volunteers offered to sacrifice themselves for the sake of providing their own skulls.

"It was a tedious process, Your Highness, and many

Wither Skeletons lost their lives—or, rather, afterlives. You see, even with a level-three Looting enchantment, the Wither Skeletons have only slightly over a five percent chance—"

"I'm well aware, Drake," Lord Tenebris cut in irritably.

"Oh, I apologize, great leader," Drake sputtered hastily, sinking into a deep bow. "By no means was I trying to imply that you were in any way—"

"Silence," Lord Tenebris hissed, cutting off Drake's babbling. "It doesn't matter. Did you complete your task?"

"Yes, sir," Drake replied, reaching into his inventory and laying several items on the ground before him. "Four blocks of Soul Sand and three Wither Skulls, all natural and obtained from the Nether, as requested."

"Excellent," Lord Tenebris replied, talking to himself under his breath. "This is most ideal. . . . When they're made with natural materials, they're so much easier to control than synthetic ones. . . Oh, and one more thing," he said, now addressing his general directly.

"Yes, o glorious one?" Drake replied meekly.

"Your judgment in this scenario was good. Preserving the Wither Skeletons was indeed a wise decision. However," Lord Tenebris continued with a dark look on his face, "I must advise you to never again disobey my orders."

"Oh, my lord . . . I am so sorry!" cried out Drake, tears streaming down his face.

"Don't fret, Drake, I won't punish you this time," Lord Tenebris replied lazily. "However, watch yourself in the future. I must be sure that all my subjects are unwaveringly loyal to me. If they're not, then they are a threat to the Alliance and must be destroyed. And you know that I will not hesitate, Drake. Just look at what happened to Minotaurus and Blackraven if you need more proof."

As Lord Tenebris gave an evil laugh and Drake cowered in fear, Kat felt a whiplash of shock hit her. What *had* happened to Blackraven and Minotaurus? Were they . . . did that mean . . . that they had betrayed the Noctem Alliance? Had Lord Tenebris killed them?

"Leave me now, Drake," Lord Tenebris commanded. "Await my next command outside. And send the villager in."

Drake stood up and, with his head still bowed, he backed out of the room through a door next to the Nether Portal that Kat hadn't noticed before. Moments later, another figure stepped out of the door, and Kat gasped. Into the centre of the room walked Oob, his skin sickly green with red eyes and tattered brown robes. The Zombie villager walked to the front of Lord Tenebris's throne.

"Villager," Lord Tenebris said calmly to Oob. "Whatever I say, I am going to need you to repeat in your vernacular. Do you understand, villager?"

"Oob . . . udder . . . stand . . ." Oob croaked out.

Kat's head was spinning. Oob was there! He was still alive! And . . . he was working with Lord Tenebris?

All Kat could do was watch in horror as Lord Tenebris stepped down from his throne and gathered the materials that Drake had left on the ground. Lord Tenebris assembled the dark-brown blocks—Drake had called them Soul Sand—into a T shape. Kat glanced at Cassandrix. Although her partner's face still showed absolute terror at the mere sight of Lord Tenebris, Kat also detected a slight element of confusion; she didn't know what was happening either.

The two girls watched as Lord Tenebris placed each of the tiny grey Wither Skeleton skulls on top of the Soul Sand formation. After he fastened the last one in place, Lord Tenebris took a step back and stood directly in front of his throne. Kat watched with bated breath as the eyes of the skulls glowed white, getting brighter and brighter, until finally a flash of light illuminated the room. In the moment of blindness, a horrible suction sound filled the room, like a demon taking its first breath. When Kat's vision returned, she saw a sight that made her heart drop into her stomach.

A mob stood in front of Lord Tenebris, but it wasn't just any mob. It was huge, almost the size of a Ghast. Its body consisted of nothing but a black spine, trailing off into a tail and wrapped in the center by a dusky black rib cage. Atop this skeletal body were three heads, perched on a wide, bony structure. The heads were black skulls, and they all looked around in different directions. The skulls all had empty white eyes and mouths, and they were taking deep, husky breaths. The creature was the most terrifying thing that Kat had ever seen.

"Behold, villager," Lord Tenebris spoke out, a half smile flashing across his face as he gazed adoringly at the newborn demon. "The Wither."

Suddenly, the creature began to flash blue and white. Cassandrix and Kat were transfixed on the beast in horror, wondering what this monster, the Wither, was going to do next. Kat started to perceive a change around her. She couldn't quite put her finger on what it was, but it was almost as if all the light, warmth and energy in the room were being sucked out, and were condensing toward the Wither. Kat saw Lord Tenebris take a deep breath and raise a hand in front of him, and suddenly, she guessed what was about to happen. As the Wither gave another ghastly moan, Kat ducked totally behind the pillar, pulling Cassandrix along with her, and covered her eyes and ears.

"What are you . . ." Cassandrix hissed, before she was cut off by the explosion.

A thousand megatons of light and sound bombarded the area around Kat and Cassandrix, only missing them because of the indestructible bedrock pillar in front of them.

Kat could feel the incredible rush of energy that engulfed the area around them. It felt like she was standing inches away from a passing bullet train. Only when the light and sound had completely died down did Kat dare peek her head back around the side of the pillar.

The monster was now floating in midair. The three heads glanced freely around the room, taking in all that was around it. As the heads of the Wither basked in their newfound existence, Kat couldn't help but feel as if she were looking at the very faces of evil itself, which sucked all that was good in the world into a void of darkness.

Suddenly, six eyes of the Wither focused on Lord Tenebris, still standing in the open alongside Oob, both of them somehow totally unharmed by the blast. He smiled.

"My name is Lord Tenebris," he said smoothly. "I am your creator, and I am your master."

Oob let out a loud Zombie roar, and the Wither Skeleton glanced at him, seeming to understand. The three heads looked back and forth between one another, and then back at Lord Tenebris. Then, all of a sudden, the mouth of the middle and largest Wither head opened and expelled a small black projectile, which sped at rocket speed toward Lord Tenebris.

The Noctem Leader didn't move. He simply stretched out his hand, and when the projectile made contact, it exploded, engulfing him in smoke. Moments later, the smoke cleared, showing Lord Tenebris totally unharmed.

Kat couldn't process what she had just seen. This Wither had just shot an explosive projectile from its mouth at Lord Tenebris. And he hadn't even been hurt by it.

The middle Wither head let out a raspy roar of fury, and spit even more skulls in Lord Tenebris's direction. Again, he simply held out his hand, and the black projectiles, which Kat could now see as tiny skulls, were simply rupturing on contact, leaving no damage whatsoever. Before long, the other two Wither heads joined in as well, sending a constant barrage of three streams of explosive Wither skulls directly at Lord Tenebris. And yet he continued to take the punishment as effortlessly as if they were blowing wind at him.

Kat didn't know what she found the most alarming about what she was witnessing. On the one hand, the Wither was clearly an incredibly powerful mob. She could feel the force of its blasts from behind her pillar. The explosions were far stronger than those of the Creeper, and the Wither was dishing them out like machine-gun fire. And on the other hand, Lord Tenebris, their archenemy, the one they had vowed to destroy, was totally unfazed by this onslaught of destructive power.

Then, without warning, Lord Tenebris raised his right hand and pointed it directly at the Wither. Instantly, the mob stopped firing on Lord Tenebris and gave a shallow moan of pain. Kat looked on, having trouble convincing herself she wasn't in the midst of a nightmare, as Lord Tenebris lowered his left hand. As he did, the Wither floated downwards, still squealing in agony, until it was finally forced onto the ground.

A serious frown crossed Lord Tenebris's face. "I said, I am your master. Should you disobey my commands, you will be subjected to this."

Lord Tenebris waited for Oob to finish translating and then he squeezed his fist. Instantly, the Wither gave the highest, loudest and most ear-piercingly shrill cry of all, as it squirmed on the ground in excruciating pain.

Kat knew that she ought to feel sorry for the killer beast, but she was too busy dealing with overwhelming dread as she watched Lord Tenebris exercise his mysterious powers. She hadn't been prepared to deal with anything like this. Whenever she had imagined Lord Tenebris, she had pictured a master swordfighter, with an army of soldiers at his command. But this . . . Kat knew that no player in all of Elementia could stand a chance against whatever Lord Tenebris was.

After a moment, Lord Tenebris released the Wither. The giant mob floated back into the air, a tangible element of fear now in its six white eyes.

"Do you understand?" Lord Tenebris asked, followed by a grunt by Oob.

Instantly, the middle head of the Wither let out a brief moan while looking at Oob. The Zombie villager turned to Lord Tenebris and spoke.

"It . . . udder . . . stand."

Lord Tenebris smiled. "Good. Now, come here behind me."

At Oob's command, the Wither proceeded to levitate over Lord Tenebris's head and make an about-face until it was floating behind him. Lord Tenebris turned his head to face the door next to the Nether Portal.

"Enter, Drake. And bring the prisoners with you."

The iron door swung open, and Kat's heart lifted. Through the door, and into the main hall of the bedrock room, marched Charlie and Commander Crunch, followed by Drake holding a diamond sword to their backs.

Although Kat had never met Commander Crunch before, he seemed to be holding up relatively well. Even though he did look tired, his uniform torn and his beard unkempt, he still walked with a strong spirit to him. He glanced around the room in a wily manner, as if plotting out the best method of escape.

Charlie, on the other hand, looked absolutely terrible. His face was covered in bruises, his clothes were tattered and worn out, and he limped into the room, barely able to stay up on his own feet. Kat was beside herself with worry the second she laid eyes on him. Clearly, the time in the prison had taken a heavy toll on him, and the torture of the Noctem Alliance had been nothing short of ruthless.

"Argh, 'tis *you* again!" bellowed out Commander Crunch in his gruff voice as he caught sight of Lord Tenebris. "Don't ye know when enough be enough, ye great bloated fool?"

"Oh, you're in no position to be insulting me, Commander," Lord Tenebris said coolly. "You see, I've found a new method of persuading you to tell me the information that you've been withholding from me."

"Sink me, ye mean that thin'?" laughed Crunch, gesturing to the Wither levitating high above the head of Lord Tenebris. "Ye reckon some giant mutant worm wit' th' face o' th' Jolly Roger will intimidate me? Reckon again, ye scallywag! I'll die before I break, I tell ye!"

Although Commander Crunch was laughing like a lunatic, Charlie was a different story. He glanced up at the Wither in a state of total panic. Kat could see him hyperventilating, clearly terrified as he imagined what the three-headed skeletal demon could do to him.

As Commander Crunch cackled on and Lord Tenebris whispered something in Oob's ear, Kat ducked back behind the pillar. She spun Cassandrix, who had been watching the process with a sickened look on her face, to face her.

"We have to do something," Kat whispered urgently. "They're gonna use that thing to torture Charlie and Crunch!

We need a plan, right now! Any ideas?"

"Well . . . it's not much of an idea . . ." said Cassandrix slowly.

"We can't waste time!" Kat hissed, panic ripe on her face. "If you have even the stupidest idea in the world, tell me now!"

"OK," said Cassandrix, taking a deep breath, and shaking her head clear of the sickening feeling that had overtaken her since she had first seen Lord Tenebris. "Here's what we do. I noticed that there's a lever on the wall at the far end of the room."

Kat glanced down to the other end of the room, opposite where Charlie and Crunch were being forced to their knees by Drake. Indeed, Cassandrix was right. There was a switch on the far wall, and furthermore, the wall wasn't made out of bedrock like the rest of the room. Rather, it was made out of stone, and Kat could see that multiple pistons were positioned on the top and bottom of the wall itself.

"I think that wall," continued Cassandrix hastily, "might be an opening, like a hangar door, so the Wither will be able to fly out of here. If we can get to that lever and open the door, this place will get filled with sunlight, which will give us a distraction for a second."

"OK . . . and what do we do with that distraction?" Kat asked eagerly.

"I don't know!" exclaimed Cassandrix. "I told you it wasn't much of an idea . . . more of a notion, really . . ."

"Aaaarrrgh!"

The growl of pain echoed throughout the bedrock chamber. Kat poked her head around the pillar and saw the two prisoners on their knees. Commander Crunch was gnashing his teeth together with his face screwed up, and wispy black smoke rising off his back. Lord Tenebris whispered something to Drake. Then, with one last look at the Wither, Lord Tenebris disappeared, teleporting back to wherever it was he had come from.

Then, Kat watched in horror as the Wither opened its mouth, and a black skull shot out and exploded onto Charlie's back. A scream of pure agony burst forth from Charlie, and he collapsed to the ground, crying and sputtering as the smoke rose from him.

Kat had to do something now. She couldn't allow this to go on. Even if it was suicide, there was no way that she could just stand by idly and watch this happen. She turned back around to face Cassandrix.

"Get down to that switch," she commanded her friend. "I'll distract them." And without waiting for a response, Kat dashed behind the rows of pillars, finally stopping when she was at the pillar closest to the players. Not even ten blocks away, her friends were being physically abused by Drake for more information. She was so close, and yet so far.

Kat checked to see what she had left. Her inventory had been emptied while she was unconscious, so she no longer had any *mêlée* weapon. The two soldiers she and Cassandrix had killed hadn't been carrying much besides food, but there were a few important things.

The first of these was a bow and a stack of arrows, which she kept on hand, ready to fire. There was also a compass, which would prove invaluable should they escape. She had also managed to come across one single Ender Pearl. This item was of the utmost importance; all she had to do was get to Charlie and Crunch without being killed by Drake or the Wither, and she could warp the three of them straight to the door. Kat thanked her lucky stars that Lord Tenebris wasn't there any more. She had no idea where he had warped off to, but as long as she didn't have to deal with him now, she didn't really care.

Kat glanced down at her bow, and suddenly an idea struck her. She didn't know if it would work, and if it didn't then it would only reveal her and result in far more pain to her friends. But then again, it was the only idea she had, and so she decided to go with it. She drew an arrow in her bow, and peeked around the corner of the pillar. She took a deep breath. These next few shots would not only have to be extremely accurate, but they'd have to be fast, too.

In front of the throne, Drake kicked Commander Crunch to the ground and snarled.

"Fine then," he growled. "If you don't want to talk, let's see if my little friend can convince you otherwise. Villager, order another attack, but don't use minimal power this time . . . make it hurt more."

As Oob growled ferociously, a wave of ice chilled Kat's heart as she realized that she would have to leave Oob behind. She wanted nothing more than to cure the little guy, not just for the sake of taking control of the Wither and the other mobs from the Alliance, but also to get her friend back. Kat shook her head of this feeling. With the operation she was about to attempt, it was no time to be getting emotional.

The Wither Skeleton's middle mouth began to glow, and Kat felt an intake of the energy around the room. She let the arrow fly, just as the projectile left the Wither's mouth. The arrow collided with the airborne black skull, and it exploded in a giant burst of light in the centre of the Wither's face. The monster screamed as it careened backwards from the blast, crashing into the bedrock wall of the room and tumbling to the floor with a thud.

"What is the meaning of this?" Drake bellowed at the stunned monster. "UP! Get UP! Villager, tell this . . . AUGH!"

Drake shouted in pain as an arrow sunk into his right arm. He whipped his head around to see where it had come from, just in time to see Kat flying towards him. Her fist slammed into his jaw like a cannonball, and he reeled backwards, cracking his head against the obsidian throne and slumping unconscious to the ground.

Kat would have loved to take the opportunity to take him out for good, but she had a mission. Crunch, who had tightened his muscles in preparation for the Wither's next strike, whipped around to see Kat sprinting towards the two of them.

"Who are ye?" the Commander asked, eyes wide. "Aren't ye that lass from . . ."

"I'm from Element City, yes. I'm here to get you two out," Kat spat out distractedly, digging the Ender Pearl from her inventory as the Wither slowly levitated back upright.

"Oh, aye . . . uh, that's wha' I was about t' say . . ." Crunch replied awkwardly.

"Kat?" asked Charlie deliriously, his eyes struggling to stay focussed on her. "Is that . . . is that really you?"

"Yeah," Kat said, looking over her shoulder to see that Zombie Oob was almost upon them. She stood up and spun around to face him.

"Sorry, buddy," Kat grunted as she punched Oob in the chest as hard as she could. The villager reeled backwards before tripping and tumbling to the ground next to Drake. Unlike Drake, though, he immediately started to recover.

"Get ready, boys . . . we're warping out of here," Kat

shouted, and she pitched the Ender Pearl as hard as she could towards the exit before grabbing the two prisoners around the shoulders. Suddenly, Kat heard a raspy groan behind her, and saw that the Wither was airborne yet again, and all three white mouths were glowing and hissing.

"CASSANDRIX, DO IT NOW!" screamed Kat at the top of her lungs, as she desperately looked up at the monster about to blow her to smithereens. An instant later, Kat had to squint her eyes as the pistons whirred and the entire bedrock chamber flooded with daylight. The Wither reeled back, surprised, and three skulls shot from its mouths in random directions, creating massive explosions across the roof of the chamber.

As Kat watched the Wither adjust to the light, she felt the familiar feeling of warping for a split second before tumbling to the ground at the opening. Kat could see Cassandrix standing next to the lever, which had been pulled down. Outside, a short drop down a steep mycelium hillside led to the edge of the ocean.

"What now?" Kat asked, turning to face Cassandrix as she heard an alarm go off somewhere in the distance. "That was as far as I got in my plan!"

"I have two boats that the soldiers dropped in my inventory!" Cassandrix replied, as Commander Crunch pulled himself to his feet and Charlie lay motionless on the ground.

"OK, sounds good. Everyone, down the hill!" Kat bellowed. As Cassandrix hopped her way down the slope, followed by Crunch, Kat knelt down and shook Charlie, trying to get him to come around. It was no use. He had been totally spent by Drake's torture, and the landing of the teleportation had knocked him out cold. Kat took a deep breath and hoisted Charlie on her back, resigning to carry him down the mountain herself.

As Kat hopped off the smooth bedrock floor of the cave and onto the jagged mycelium cliff side, two black Wither skulls rocketed over her head, her hair blowing in their tailwind. Realizing that the Wither would likely be in hot pursuit of them, Kat shrugged Charlie off her for a moment and knocked the switch of the wall with a well-placed arrow. With no flow of redstone energy, the pistons returned to their off position, closing the hangar door. Even from outside the prison, Kat could still hear the explosions inside. She knew that it wouldn't be long before the Wither blasted its way through the door, so she picked up Charlie once again and hopped her way down the hill.

The trek down the hill was one of the most strenuous things that Kat had ever done. Beyond the fact that she was sprinting as fast as she could down an uneven slope while carrying another unconscious player on her back, Kat's legs still had an ache in them from the teleportation, which only grew worse and worse with each step down the mountain. By the time she reached the final expanse of mycelium leading to the beach, her legs were killing her, while Cassandrix and Crunch had already managed to make it to the shore.

As they set up the boats, Kat suddenly heard a whooshing sound, and an instant later an arrow stuck into the ground beside her. She strained her neck to look over her shoulder and saw to her dismay that the entire outside of Mount Fungarus was now covered with black-clad Noctem troops, all firing at her. Kat looked forward again, and tried as hard as she could to zigzag back and forth, making herself a harder target.

Then, when she was just ten blocks away from the boats, Kat felt a sharp sting on the back of her right thigh, and she knew she'd been hit. Gritting her teeth, Kat hit the spongy mycelium ground hard, flopping face-down while Charlie tumbled off her back and towards the shoreline. Kat forced herself to get back up to her feet as she became aware that Crunch and Cassandrix were dragging Charlie back to the boats.

Then, as Kat finally got up, she heard a sound behind her, like a car coming closer and closer. She looked over her shoulder, and her heart stopped. The Wither had blasted a small hole through the front of the hangar door. Through that hole, a black Wither skull was flying directly towards her, and it was now less than ten blocks away from her.

Kat had no time to dodge. She had no time to duck. There was nothing she could do as the skull sped towards her at breakneck speed. Kat took a deep breath and closed her eyes, preparing for the end.

Kat heard the explosion . . . but she didn't feel any pain. She felt the wave of force knock her to the ground. Lying there on the mycelium ground, Kat knew that, somehow, the Wither skull had exploded before it reached her. And oddest of all . . . she wasn't dead.

She opened her eyes. Sure enough, the cloud of smoke from the explosion hung right there in front of her. She couldn't see anything through the black cloud, not the island, not the mountain above her, not the Wither, not even the sky. The only form that Kat could make out was a black figure, with a cloak draped over his head, vanishing into the cloud of smoke.

For some reason that she could not explain, the name Black Hood entered her mind.

Kat didn't take the time to question what had just happened, though. She sprinted the last few steps across the shore and climbed hastily into her boat, alongside the unconscious Charlie. By the time the smoke of the skull's blast had cleared, the four players were already dozens of blocks from the shoreline, arrows from the island were falling far short of reaching them, and Kat could hear cries of indignation and fury from the prison guards they were leaving in their wake.

It wasn't until the Mushroom Islands had completely vanished from their view that Kat finally allowed herself to breathe. She glanced over at Cassandrix, piloting the boat beside her with Commander Crunch snoring behind her.

"Hey, Cassandrix?" Kat said.

The girl returned her look, and raised her eyebrows in response.

"Good job in there today."

Cassandrix looked across the water at Charlie's unconscious form, then behind her to the sleeping Commander Crunch, and then back to Kat again.

"Thank you, darling," Cassandrix replied, before setting her sights back out to the open ocean.

Kat sighed, but then smiled a little to herself. She supposed it was a bit too much to ask for Cassandrix to return her compliment. She *had* managed to get a thank you out of her, with no snide remarks to accompany it.

At the very least, that was something.

It was plain that neither of them were in the mood to talk after all they had been through, and so Kat focused on piloting the boat yet again. However, as she tried to turn her mind off and allow her brain to slip into autopilot, she found that a certain question couldn't stop nagging her in the back of her brain. Finally, she turned to Cassandrix yet again.

"Hey, I have just one more question," Kat said slowly.

Cassandrix nodded, still looking straight ahead. Kat spoke on.

"When . . . when that Wither skull almost killed me . . . did you . . . or did anybody . . . block it?"

Cassandrix looked puzzled for a moment, and then turned to look at Kat again.

"Of course not, darling," Cassandrix replied, as if it should be obvious. "The Commander and I were pulling Charlie onto the boat, and there was nobody else on the beach. Why? Did you see somebody?"

Kat thought back to that moment, less than an hour ago. The explosion had gone off right in front of her. She was being struck by waves of force, light, and sound, and in the centre, she clearly remembered a figure silhouetted in the smoke, wearing a black cloak, with a sword held in a block . . . as if the player was defending her . . .

"No," Kat replied, shaking her head and glancing down at her reflection in the water. "I'm sure it was nothing. . . ."

I gotta admit," Jayden mumbled to G as they filed along with the rest of their class of recruits into the rec area, "I'm a bit surprised that I didn't hate that lesson more than I did."

"Agreed," replied G, pulling the door closed behind them. "I mean . . . I know that the stuff they're showing us is being used against Elementia troops," he murmured under his breath, "but still, I think those interrogation techniques might actually turn out to be pretty useful."

Jayden nodded, and he sat down on a wood block on the floor and watched the other players in their group having fun around the rec room. Truth be told, G was finding it difficult to look around the room without squinting, since everything was almost entirely white.

On the most recent update to Minecraft, quartz had been added in veins throughout the cave of the Nether. In order to flaunt their dominance over the dimension, the Noctem Alliance had apparently taken it upon themselves to mine as much quartz as possible and incorporate it into their buildings. In fact, G had heard Tess saying that their group of recruits would be going into the Nether before long to mine quartz. As of now, there was only one small part of the rec room that was still made out of chiselled stone blocks, not having been remodelled yet.

G ignored that, though, determined not to let the white quartz distract him from the game of Spleef being played in the rec room's miniature arena between several of the recruits. After all, Spleef was enjoyable to watch no matter who was playing, and G felt that he and Jayden deserved some downtime after all their hard work.

In just the last few days, they had managed to learn crucial information about the Capitol Building, and where the hostages may be. They had narrowed it down to three hallways in the building, and all they needed now was some way to check them. How they would do that, they had yet to figure out. Still, they were doing good work, and G was looking forward to an afternoon of relaxation.

As the Spleef match was coming to a close, the wooden door of the rec room swung open. Through the doorway walked General Tess, still dressed in full uniform, her pink face as unreadable as ever.

"Good evening, recruits," Tess said, in a voice that wasn't particularly loud, but nonetheless caught the attention of every single player in the rec room. In an instant, every player dropped what they were doing and stood up, including the two remaining Spleef players. They turned to face Tess, and stood at full attention.

"Good evening, General Tess," all the recruits replied in unison.

"At ease, soldiers," Tess said, still not cracking a smile, or showing any emotion for that matter. "I've only come for one of you. MasterBronze, would you come with me, please?"

G's heart skipped a beat. *Me? She wants me? What does she want with me? Does she suspect me?* Despite his racing thoughts, he tried to keep a determinedly calm and respectful demeanour as he marched over to join the general. He shared one last baffled expression with Jayden before the door closed behind him, and he found himself standing alone in the hallway with Tess.

"What may I do for you, ma'am?" G asked, standing at full attention.

"Did you not hear me before, soldier? I said, at ease," Tess repeated, and she watched as G let his hands hang loose by his side. There was a moment of awkward silence before Tess spoke again.

"What level are you, soldier?"

"Um . . . I'm sorry?" G stammered. *She must suspect me . . .*

"I asked you what your level is."

"I'm level sixty-four," G answered, not sure what it had to do with anything. "I would be higher, but these are tough times, and you of all people must know how necessary it is to have enchanted weapons on hand."

"As I suspected," Tess replied and, to G's amazement, she actually smiled. "A master Minecrafter like you? It doesn't shock me at all that you've got a good number of levels under your belt, even for someone in this Alliance."

"I'm sorry?" G replied, not following.

"Soldier . . . actually, let's drop the formalities for now . . . can I call you MasterBronze?"

"I, uh . . . suppose so . . ." G answered clumsily.

"Soldier, even at ease, I'm still your commanding officer," Tess said, her voice suddenly stern again. "When I ask you a question, you will respond with 'yes, ma'am,' or 'no, ma'am.'"

"My apologies," G said, taking a deep breath to overcome his discomfort. "Yes, ma'am, you may call me that."

"Good," Tess replied, smiling once again. "MasterBronze, ever since you won that Aptitude Tournament a few days back, I've been keeping my eye on you, and I must say, as a soldier I see some real potential in you."

"Oh. Well, thank you, ma'am."

"Besides already being well versed in fighting, I see that you have a drive to you. In every training exercise that we've done so far, you in particular have given all your energy to it. You do this in every area, from your fighting to your skills training."

"Thank you, ma'am."

"And because of that, MasterBronze, I would like to personally appoint you as my apprentice."

"I'm . . . I'm sorry?" replied G, taken aback. "What exactly do you mean?"

"Well, to be honest, it's a bit unorthodox," Tess replied. "No general in the Noctem Alliance has ever handpicked a student to personally train before. However, I've never seen any recruit come through this programme with more potential than you, MasterBronze. Therefore, after initial training sessions are completed each day, I would like to train you myself in various high-level tasks.

"None of the other students will have the opportunity to do this, and it is more than likely that you will advance much faster through the ranks of the Noctem Freedom Fighters than any of your fellow recruits. What do you say, MasterBronze? Does that sound like something that you'd be interested in?"

"Of course, ma'am," G replied enthusiastically, a huge smile breaking across his face. *This is fantastic,* he thought to himself. *The faster I can get access to high-level Noctem information, the better!*

Tess smiled even wider. "Excellent. We will begin tomorrow. For now, you may return to the rec room."

And with that, General Tess turned on her heel and

walked back down the hallway. G pumped his fist in ecstasy, and strutted proudly back towards the rec room. He couldn't wait to tell Jayden the great news that he was one step closer to uncovering the Noctem Alliance's deepest, darkest secrets.

"OK, noob," Sally said, flying high in the sky. "Let's do one more drill, and then we can take a break. All right?"

"Sounds good to me!" Stan shouted from the ground about a hundred blocks away.

"Here's how this goes," said Sally. "I'm going to try to catch up to you. I won't go at full speed, but I won't go slow, either. Your job is to try to keep away from me for as long as possible. You can use anything that you've learned so far to slow me down. For now, I'll come directly at you, which means I won't, like, loop around anything you put up, I'll go through it instead."

"All right!" Stan shouted back.

"Are you ready?" asked Sally, a devious glint in her eye.

"Just a sec," replied Stan. He took a deep breath, focussed as hard as he could on feeling weightless, and, with all his might, he launched himself into the air. Stan flew upwards until he was at the same eye level as Sally, and then just floated there, looking back at her.

"OK," he shouted back to her, a diamond axe popping

into his right hand as a manic grin crossed his face. "Come at me."

Sally flew directly towards Stan, a diamond sword appearing in her own hand. Stan stretched out his hand and, through the power of his mind, he summoned a giant wall of bedrock directly in front of Sally. While she was punching through, Stan focussed harder, and a flow of lava appeared at the top of the wall. When Sally burst out through the wall of lava, she gave a short scream of pain as she caught on fire.

"Nice one, noob," she chuckled after the shock wore off, and she swigged down Potions of Fire Resistance and Regeneration. "I've gotta admit, I didn't see that coming."

Stan smirked, and he swept his hand through the air, causing a cascade of gravel blocks to appear above Sally and immediately fall back down onto her. Without flinching, Sally dived to the ground but wasn't expecting to see the grid of sand and cacti that Stan had summoned directly beneath her. Sally did a U-turn in midair and barrelled back up through the falling gravel, squinting her eyes as she did so, only to get caught headfirst in the mess of gooey cobweb blocks that Stan had summoned directly above her.

"Well, I give you points for resourcefulness, noob," remarked Sally in a muffled voice as she hacked through the mess of cobwebs with her sword.

"I'm not done yet." Stan laughed as he focussed all his

energy on a spot right next to Sally. A moment later, with a pop, a Blaze appeared out of nowhere. The spinning inferno of a mob fired off three tiny fireballs, which hit the cobwebs and engulfed Sally in flames.

There was a teleporting sound as Sally warped out of the disordered cobwebs, floating above them instead. She squinted her eyes, clearly focussing hard, and all of a sudden, there was a crash of thunder as the sky turned grey, and heavy rains started to fall from the clouds in waves. The fire of the Blaze was instantly extinguished, and a moment later the mob itself fell dead from the sky, leaving only a single blaze rod to fall to the ground.

As he watched it fall, Stan felt himself clutched in the grasp of an invisible power as Sally stretched out her hand towards him, followed by a mischievous leer. Try as he might, Stan couldn't break free of her hold, and she levitated him towards her until finally they were close enough for her to poke him in the forehead.

"I win," she replied cheekily. With a pointed blink from Sally, the weather instantly turned back into sunshine again. She released Stan from her telekinetic grip, and, totally unprepared, he plummeted towards the ground, flailing for a good few moments before he caught himself in midair.

"Hey, no fair," Stan laughed. "You weren't supposed to use powers I haven't learned yet."

"Noob, if life were fair," replied Sally coolly as the two of them levitated back to the ground, "then my personal online business that sells pants with built-in life preservers would have taken off by now, and I'd be a multibillion-dollar entrepreneur rather than some chick who stays home all day hacking Minecraft servers."

Sally focussed on her hand, and instantly two pumpkin pies appeared.

"Eat up, noob," Sally said with a smile, tossing Stan one of the pies, which he caught in his outstretched hand. "You've earned it."

And with that, the two players both conjured up blocks for themselves to sit on—Stan's block being a block of iron, and Sally's being a block of obsidian—as they began to eat. There was a long stretch of silence as the two players stuffed their faces with food, tuckered out by the long work session. After a while, Sally finally spoke.

"So, how're you doing back in Elementia, noob? Has the Alliance been giving you too much trouble?"

"Actually, no," Stan said, his pleasant surprise at this truth reflected in his voice. "I mean, I had a run-in with Leonidas a few days ago, and I thought I was a goner then . . . but I guess I must have hurt him more than I thought I did, because I haven't seen him or any other Noctem troops since then."

"Well that's good," Sally replied. "You managed to make it back to the mainland yet?"

Stan forced the final bite of his pie down in a giant gulp before responding. "No, not yet, although I am making good progress. I found an island with some trees on it yesterday, so I was able to make a boat for myself and that's really sped the travel up. I also killed some monsters, and got some supplies from them. I'm actually camping in the Taiga Archipelago right now, which means I'm getting pretty close to Diamond Bay. Unfortunately, if my hunch is correct, then it won't be safe to go back to the city through there."

"And what is this brilliant hunch of yours, exactly?"

"Well, I've been out of contact with everybody in Elementia for a while now, so I have no way of knowing anything for sure. But one thing I did find out before leaving the Mushroom Islands was that Blackraven was leaking our plans to the Noctem Alliance, so our attacks almost certainly failed. Element City was probably hurt pretty badly in the attack, so I wouldn't be at all surprised if the Noctems managed to take Diamond Bay."

Sally nodded gravely. "Makes enough sense, I suppose. Well, I'd definitely head for the swampland peninsula, if I were you. Better safe than sorry, you know."

"Yeah, that's what I was planning on doing. I mean, I don't know the swamp well or anything, but I figure it's probably better to go somewhere it's easier to hide than to be a sitting duck out in the ocean."

Sally nodded, and spawned a steak from her inventory. Stan was still hungry, but not *that* much, and so he opted to summon an apple for himself. As he bit into the red fruit, an old thought started to float to the front of his mind.

There was a question that had been eating away at Stan for months now, from even before he had defeated King Kev. Since he had become president, he had found that he had become far too busy to give it any thought. However, having been alone for so long over the past few weeks, Stan had finally had the time to think about it, and it occurred to him now that, just maybe, Sally could help him find the answers he was looking for.

"Hey, Sal?"

"Waddup, noob?" Sally managed to get out as she scarfed down the last bits of her steak.

"I've been thinking . . . about some stuff . . ."

"Oh, come on, noob, don't start with me. You know how much I can't stand sentimentality."

"No, no, it's not that!" cried Stan, shaking his head as if he were trying to shake off a bug. "It's just . . . I have a question. About myself. And I was wondering if you could give me your perspective on it."

"Well, sure, I can give you my perspective, noob," replied

Sally, shrugging. "I mean, I can't guarantee it'll be any good, but you can try me."

"Well, OK then. Hmm . . . how do I say this . . . Do you remember right before the Battle for Elementia, how you told me that I was special, and I was on a higher level?"

"Yeah, what about it?"

"Well . . . what exactly did you mean by that?"

Sally paused for a moment, and a pensive look crossed her face. After a while, she spoke. "Well . . . to be honest, I'm not entirely sure, noob. It was just . . . in that moment, I felt like there was something about you. I couldn't put my finger on what it was, but it seemed like, somehow, you were definitely on some sort of higher plane than the rest of us. And then, when you came up with that amazing speech off the top of your head . . . well, at the time that seemed to confirm it."

"But the thing is," continued Stan, talking faster now, "that you weren't the only one who told me that. During my training session in the Adorian Village, Crazy Steve implied that he could sense something like that in me, too. And then later, in the middle of the Ender Desert, Kat told me that she could feel it, too . . . it's like they felt I was some kind of chosen one or something . . . as if I was destined to defeat King Kev and become the president of Elementia. I mean . . . do you think that that's possible? Do you think that I might be some sort of chosen hero or something like that?"

Stan looked at Sally expectantly, waiting for an answer. None came. Sally simply sat on her obsidian block, hand pressed against her forehead. Finally, after a full minute of silence, she responded.

"Well, let me start by saying this, Stan: no. No, I don't think that you're a chosen one, with your destiny written in the stars or any of that crap."

The breath that Stan had been holding in gushed out of him in a wave. He wasn't entirely sure what to say next. Luckily, he didn't have to answer, as Sally wasn't done yet.

"That being said, I still believe that you're something special."

Stan was confused. "But you just said—"

"Stan, let me spell it out for you," Sally said slowly, turning to look him in the eye. "There are a lot of people in the world who are talented. There are a lot of people who are willing to work hard. And there are a lot of people who care about those who can't help themselves, and want to do all they can for those people. Most people have at least one of those qualities, and if you looked a bit, you could find somebody with two of those qualities without too much trouble. But Stan, let me tell you . . . it's extremely rare to find somebody who has all three of those qualities. And you're one of those people."

Stan smiled. "Do you really think so?"

"Of course," replied Sally, as if it were the most obvious thing in the world. "And I think that the thing that so many people see in you, Stan, that makes you stand out even more, is that not only do you have a ton of all three of those traits, but you also have a habit of influencing people around you."

Stan raised his eyebrows. "What do you—"

"Oh, come on, Stan, look at your two best friends!" sighed Sally in exasperation. "When you first met Charlie, he had talent, and he wanted to help other people, but what happened every time he tried?"

"Well," mumbled Stan awkwardly, "usually he would just end up too scared to be much help . . ."

"Exactly!" exclaimed Sally. "And what was it that finally forced him to buck up and fight for what he believed in?"

Stan scratched his head, forcing himself to think back to their quest across the Ender Desert all those months ago. "Well . . . I guess it was in the NPC village . . . when I made him face that Spider Jockey . . ."

"Right, Stan, *you* did that! You saw that he had potential for greatness, and you gave him the little extra shove he needed to turn into the amazing warrior he is today!"

"Well, I guess . . . I mean, I hardly feel like I deserve all, or even most of the—"

"And look at Kat!" Sally cut in. "I'm sure you remember

what she was like when you first met her, right?"

"Well, I seem to recall that she might have tried to kill me a little bit . . ."

"So you met up with this girl. She had the raw talent, and she was a fearless and hard worker, but her priorities were all in the wrong place. She was using all her potential for her own ends, just trying to claw her way up in the world and not caring who got thrown under the bus because of it. And do you know how she realized that she was wrong?"

"No," Stan replied sceptically. "Do you?"

Sally scoffed at him. "Oh, give me some credit, Stan. You don't think that you were the *only* one I talked to during that training week before the Battle for Elementia, right? I talked to Kat and Charlie, too . . . come to think of it, I probably talked to Kat *more* than I talked to you! I was training her in dual sword fighting, remember?"

"I guess you're right," replied Stan. It was amazing how many details of their campaign to take down King Kev he had forgotten during his last five months as president.

"I'll tell you, Stan . . . it was *you.* Do you have any idea just how much Kat respects you, not just as a friend but as a person? By taking her with you on your journey, even after she'd attacked you, changed her life, and you showed her by example how to be a better person who cares about other people.

"That's the reason that you're special, Stan. It's not any kind of prophecy, or destiny, or anything like that. Simply put, you're one of the best all-around people that I've ever met, and it rubs off on the people you know."

As Sally finished her speech, she took a deep breath, let it out, and pulled an apple out of her inventory to eat. The two players sat there for a while in silence. But as the sun set on the infinite expanse of totally flat grass, a single tear of happiness rolled down Stan's cheek. All he had ever tried to do was be the best person he could be, and every once in a while, it was nice to know that he was doing a good job.

As the sun finally sank out of view, Stan stood up from his block.

"Thanks for the advice, Sally," he said with a smile. "It means more to me than you know."

Sally chuckled and looked up at him affectionately. "You know I meant all of it, noob. You gonna head back to Elementia now?"

Stan nodded. "This has been a great day, Sally, both in training and in talking to you. But I have to get back to my server now. My people need me."

Sally smiled. "Do what you have to do. I'll call you back here tomorrow, OK?"

"Deal," Stan replied. And with that, he turned his back to Sally, and looked straight into the eternal expanse of the starry night sky. He took a deep breath, and before long, the words popped into his head yet again.

DISCONNECT FROM SERVER?

"Yes," Stan replied out loud, and with a faint pop, he disappeared from SalAcademy.

Stan felt his body once again as he rejoined Elementia. The frigid air of the taiga was soothing to his skin, far more pleasant than the biting gales of the tundra. Stan opened his eyes.

All around him, the tall spruce trees protruded into the night sky from the snow-covered ground. Small hills of dirt topped with snow were scattered about the island. In the distance, a ring of ice expanded around the shoreline of the island, beyond which the azure ocean stretched forever until it merged with the starry night sky. And right in the centre of all this, standing not two blocks away from Stan and looking him straight in the eye, was another player.

"Hello, Stan," said Leonidas with a smile. "Glad to see that you're back."

11

THE DUSK OF HOPE

There was a moment of silence as Stan stared at Leonidas in disbelief. Leonidas looked Stan in the eye, praying that he wouldn't panic.

Then, without warning, Stan gave a shout of fury as he whipped a diamond sword out of his inventory and swung it as hard as he could. Leonidas just barely managed to leap out of the way as he felt a shockwave leave the sword and brush right by his head. He was forced to hop backwards twice more to avoid the two follow-up attacks.

"Stop it, Stan!" cried Leonidas, raising his hands over his head. "I ain't gonna fight ya!"

But Stan paid no attention. He thrust the diamond sword forwards, directly at Leonidas's stomach. He was forced to lean backwards, his stomach just moving out of the range of the sword jab, but the pulse of Knock-back energy that shot off the sword hit him squarely in the stomach, sending him flying backwards. Leonidas landed with a thud on the snow-covered dirt right on the shore of the island. He glanced back up and saw Stan, flying through the air with sword overhead, on course to plunge it directly into Leonidas's heart.

As much as he hated to counterattack, Leonidas knew that he had no choice. With great agility, Leonidas rolled onto his back, and when Stan was over him, he kicked his feet into the air and directly into Stan's stomach. Leonidas flew up off his back and landed on his feet, as Stan was launched backwards and skidded to a stop on the ice surrounding the island.

"Stan, I refuse to fight ya!" shouted Leonidas again as Stan struggled his way to his feet, battling the slippery ice underfoot. "I just wanna talk to ya."

"Yeah, well I just want to get home without running into any more Noctem troops. Life isn't fair," grunted Stan, no mercy on his face as he sunk to one knee, driving his sword into the ice block he was standing on. The ice shattered with a crack, and Stan sunk down through the ice and into the water below.

Leonidas glanced wildly around the ice field, squinting to try to figure out where Stan had gone. In the faint moonlight, Leonidas saw no indication of where Stan was going to pop up next. Then, all at once, Leonidas noticed a dark figure directly under his feet, getting larger and larger by the second. Leonidas leaped back towards the island in alarm as a glowing diamond sword drove up out of the ice, missing him by inches. He jumped and leaped back and forth in desperation, narrowly avoiding the jabs of the sword that Stan was sending up through the ice.

Leonidas felt the crunch of snow under his feet, and realized that he had reached the island yet again. He glanced at the edge of the ice, where Stan had burst out of the water and landed. Immediately, Stan's steely eyes locked onto Leonidas, and he began to sprint as fast as he could toward Leonidas. Unfortunately, he had forgotten what he was standing on; Stan slipped on the frictionless ice blocks under his feet and tumbled to the ground. Leonidas seized the opportunity to turn around and flee back onto the island.

"Come back and fight, you coward!" bellowed Stan in outrage, but Leonidas sprinted across the snowy dirt of the island, weaving his way through the grove of spruce trees. *I need to talk to Stan,* he thought to himself, his mind shifting into strategy mode. *And if I'm going to do that, I need to get myself somewhere where he can't attack me.*

Leonidas ducked his way behind a particularly wide spruce trunk, and he glanced over his shoulder. Stan was prowling through the forest in his wake, lunging behind every tree in search of Leonidas. Leonidas was relieved. He had a minute to catch his breath and figure out a plan before Stan was upon him. He turned to look straight ahead and found himself staring directly into the eyes of an Enderman.

The monster was standing about fifteen blocks away from Leonidas, but he could feel the creature's purple eyes piercing into him like knives. Leonidas's heart had stopped dead in its tracks at the sight of the dangerous mob, but it now began to race in panic as the Enderman's mouth opened, revealing its jagged black teeth. It began to tremble in preparation for attack. Slowly and calmly, Leonidas notched an arrow in his bow. He knew that if he were to shoot an arrow at the Enderman, it would just teleport out of the way. He had to wait until the monster moved of its own volition, and when it was upon him, fire the arrow at point-blank range.

Leonidas's eyes began to water. He didn't dare look away from the Enderman, or even blink, lest the monster vanish and catch him totally off guard. Leonidas held the eyes of the open-jawed, shuddering Enderman for another half a minute. The monster refused to let up and, finally, he could take it no more. He blinked for a split second, and when he opened his eyes, the Enderman had vanished.

Leonidas cursed under his breath, and he slammed his back against the tree, bow raised. He glanced around in a frenzy, trying to see the entire area around him at once. The Enderman was going to reappear any second now, and he had to prepare for anywhere that it could possibly . . .

Without warning, Leonidas felt a pair of hands wrap around his throat. As he coughed and sputtered in a panic, Leonidas saw two long, spindly black arms out of the corner of his eye, reaching around from behind the tree. Leonidas kicked and struggled to no avail as the black hands pressed harder into his throat, beginning to pull him up the tree trunk by his neck. Leonidas could hardly see nor feel anything any more, besides an overwhelming feeling of helplessness as the demon choked the life out of him. Then, from somewhere in his collective instinct, Leonidas became aware of the arrow still grasped in his right hand. Without thinking, acting purely on base impulse, he drove the arrow into the Enderman's hand.

The monster gave a shriek of alarm and vanished, dropping Leonidas to the ground with a thump. Leonidas gasped for air, and the world seemed to be going in slow motion as his senses returned to him. Then, all at once, the Enderman was standing above Leonidas, drawing back its black hand, still stuck with the arrow, in preparation for the final blow. Leonidas loaded his bow as fast as the warped lethargic reality around him would allow, and just as the slow-motion punch made contact with Leonidas's left arm, the arrow entered the Enderman's chest.

Although the slender black body fell to the ground and faded to nonexistence, Leonidas had to bite his tongue to refrain from uttering a holler of agony. The Enderman's punch, imbued with the monster's dark magic, had burned a hole in Leonidas's leather armour, and the pulsating pain coursing through his arm was unfathomable. As he clenched his teeth nearly to the point of cracking, Leonidas attempted to move the arm. Only by the highest willpower imaginable did Leonidas not bellow as indescribable pain engulfed his immobile limb.

Taking a deep breath, Leonidas grabbed the tree trunk with his good arm, pulling himself to his feet and wincing as his left arm swung back and forth limply. *Wow,* Leonidas thought to himself, cringing. *I guess they really* did *make the monsters' AI better on the last update.*

"You've got five seconds to tell me if there're more soldiers with you."

Slowly, Leonidas turned his head to the left, an exhausted look taking to his face. There, pointing his diamond sword directly at Leonidas's heart, stood Stan, his face ugly with hatred.

"Two seconds left," Stan spat out in disgust.

Leonidas sighed. To be honest, he was really sick of finding himself in these situations. No matter where he went, he could never catch a break. Never once had things ever gone his way, and he had always walked in the worst place possible. He was tired of it. Maybe . . . just maybe . . . it would be worth it to just let Stan run him through, and allow all his problems to just end . . .

"Answer me, you monster!"

The shout jolted Leonidas out of his trance. His eyebrows creased, and adrenaline shot through his body. *No. I've come too far. I'm too close to give up now.* Leonidas gave a shout of fury, which Stan clearly wasn't expecting. The distraction allowed Leonidas to raise his good arm and knock the sword to the side. He desperately searched for a plan, when his eye fell upon a turquoise orb lying in the snow.

Finally, Leonidas smirked to himself. *Something goes my way.*

Leonidas snatched the Ender Pearl from the ground, pitching it fastball style toward the limb of a tall spruce tree as Stan recovered. Leonidas closed his eyes, and before Stan's sword could harm him, Leonidas felt himself be sucked through the vacuum of space and land on the cushioned, snow-covered leaves of the tree.

Leonidas paused for a moment to catch his breath as Stan looked around wildly in confusion. In the moment of peace, the adrenaline began to drain from Leonidas, and the stinging pain in his arm became more and more prevalent. Leonidas gritted his teeth and realized that now was as good a time as any to talk to Stan.

"Hey, Stan! I'm up here!"

Stan whipped around to face Leonidas, and their eyes met. Instantly, Stan's befuddled face morphed into a scowl, and, with no words, he drew a bow.

"Don't, Stan!" bellowed Leonidas, his heart skipping a beat. "I already said, I don't wanna fight ya!"

"I'm not interested in anything you have to say, Leonidas!" grunted Stan as he notched an arrow and aimed at Leonidas's heart.

"Well, fine then! Kill me! But I refuse to fight!" shot back Leonidas. Taking a deep breath and praying that it wouldn't come back to bite him, Leonidas extracted his bow from his inventory and, before Stan could react, he pitched it down off the tree. It landed on the snow right in front of Stan's feet. Stan stared at the weapon.

"What're you playing at?" growled Stan, his brow creasing further as he glared back up at Leonidas.

"Nothin'," replied Leonidas, sounding much braver than he really was. With no bow in hand, he felt almost naked, and incredibly helpless. "I just don't want to fight you or your friends ever again."

"What're you talking about?" spat Stan.

"Exactly what it sounds like, Stan. I quit the Noctem Alliance already, and I wanna join you and fight for Element City."

"Ha!" laughed Stan bitterly. "There's no way you're gonna lower my guard by lying . . . where're your other guys? Are they getting ready to ambush me? Are they watching now with Invisibility Potions?" Stan's eyes flickered around the snowy island nervously before returning to the now angry Leonidas.

"No, Stan, I'm bein' serious! I was wrong to ever follow anythin' the Alliance said! They're a bunch of no-good, vile murderers with twisted ideals and horrible methods. I never believed in anythin' they said, and now I've broken free and want to fight for ya!"

"Give me one good reason that I should believe you, and not shoot you right now," Stan spat out in disgust.

"Well, how's this?" Leonidas replied, thankful that at least one good thing had come out of the fight from a few minutes ago. "All the mobs in the game are fightin' for the Alliance now. If I was still with the Alliance and had guys with me, how come I got attacked by the Enderman just now?"

Stan's mouth opened for a moment, then closed. He looked confused, and Leonidas grinned, realizing that he had gotten the point across.

"Well . . . that's . . ." sputtered Stan, " . . . maybe . . . that was just a rogue Enderman that you just so happened to come across! I mean, come on, Leonidas! You expect me to believe that you realized overnight that you were fighting for the most evil organization in the history of Minecraft?"

"Course not!" cried out Leonidas in indignation. "Stan, I told ya this the last time we met, and I'll tell ya again . . . I didn't *choose* the Alliance, the Alliance chose *me*! The only reason I *ever* joined those evil cretins is 'cause I had to! When I was a noob, they threatened my family and said that if I didn't join . . ."

Suddenly, Leonidas found that he couldn't continue. Although he was sure that he was about to win Stan over, it finally occurred to him who he was talking to. Stan was well known for being very friendly towards, and extremely protective of, the NPC villagers. If anybody would know what Leonidas so desperately needed to, it was him.

"Stan . . . the moment that I quit the Alliance," Leonidas continued slowly, his voice trembling with emotion, "was the moment . . . when they told me they had attacked the NPC Village. I never did hear . . . what the casualties of the attack were, before I left. So . . . I'm so sorry, but I have to ask you . . . did Moganga survive?"

Stan's eyebrows, which had been slightly raised at the sheer levels of poignant sadness in Leonidas's voice, now shot up, and his mouth hung open. How did Leonidas know Moganga by name?

"Um . . . no, she didn't . . ."

"Then what about Ohsow? And Leol? And Vella?" Leonidas was desperate now to hear the news that even one member of his family had survived the raid. "Stan . . . what about Mella and Blerge? What about their sons?"

Stan couldn't believe his ears. Leonidas knew the names of the villagers? How was that possible? And Stan recognized the tone of Leonidas's voice as strikingly . . . sincere. And . . . if that was true . . . could it possibly mean that Leonidas really . . .

Suddenly, Stan flashed back to his fight with Leonidas in

the Jungle Base. During that fight, too, Leonidas had spoken with true emotion in his voice, trying to make it seem like he was an actual human being with feelings . . . right before he had sunk an arrow into Charlie. This was clearly just Leonidas playing another mind game with him. Surely there was some other explanation for how Leonidas knew the villagers' names. Stan was about to release the string of his bow and let the arrow fly when, from the other side of the island, he caught the tone of faint whispering.

Stan whipped his head to face the source of the noise, instinctively sinking to his knees to make himself as inconspicuous as possible. As he glanced through the tall, spruce-wood tree trunks, nearly black in the midst of the night, he didn't see anybody. Then, without warning, a dark figure emerged from behind one of the trees. Without hesitation, Stan drew an Ender Pearl from his inventory, and, praying he wouldn't be seen, he pitched it upwards into the boughs of the nearest tree. A second later, Stan found himself comfortably perched in a hollowed-out den of leaves in the top of the tree. He looked up and realized that he could see Leonidas, crouching up in another tree.

Becoming aware that somebody was staring at him, Leonidas whipped his head around, only to realize it was just Stan. The two locked eyes for a moment before Stan hastily looked away. Leonidas didn't care. Although he truly had been emotionally invested in his own speech, he had shifted right back into hiding mode the instant that Stan had realized that there was somebody on the island. Right now, the fate of the village didn't matter to Leonidas as much as ensuring that he and Stan gave this mysterious figure, whoever he was, the slip.

As Leonidas glanced down onto the dark snowy ground, he realized with a start that not one but three figures were walking across the island. The three of them stopped in a clearing in the trees, not too far from where Stan had been just moments ago. In the faint moonlight, Leonidas could make out the bodies of all these players.

One of them had the exact costume of a Spider, and an intrigued look on her face. The second player resembled an Enderman almost perfectly, but she had blue eyes and a black ponytail down her back, her face seeming a bit unfocussed. The final player had the body and face of a skeleton, with a mop of white hair, tinted black on top. This player's face looked stony and stoic.

Leonidas's heart dropped. He knew these players. He knew them well. And he knew just then how much trouble he and Stan were in.

Arachnia looked around the clearing, surveying the trees and landscape. Enderchick opened her mouth to say something, but Arachnia raised her hand, and her mouth immediately closed. Arachnia took a deep breath and closed her eyes, focussing intently on something. After a moment of silence, she opened her eyes.

"Somebody's on the island," she whispered, looking to Enderchick and the skeleton-player, who Leonidas knew to be called Lord Marrow. "I can't tell where, exactly . . . but they're not going anywhere."

Leonidas inhaled sharply, praying that Stan wouldn't hear this and take it to mean that he should run. Nothing could be further from the truth; they both had to stay put, lest Arachnia sense them.

Back when Leonidas had been commanding troops in Nocturia, Drake had told him about some old friends of his, bounty hunters who they could hire if they ever needed any extra hands. He had told Leonidas that this team, composed of five players named Arachnia, Enderchick, Lord Marrow, Creeper Khan, and Zomboy, was known as the Elite Legion of Mobhunters, or ELM. A mobhunter, Drake had explained, was a type of hacker who took on the skin of a mob in the game, and used cheats and mods to give themselves all the abilities of the mobs they were disguised as.

Drake had pointed out that Arachnia, for example, was a mobhunter dressed as a Spider. Therefore, she had given herself the ability to poison others on contact, high agility and wall-climbing abilities, and the ability to sense when others were around if she devoted all her focus to it.

At that point, Leonidas told Drake that he'd consider hiring them if need be. Now, Leonidas hated himself for not having Drake go into more detail as to what exactly the other mobhunters of ELM were capable of. Leonidas assumed that Enderchick had some sort of teleportation ability, and Lord Marrow was most likely a skilled archer, but he still couldn't guess exactly what these players could do. And he had no idea where Creeper Khan and Zomboy were . . .

"You know what to do, Enderchick," whispered Arachnia. Leonidas couldn't see Enderchick's face, but she nodded her head and then, in a puff of purple smoke, she was gone. Leonidas's heart sank; she *was* able to teleport.

Leonidas tried to keep his breathing as silent as possible as he heard the sound of teleportation go off every few seconds below him, indicating that Enderchick was clearly scouting out the island. He glanced up at Stan, in the tree directly across from him. Stan appeared to have the right idea and was crouched down, sword in hand and trying to be as inconspicuous as possible. Leonidas sighed in relief, and hoped that Stan would stay that way before the mobhunters managed to find him.

Enderchick appeared back in front of Arachnia in another burst of purple smoke.

"He's, like, not underground or anything, Arachnia," Enderchick chirped softly, a ditzy, Valley girl tone to her voice. "All the blocks on the island still have, like, snow covering them and stuff. Also, just over behind those trees, I found this thingy."

Enderchick reached into her inventory and pulled out a bow. As she handed it to Lord Marrow, Leonidas realized in horror that she was holding his own bow. Beyond being terrified that ELM now had evidence that somebody was indeed on the island, the feeling of helplessness that came with being unarmed crashed over Leonidas once again.

"Lord Marrow, what do you think?" Arachnia asked, as she and Enderchick turned to the skeleton-skinned mobhunter. "Has this bow been used recently?"

There was a moment of silence. Lord Marrow turned the bow over in his hand, and held it up to his eye level, examining it. Then, without a word, he turned to Arachnia, and nodded.

"All right," Arachnia replied, a grin cracking on her face. "He's here. Enderchick, please bring over our little friend."

Enderchick disappeared and reappeared an instant later,

holding another player by the shoulder. As Leonidas looked closer, he realized that she wasn't holding another player; this was a Zombie villager. As he got a closer look, Leonidas wondered in horror if this could be a citizen of the NPC Village he had once called home.

"Villager, give the command," Arachnia ordered. Leonidas was puzzled. What did that mean?

The villager gave a series of short roars, sounding vaguely similar to hacking coughs. There was a moment of silence as the three mobhunters and the Zombie stood there, and Leonidas wondered what was going on. Then, the sounds of Zombie moans, Spider hisses and rattling bones caught Leonidas's ear as he watched dozens of hostile mobs appear and begin to swarm between the tree trunks, clearly searching for someone.

"I still think that this is, like, a totally suh-*tupid* idea," whined Enderchick, sticking her tongue out in disgust. "We could, like, totally find him ourselves, Arachnia."

"I know that we could," replied Arachnia, "but trust me, the mobs will find him much faster."

Leonidas sighed, and looked down at the leaf blocks he was sitting on. If they were using the mobs to search, then he was probably safe. The only real danger would be if he looked an Enderman in the eye, so if he just kept staring down, he'd more than likely stay undetected. Leonidas gave a quick glance up at Stan, to ensure that he, too, had the same idea. Indeed, Stan was still in the same position, crouched and ready to strike if need be, keeping his gaze fixed on the mobhunters below. Leonidas was about to return to looking down when, out of the corner of his eye, he noticed something.

Crouching on top of another spruce tree, not too far from where Stan was, was another player. Leonidas's heart stopped for an instant, as he feared that he was being surveyed by another mobhunter. Yet, as he got a closer look at the player's features in the faint moonlight, Leonidas realized that this player was quite different.

The figure had dark-coloured trousers, and his upper body was covered by a black cloak that draped down over his head, obscuring his face. Leonidas could still see a pale mouth.

Leonidas remembered back to days ago, when the same mysterious player had appeared out of nowhere to defend him from Spyro. The Black Hood had returned.

Leonidas had no idea what to do. He had no idea why this player was following him. And he had no idea why the Black Hood continued to stare directly at him. Leonidas raised his eyebrows at the player, eyes wide, as if trying to ask, *Who are you? And what do you want?*

The hooded figure—the Black Hood—said nothing.

Instead, he simply raised his pale hand and pointed directly above Leonidas's head.

Leonidas glanced up behind him and immediately rolled out of the way to dodge the Spider that was dropping down from the leaves above him. The arachnid landed next to Leonidas with a clicking hiss, and Leonidas cringed, as the pain in his arm had flared up yet again from the sudden motion. He had no time to tend to his wound, though. The Spider had already hopped into the air and was about to land on Leonidas, teeth bared. Without flinching, Leonidas drew back his good hand and sunk it as hard as he could into the airborne Spider's stomach.

On contact with Leonidas's fist, the Spider hissed in pain and flew further into the air. Then, to Leonidas's dismay, the mob fell down off the tree and directly toward the mobhunters down below. Leonidas turned in a panic back to the Black Hood, wondering if the mysterious stranger could help him in any other way. But the Black Hood had vanished. And out of the corner of his eye, Leonidas saw something that made him immobile with alarm.

Stan was still in his same position in the tree, crouched and ready for action. He was staring down at the mobhunters, completely oblivious to the Spider leaping down towards him from above. Leonidas waved his hands around in desperation, trying to catch Stan's attention. He looked up at

Leonidas with a look that questioned Leonidas's sanity, right as the Spider slammed into Stan's back, and he tumbled down out of the tree, landing with a thud on the snow-covered dirt below.

The mobhunters, who had all been preoccupied with the Spider that had fallen on them, now turned on their heels to face this player who had fallen on the ground. Arachnia took a step forwards and glanced down at the player in surprise before a wild grin of victory crossed her face. The Spider reared up behind her and prepared to strike, but she cut the beast in half with a diamond sword without even turning around.

"Well, well, well," Arachnia chuckled, elation flowing through her voice. "If it isn't the great and powerful President Stan2012 of Elementia."

Stan, winded from the sudden fall to the ground, struggled to push himself up and look her in the eye, a pained expression on his face.

"Enderchick," Arachnia said, looking to her black-skinned companion. Without hesitation, Enderchick disappeared in a puff of purple smoke and reappeared with her foot on Stan's back and a wild, sadistic look in her eye as she forced him to face-plant back into the snow.

"Try anything funny, Stan," Arachnia spoke softly, as Lord Marrow drew a bow and notched an arrow, which instantly began to swirl with strange, dark magic as he loaded it, "and we won't hesitate to kill you."

Stan gave a tiny grunt but no other response. He seemed totally unable to move as Enderchick ground her foot harder into his back. Arachnia raised her fist and clenched it. Before long, the fist began to swirl with blue-grey smoke. Slowly, Arachnia brought her hand lower and lower, towards the back of Stan's head.

Then there was a roaring sound from out of nowhere. Arachnia barely had time to turn around before Leonidas's right arm struck her across the forehead. As Leonidas landed on the ground, a sickening crunch emanating from his legs, Arachnia fell unconscious to the ground. His limp left arm struck Lord Marrow against the back of the head, sending his bow tumbling to the ground, the dark arrow flying into the night sky. Leonidas gave a scream of agony and fell to the ground as Enderchick, shocked by the sudden attack, warped away from Stan, appearing a few blocks away. As she drew her sword for self-defence, Stan leaped up onto his feet, drawing his diamond sword and surging forward to attack Enderchick.

Leonidas was vaguely aware of Stan and Enderchick beginning to fight, but he was in too much pain to fully comprehend what was going on around him. Beyond the stinging in his legs from jumping off such a tall tree, his left arm, which had struck Lord Marrow across the head, was now in such agony that he found himself unable to move. And as Leonidas gritted his teeth, tears streaming down his face, he realized there was no reason to move. Arachnia and Lord Marrow were both down for the count, and Stan was fighting Enderchick—there was nobody left to harm him.

Then, all at once, Leonidas became aware of the monster directly above, preparing to bear its fangs down into him. His deflating adrenaline levels suddenly pumped up to maximum yet again. Leonidas reached into his inventory and threw the bottle of Potion of Weakness, which he had been saving for weeks now, directly into the face of the Zombie villager. As the monster flinched, Leonidas plunged his hand into his inventory again, and forced the golden apple into the mouth of the Zombie.

As soon as the glimmering fruit disappeared into the mouth of the mob, it stopped trying to attack Leonidas. After a moment of standing still, the Zombie villager fell backwards onto the ground, no longer pursuing Leonidas but rather shuddering as the wisps of smoke curled up off its body. Realizing that his job was done, Leonidas flopped back onto the ground, taking in the joy of lying still as he tried to catch his breath.

"You seem like you're having a totally awesome time, Stan!" giggled Enderchick, as she warped around Stan, dodging every strike of his enchanted diamond sword.

Stan panted with exhaustion, a slight growl of frustration escaping his mouth. He had no idea who these people were, and he was baffled as to how this player named Enderchick apparently had gained the ability to teleport at will. The one thing that he did know, however, was that he was beginning to tire, and he hadn't landed one single hit on her yet.

"You know, sweetie, if you just surrendered," simpered Enderchick, "then we could stop all this right now and just, you know, cut to the chase and stuff."

Stan's vein pulsed in his temple as she gloated, and he rushed towards her at top speed. Drawing back his sword, he launched himself into the air and spun around like a blender, trying as hard as he could to emulate the technique that he had invented on his day of axe training in the Adorian Village. Shockwaves shot out of the spinning sword, and one of the Knockback blasts slammed into Enderchick, who had teleported to avoid Stan's attack. Caught unaware, she toppled to the ground, giving Stan a free shot to her right leg before she warped away.

Suddenly, Stan sensed something approaching behind him, and he ducked to avoid the arrow that flew past his head. The glowing projectile stuck into a nearby tree, and the wooden block caught fire. Realizing that the other player must have a bow with Flame on it, Stan spun around to face the archer, who he had heard Arachnia call Lord Marrow. He was loading another arrow, but Stan saw that this one was different. As he squinted at it, he realized that the tip of this arrow had a tiny Creeper head on it. Baffled at what that could mean, Stan found himself forced to sidestep the arrow. It landed not too far from Stan, and there was a massive explosion at the spot where it landed. Stan had to raise his hands up to block the force of the blast, and he turned to face Lord Marrow again.

A horrible realization dawned on Stan. These players must be hackers! And Lord Marrow had several deadly types of arrows in his arsenal.

Frightened by the idea of what these arrows could do, Stan clutched his sword tightly and prepared to approach Lord Marrow. He knew how to approach archers; he had done it before. And if he could just get into close range, he would have the advantage.

Stan rushed forwards as Lord Marrow fired another arrow directly at him, this one trailing purple, Enderman-like smoke behind it. Stan ducked under the arrow and it curved downwards in midflight, still aiming for his head. The smoking projectile snagged onto Stan's black leather cap, pinning it to the snowy ground behind him.

Stan was too stunned to speak. Did he see that correctly? Did Lord Marrow have homing arrows?

He had no intention of sticking around to find out as Lord

Marrow readied his next shot. Stan ducked behind a tree to avoid another purple-smoked arrow, this one also curving off its path to find him but sticking in the corner of the tree before it could. Stan sprinted between the trees, as arrow after arrow flew after him. Some zigzagged their way through the branches, missing him by inches. Others connected with the trees in a massive explosion, clearing the woods of places for Stan to hide. And still others set the trees on fire, causing entire groves to go up in flames in a matter of seconds.

It wasn't long before Stan was exhausted, and he ducked behind a tree trunk that had avoided the blaze to dodge another homing arrow, this one coming within a centimetre of his foot. Stan glanced up, seeing what type of arrow Lord Marrow was going to fire next—an explosive one. Stan readied himself to dash out of the way, when suddenly, a shout rang out through the burning forest.

"Hey, Lord Marrow! Check out what happened to our little villager pal!" Enderchick screamed, her voice sounding bitter.

Stan's heart skipped a beat, and he peered around the side of the stump, preparing himself for whatever may have happened to the Zombie villager. But to Stan's total shock, the villager, who he didn't recognize, was now completely cured, no longer showing any signs of Zombie-hood. He merely looked around in a confused sort of way, the typical behaviour of a villager.

"He's, like, totally useless to us now," Enderchick spat in disappointment. "Hey, Marrow, you should totally take a break from Stan for just a sec . . . take care of that villager for me, will ya?"

And Stan watched in horror as Lord Marrow loaded his bow with another arrow—a new type, this one sparkling with electricity—turned his back to Stan, and took aim at the villager. He let the arrow fly, just as the cry "NOOOO!" escaped from Stan's mouth.

And yet, to Stan's surprise, relief and alarm, he wasn't the only one to utter this cry. He looked on as Leonidas dived out of the shadows of the forest, flying in front of the oblivious villager right into the path of the arrow, which sunk into his stomach. There was a massive crash of light and sound as, without warning, a bolt of lightning dropped out of the clear night sky through the power of the hacked arrow, striking the dark form of Leonidas. He went through a short fit of spasms in midair before he finally fell lifeless to the ground, smoke curling off his singed black leather armour and sparks dancing around his body.

Stan acted without thinking, moving purely through some primal, animal instinct as he charged into the clearing, a war cry escaping from his mouth. He sliced his sword across the unarmoured back of the totally unprepared Lord Marrow. The archer tumbled across the clearing of snow, his pained face illuminated in the light of the burning forest, and he landed with a thud next to Enderchick, who was nursing her leg beside the still-unconscious Arachnia. When she saw Stan rushing towards them, sword raised and eyes blazing with unfathomable hatred, Enderchick, with a shriek of horror, grabbed on to both of her companions and disappeared in a cloud of purple smoke, leaving Stan to sink DZ's sword into nothing but dirt.

Stan didn't care that the players had escaped. He didn't even care right now why they had come in the first place. All that mattered to him was the player lying in the snow, covered in the soot of the lightning blast, the rising and falling of his chest slow and strained. In desperation, Stan pulled off Leonidas's charred chestplate. There was a noticeable wound on his left arm, where Stan assumed the Enderman from earlier that night had probably hit him. His leather chestplate had stopped the arrow from entering his body, and the place where the lightning had struck him bore a scar in the shape of a snowflake-like pattern, directly over his heart.

"Leonidas? Can you hear me?" Stan asked, desperate to hear a response.

"Yeah," Leonidas breathed, with no hesitation, "I . . . can hear ya, Stan."

Stan's heart flooded with relief, and he let out the massive breath he had been holding in.

"Leonidas . . . that was . . ."

"Pretty stupid of me?" Leonidas asked with a faint chuckle, followed by a raspy cough.

"No . . . it was amazing," Stan replied, tears of joy streaming down his face.

Leonidas gave a faint smile, immediately followed by continued coughing and wheezing. Stan reached into his inventory and pulled out a raw pork chop, the only bit of food he had left. He put it into Leonidas's mouth and, slowly but surely, Leonidas began to chew, and eventually the entire piece of meat entered his system. Leonidas sighed in relief.

"Thanks, Stan," said Leonidas softly, though noticeably stronger. "That helped."

"You're welcome. Leonidas, do you think . . . are you gonna . . ."

"I'll be fine, Stan," Leonidas cut him off, his breathing now more even. "I've survived a lot worse than this. Just give me a couple hours to heal up, and I'll be ready to move again."

Stan smiled, not believing that he was feeling so thankful, relieved, and even overjoyed that Leonidas, who he had once called the most savage player in all of Elementia, was going to live. Finally, Stan managed to speak.

"Leonidas . . . did you mean what you said before? Do you really want to help me?"

Leonidas took a deep breath, and let out a heavy cough before responding.

"Stan, I'll tell it to ya one more time . . . I didn't choose the Alliance. The Alliance chose me. But now, it's about time that I start makin' my own choices. And ya know what, Stan? I choose the NPC villagers. I choose Elementia. And . . . I choose you."

With that, a smile crossed Leonidas's face, his head rolled to the side, his chest rising and falling in the peaceful rhythm of sleep.

Stan noticed something lying beside him, and he picked it up. It was Leonidas's bow, the one Lord Marrow had picked up before Leonidas had knocked it out of his hand in the sneak attack. Stan turned the bow over, examining it for a moment, before looking back down at the sleeping player beside him.

Stan reached into his inventory and pulled out an arrow, half-aware of the villager still wandering around aimlessly behind him (he did not recognize the villager but would be sure to point him towards his home in a little while). He notched it in the bow and got into a crouching position, ready to fire. When Leonidas had healed and he finally woke up, Stan would give the bow back to him. Until then, however, Stan stood crouched in the snow in the midst of the burning forest, ready to take down anyone or anything that attempted to harm his new ally while he rested.

Even now, as Bob entered the courtyard of Element Castle, he could hear the sounds of hard labour taking place outside the castle walls. The sounds of toil and ruthless work were occasionally interspersed with cries of suffering as the citizens of Element City worked as hard as they could on their mandated task. These sounds alarmed Bob, and he prompted Ivanhoe to run faster as they entered the main hallway of the castle.

As he steered Ivanhoe up the stairs, Bob thought about what was going on outside. He knew that what was going on was definitely necessary. While the Element City walls were still holding up, all it would take was one breach of the defenses for Element City to fall to the Noctem forces. Should that fateful day arrive, the citizens would need somewhere to stay safe, and the Mechanist's solution was indeed a brilliant one, as his solutions usually were.

For the past few days, under the authorization of the Mechanist and the oversight of Bob and his brothers, all citizens of Element City had been recruited to take up their shovels and pickaxes and construct a defensive bunker underneath the city. While the underground of Element City already held a series of mines from its founding days, the Mechanist had ordered these tunnels to be strengthened, fortified with defences, and enlarged so that the entire population of Element City could be safe underground.

However, in his messages relayed to the police chiefs from Element Castle via soldiers, the Mechanist's orders had become increasingly demanding. The Mechanist had commanded the citizens to work through the night, constantly digging and building to upgrade the tunnels as quickly as possible. Countless citizens had collapsed from fatigue, unable to work any longer. In the dark mines, dozens of citizens had been wounded by mob attacks, lava flows and falling gravel, including one player who had died via a TNT blast set off by a miner who was delirious with exhaustion. It was this player's death that had finally made Bob realize that he had to confront the Mechanist.

As he reached the top of the stairs, Bob and Ivanhoe dashed down the stone-brick corridor until they came to a stop at the door to the council room. Bob took a deep breath and gave three sharp knocks on the door. After a moment, a growling, irritated voice rang out.

"Whaddaya want?"

Bob was taken aback; he wouldn't have been surprised if the Mechanist had sounded exhausted, or even hopeless, but he hadn't been expecting any brashness. Tentatively, Bob pushed the door open. The Mechanist was sitting at the table, a mess of papers strewn out haphazardly before him, and, for whatever reason, he no longer seemed irritated. In fact, he was smiling in a goofy way.

"Ah, look who it is!" the Mechanist cried, despite the fact that Bob could hear him perfectly fine. His voice was slurred and giddy, and his Texas accent had all but vanished. "It's always a pleasure to see my favorite little pile of pork . . . oh, and you, too, Ivanhoe!"

The Mechanist burst out laughing, clutching his sides and falling out of his chair as he banged the ground with his fist. Bob looked on, feeling extremely uncomfortable. Was this the same player they had agreed would run their city?

"OK, OK," the Mechanist slurred after a moment of hysterics, grabbing the stone table and pulling himself to his feet. "All . . . *hic* . . ." A tiny hiccup escaped the Mechanist's mouth before he continued. "All hilarious comedy aside, how're you doing, Bob? Are the front lines holding up OK? And what about the tunnels? How're"—the Mechanist gave a huge, open-mouth yawn—"how're those coming along?"

"Well, uh," Bob said slowly, trying to keep his composure after the display that he had just seen. "Well . . . the front lines are holding up just fine. Our resources are starting to run a little low, but we won't have anything to be concerned about for a while. As for fortifying the old mines . . . well . . . that's actually what I came in here to talk to you about."

"Oh, don't tell me something went wrong!" cried the Mechanist, jumping to his feet, an infuriated look flashing over his face. "We need those mines fortified as fast as possible, we can't afford any setbacks!"

"Calm down!" replied Bob in hasty alarm. He was totally caught off guard by the rapid mood swing. "There hasn't been any setback! As a matter of fact the work on the mines is going at just the speed that you wanted."

"Well, then what's the problem?" spat the Mechanist as he plopped back down in his chair, no longer furious but rather agitated.

"Well, to be honest, I've come to request that you order the work schedule to slow down," said Bob, deciding that it wasn't worth it to beat around the bush. "The citizens are exhausted. They've been working nonstop, and they just need a break. Not to mention that several people have been injured, and a girl actually died earlier today."

"I'm sorry," replied the Mechanist, glaring at Bob and not missing a beat, "but do you realize what we're up against here, Bob? You're the *Chief of Police* . . . you must realize that the Noctems are coming closer and closer to breaking through our walls every day."

"Well, I—"

"And surely you realize that the second the Noctem Alliance breaks through that wall, they're going to try to take as many Elementia citizens hostage as possible. And that underground tunnel is the only place that will be safe—if you designed it the way I told you to, that is," the Mechanist spat.

"Of course I realize—"

"Then you should *also* realize," the Mechanist cut in, sounding more irritated by the second, "that completing those tunnels is incredibly important! Frankly, I don't care if a few people get hurt just so the tunnel gets done faster. If it means that the people of this city have somewhere safe to go when we get overrun by Noctem troops, then it's totally worth it! And I'll thank you to shut up and not question my logic, because I've spent far more time alone in this room thinking about what's best for this city than anybody else around here! Now go down there and get back to work! I'll have the plans for the blast doors done soon, and when I do, I expect them to be installed with no hesitation! *Do you understand?"*

As the Mechanist finished his rant, nostrils flaring and eyes bloodshot, Bob was more than a little disturbed. On the one hand, he knew that the Mechanist had a point; the Noctems could only be held at bay for so long, and it was imperative that they finish the tunnels before the walls failed them. But on the other hand, it frightened him that total control over their city was in the hands of the player who had just screamed at him.

"I understand, sir," Bob finally replied. "I'll tell my brothers, and we'll be ready to go when you finish the plans for those doors." And with that, Bob steered Ivanhoe back to the door and, vowing to keep a closer eye on the Mechanist from now on, he left the council room.

The Mechanist glanced in disgust at the door where Bob had just left. Preposterous it was, the Mechanist thought, that Bob had questioned his authority. He knew what he was doing, and clearly, if the people were demanding that they slow down their schedule, he was the only one with a clear scope of the situation.

Well, I guess what they say is true, the Mechanist thought to himself. *If you want something done right, you've got to do it yourself.*

And with that, the Mechanist extracted a bottle of blue-grey potion from his inventory, took a huge gulp and wiped his mouth. When he was finished, he put the bottle down and got back to work on the designs for the blast doors.

"LAAAAAAND HOOOOOOOH!"

Kat, who had nodded off in the cramped back of the boat, jolted upright, causing the boat to rock sharply from side to side, prompting Charlie, who was steering, to cry "Watch it!" in irritation.

"Would you all shut up?" hissed Cassandrix, looking at

Charlie and Commander Crunch, who had just shouted in surprise. "I don't know if you people remember, but we still have an entire army of Noctem troops looking for us!"

"Oh, well, pardon me," growled Commander Crunch in irritation. "Ye know, I would 'ave expected that a bunch o' landlubbers like ye would've been more excited by th' prospect o' gettin' off these ships . . ."

"Oh, trust me—we are," replied Kat, staring fondly at the mass of swampland rising up out of the distant ocean. Finally, after days and days of nothing but ocean and scattered, barren islands, they were back to the mainland. Then, suddenly, a thought occurred to her. She glanced up at Charlie sitting in front of her.

"Are you . . . gonna be OK, Charlie?"

"What? Oh, yeah, don't worry about me. I'll be fine," Charlie replied, and although Kat knew he was trying his hardest to sound earnest, there was a noticeable hint of apprehension in his voice. Kat looked at Charlie with sympathy. Although she had asked him once before, he hadn't been able to talk about the exact methods that the Noctem Alliance had used to try to get information about Element City out of him. However, Kat knew that they had targeted his legs. She imagined that he was dreading the prospect of having to walk all the way back to Element City.

It wasn't long before the two boats reached the swampy

land mass that Commander Crunch joyfully identified as the peninsula that would lead them back to Element City. As they exited their boats, Kat took a deep breath and stepped onto the soggy dirt blocks. Rex, who had been paddling beside them, pulled himself out of the water and shook his fur dry. Kat relished in the feeling of finally setting foot on dry land again after so long at sea.

The sensation lasted only for a moment, though, before there was a splash behind her. Charlie had tumbled out of the boat and into the water, and Kat helped him back to his feet, despite his protests. However, as Kat had expected, Charlie moved across the swampland with a limp, and Kat wondered how much of the damage would heal over time . . . and how much was permanent.

Without hesitation, all four players set to work. Kat and Commander Crunch broke down their two boats by hand, Cassandrix pulled out the compass and examined it, and Charlie hobbled his way over to the nearest tree and began harvesting wood. When the four of them had finished their various tasks, they walked over and met each other in a circle.

"OK," said Cassandrix, pocketing the compass. "By my estimation, we're still a few days' walk from Element City." Charlie let out a small groan. "I think that we should take a rest for now, though. We still have enough food to last us for one more night, and if we go underground then we can get materials to make some new weapons for ourselves. We'll start hiking tomorrow, after we've gotten a good night's sleep."

The four players nodded and Charlie pulled a crafting table out of his inventory. Using the wood that he had collected, he crafted some wood planks and sticks, which were soon turned into a wooden pickaxe. As Cassandrix gathered some more wood for their weapons, Charlie punched the dirt blocks on the ground until he finally hit stone. Drawing out his pickaxe, Charlie brought it down onto the stone with a mighty strike, only to wince in pain as he did so. Kat's eyebrows raised in concern. Clearly, the damage from the torture was more severe than she had expected.

"Let me see that," Kat said kindly, taking the pickaxe from Charlie's hand and intentionally avoiding his crestfallen face. It wasn't long before Kat had tunnelled down into ground, and, to her delight, came across a vein of coal ore. She harvested the black lumps, and, after she had Charlie toss a few sticks down to her, she put up torches to illuminate the cube-shaped cave she was carving out. Before long, however, the wooden pickaxe snapped off its handle, having lived out its incredibly short life span.

"Charlie!" Kat yelled. "Can you—"

But before she could finish, she watched as Charlie dropped down the hole and landed on the stone-block floor, stumbling with a grimace and an audible grunt of pain. Kat was alarmed. He shouldn't have taken any fall damage from such a short drop. She was about to go help him when Charlie looked up at her, determination in his eyes.

"Give me some stone, Kat," he grunted, pulling himself back to his feet.

"Charlie, you're hurt. Please, just let me—"

"I said, give it to me, Kat!" Charlie growled, anger coursing through his voice as he pulled the crafting table out of his inventory and slammed it to the ground in a huff. Kat stared at Charlie, taken aback by how aggressive he was all of a sudden. She handed three blocks of cobblestone to him, and he snatched them up. She looked on in shock, having trouble believing that this was the same happy-go-lucky player she was best friends with.

Kat continued to put up torches, still allowing Charlie to widen the space of their underground chamber, despite the clear fact that every stroke of the pickaxe was hurting him. It wasn't long before the chamber was a perfectly rectangular shape, large enough to comfortably hold all of them. Looking around the room, Charlie nodded to himself, drew a cobblestone block from his inventory, and placed it down, sitting on it and wiping his brow.

"All right, guys. We're done!" Kat yelled up the hole as she placed the last of the torches on the wall. "Come on down!"

Cassandrix plopped down the hole, landing gracefully next to Kat and immediately walking over to the crafting table. Then, Kat heard a yell come down from the hole in the roof.

"Ahoy scallywags, guess wha' I found!" Seconds later, Commander Crunch fell through the hole and landed next to Cassandrix and, without hesitation, he tossed a whole mess of wool blocks from his inventory onto the ground. "Thar was a flock o' sheep roamin' through th' swamp! We gonna be sleepin' comfy tonight! Well, I mean, personally, I prefer t' sleep on rigid wood planks . . . but I 'ave a feelin' that ye'll appreciate it!"

Although the prospect of a good night's sleep on a real bed did appeal to Kat immensely, it paled in comparison to the joy she felt when Cassandrix pulled a stone sword off the crafting table and put it into Kat's eagerly awaiting hands. It had been far too long since Kat had felt the wholesome completeness that came with being armed with her weapon of choice. While the bow was definitely a decent second, Kat still felt overjoyed to finally be holding a sword again.

The next couple of hours were spent mainly in silence. While her three friends stayed in the cave and crafted various necessities, Kat climbed back into the swamp and crept her way through it, gathering food for their journey with Rex at her heels, and keeping an eye out for Noctem forces hidden between the trees. As the sun started to set, Kat returned to the hole, leaping her way back in and securing a dirt block above her head before settling into the hideout.

Cassandrix and Commander Crunch were both sitting on beds that had been made from the wool, while Charlie was still sitting on the cobblestone block. All of them looked rather bored. Kat deposited the steaks she had obtained in the furnace and sat down on her own bed, stretching and giving a yawn.

Kat, not being in a particular mood to talk, simply lay down on her bed, closed her eyes, and attempted to drift off to sleep, with Rex curled up at the foot of her bed. However, try as she might, Kat was repeatedly distracted by a rumbling in her stomach. It appeared that eating could not wait until morning.

"Hey, Cassandrix," mumbled Kat to the girl in the bed next to hers. "You wanna reach into the furnace and grab a steak for me?"

After a moment with no reply, Kat continued, "Come on, Cassandrix, you're right next to it, and I really don't feel like getting up."

Still, there was no response.

"Blimey, Cassandrix!" cried out Commander Crunch, his eyebrow knitting as Kat groggily sat upright in her bed and glanced over at Cassandrix. "Th' lass asked ye a question, th' least ye can do be respond."

But suddenly, Kat wasn't interested in the food any more. Or at least, not for the time being. Rather, she was distracted by Cassandrix, who was sitting upright on her bed, her eyes glazed over and a terrified expression on her face, as if she were in some sort of trance.

"Cassandrix? Come on! Snap out of it!" cried Kat, clapping her hands together in front of her face. Instantly, Cassandrix's head gave a jolt, and she looked around in confusion, clutching her chest, before finally realizing that she was in no danger.

"Did you not hear me?" Kat demanded. "I was asking you a question!"

"Oh, quiet yourself, you impudent twit," growled Cassandrix. "Get it yourself if you're so hungry."

"What's with you?" snapped Kat. She had actually been slowly warming up to Cassandrix over the course of their journey, and she was fully taken aback by this sudden return to her stubbornness.

"Oh, that is just like you, darling . . . so ignorant, so concerned about fairness and avoiding work. Kat, do you have any idea what we're up against?" screeched Cassandrix, her eyes wide and desperate, pure, primal fear ripe in every inch of her face. "Of course you don't! You're just as ignorant as any other young player! You didn't even recognize who Lord Tenebris was, did you?"

Kat opened her mouth, then closed it. She had been about to scold Cassandrix for dwelling on what they had seen Lord Tenebris do, rather than focussing on returning to Element City. On the one hand, Kat knew that, even though they had seen Lord Tenebris demonstrate terrifying and unexplainable powers, they couldn't dwell on that now if they wanted to get back to Element City as fast as possible. On the other hand, now that Kat remembered when the two of them had first laid eyes on Lord Tenebris, Kat had definitely sensed some fearful recognition on Cassandrix's face even before he had demonstrated what he could do.

"No, I didn't recognize him," Kat finally admitted.

"WHAT?" bellowed Commander Crunch, causing them all to jump as he leaped onto his feet in outrage. "Are ye tellin' me that ye looked wit' yer owns eyes into th' most infamous, most powerful 'n' most evil demon in th' history o' Minecraft, 'n' ye didn' even recognize 'im?"

"What are you talking about?" demanded Charlie. "Of course we recognized him, Crunch . . . it was Lord Tenebris! Anybody with half a brain could figure that out!"

Rather than responding to Charlie, Commander Crunch turned to look at Cassandrix, who in turn stared back at him. Both of the older players held looks of equal disbelief on their faces.

"I don't believe it," whispered Cassandrix.

"Aye," replied Commander Crunch in an uncharacteristically soft voice. "They really don't know. . . ."

"Could you two cut to the chase already?" growled Charlie in irritation.

"Yeah," added Kat, indignant but also a little bit disturbed at her friends' reactions to her and Charlie's ignorance. "Clearly you know something that we don't, so spit it out!"

Cassandrix and Commander Crunch held each other's gaze for a long time, as if both were lost for words. Finally, Cassandrix turned to face Kat and Charlie, who had stood up and walked over next to Kat.

"The head of the Noctem Alliance," Cassandrix said slowly, as if carefully choosing her words, "is actually very well known. He's probably the most famous being in the history of Minecraft. And . . . most of the people who know of Lord Tenebris . . . know him by a different name."

"Aye," replied Crunch, giving a solemn nod. "She speaks th' truth. Have either o' ye two scallywags ever heard o' th' legend o' Herobrine?"

As the last word left Commander Crunch's mouth, Cassandrix gave a shuddery outtake of breath, and the aura of dread about her was palpable. Even Commander Crunch seemed fully absent of his usual upbeat sailor demeanor as he spoke. Charlie and Kat, on the other hand, were just confused; neither of them could recall ever hearing the name in their lives.

"No," Kat replied, quite uneasy but also intrigued. "What do you know about this . . . Herobrine?"

There was a moment of silence in which not a sound was uttered by anybody. Finally, Cassandrix spoke.

"Herobrine," she replied, taking a deep breath and trying to keep her voice stable, "is a demon. The most evil and most powerful entity in the history of Minecraft, which all but the most gullible believe to be simply an urban legend. I used to believe that as well, before I finally set my gaze upon Lord Tenebris myself."

"If it'd help ye," growled Commander Crunch slowly, his stony face flickering in the torchlight, "I jus' so happen t' know th' tale o' Herobrine's origin. 'Tis an ole tale—passed from sailor t' sailor since th' earliest days o' Minecraft—'n' perhaps, I may be able t' shed some light fer ye two on jus' wha' we be dealin' wit' in th' mastermind o' th' Noctem Alliance."

Kat and Charlie glanced at each other, then back at Commander Crunch. After a moment, Kat nodded.

"All right, Commander," Kat said, a tiny seed of fear in her heart as Charlie sat down in his bed to listen to the story. "Tell us the story of Herobrine."

And with that, Commander Crunch pressed his fingers together in front of his mouth and began to speak.

"Nigh-on three years ago, a Minecraft player posted a

message on an online message board. T' this day, nobody can say fer sure who this player was. This was back in th' days when Minecraft was in th' Alpha stage o' development, 'n' prone t' countless bugs, errors, 'n' glitches. Th' post consisted o' a simple thread o' text. Here be wha' it said:

"'I had recently spawned a new world in single-player Minecraft. Everythin' was normal at first, as I began choppin' down trees 'n' craftin' a workbench. I noticed somethin' move amongst th' dense fog . . . I 'ave a mighty slow computer, so I 'ave t' play wit' a wee render distance. I thought 'twas a Cow, so I pursued it, hopin' t' grab some hides fer armour.

"'Aye, but it wasn't a Cow.

"'Lookin' back at me was another character wit' th' default skin, but his eyes were empty, white, and lifeless. I double-checked t' make sure I wasn't in multiplayer mode. He didn' stay long, though . . . he looked at me 'n' quickly ran into th' fog. I persued out o' curiosity, but he was gone.

"'I continued on wit' th' game, nah sure wha' t' reckon. As I expanded t' world I saw thin's that seemed out o' place fer th' random map generator t' make by itself; square tunnels in th' rocks, wee perfect pyramids made o' sand in th' ocean, 'n' groves o' trees wit' all thar leaves cut off. I would constantly reckon I saw th' other player in th' deep fog, but I ne'er got a better look at 'im. I tried increasin' me render distance t' far whenever I thought I saw 'im but t' no avail.

"'I saved th' map 'n' went on th' forums t' see if anyone else had found th' pseudo-player. Thar were none. I created me own topic tellin' o' th' scallywag 'n askin' if anyone had a similar experience. Th' post was deleted within five minutes. I tried again, 'n' th' topic was deleted even faster. I received a private message from username "Herobrine" containin' one word: "Stop."

"'When I went t' look at Herobrine's profile, th' page was gone.

"'I received an email from another forum user. He claimed we were safer usin' email. Th' email claimed that he had seen th' mystery player, too, 'n' had a list o' other users who had seen 'im as well. Thar worlds were littered wit' obviously man-made features as well, 'n' described thar mystery player t' 'ave no pupils.

"'About a month passed till I heard from me informant again. Some o' th' players who had encountered th' mystery scallywag had looked into th' name Herobrine 'n' found that name t' be frequently used by a Swedish gamer. Aft some further information gatherin', 'twas revealed t' be th' brother o' Notch, th' game's developer. I personally emailed Notch 'n' asked 'im if he had a brother. It took 'im a while, but he finally emailed me back a mighty short message.

"'He said: "I did, but he be no longer wit' us.""

"'I haven't seen th' mystery scallywag since our first encounter, 'n' I haven't noticed any changes t' th' world other than me own. I was able t' press "print screen" when I first saw 'im. Here's th' only evidence o' his existence.'

"'N' attached t' this player's message," Commander Crunch continued, as Charlie and Kat listened on, intrigued, "was a picture. Th' picture showed a Minecraft world in deep fog, wit' trees, hills, 'n' a chicken. 'N' peekin' out o' th' edge o' th' fog be a player wit' navy-blue trousers, a turquoise shirt, 'n' empty, white eyes.

"Naturally, at th' time when this all came out, 'twas ignored, 'n' th' player was called out as a faker," Commander Crunch continued. "However, afore long, this mysterious, dead-eyed player named Herobrine began t' appear in other servers. Everywhere he went, he brought havoc wit' 'im, spawnin' lava in houses, creatin' mysterious structures in the worlds of unsuspectin' players, destroyin' thin's that others had created.

"He would also kill some players, playin' psychological tricks on them by leavin' items behind them when thar backs were turned, makin' bumpin' sounds in the night, makin' them feel as if they were bein' watched, 'n' slowly drivin' them further 'n' further into madness afore finally endin' them, 'n' corruptin' thar entire Minecraft server once 'n' fer all.

"It wasn't till a few famous Minecraft players had Herobrine appear on thar livestreams that scallywags finally began t' share thar tales. Since then, Herobrine has become somethin' o' an icon t' Minecraft. 'N' as soon as he became famous, thousands o' scallywags started t' fake sightin's o' 'im, eager t' get thar fifteen minutes o' fame by convincin' scallywags that they've got th' real proof that Herobrine exists.

"They be a bunch o' no-good leeches, be wha' they be, nah takin' th' demon seriously jus' 'cause they wants a good laugh. They don't care fer th' scallywags who really 'ave lost entire servers full o' players t' th' scourge o' Herobrine.

"Oh, 'n' if ye're feelin' sceptical, 'n' don't believe that Herobrine exists, then I ask that ye look no further than Minecraft itself. Every time a new update gets released, they'll also put out a list o' all o' th' changes t' Minecraft in th' newest version. 'N' at th' end o' every single list, ye'll always find th' same message: 'Removed Herobrine.' They keep on removin' Herobrine from th' game . . . but he keeps comin' back. I rest me case."

"I know that it's incredibly hard to believe," cut in Cassandrix, sounding stressed. "Trust me, I never believed it for a second . . . I always assumed that all Herobrine sightings were hoaxes, and when Mojang said that they'd 'removed Herobrine' from Minecraft, they were just going along with the joke. But when I saw Lord Tenebris sitting on his throne, I knew that he wasn't a player, not even a player who was using mods. There was something about him that was . . . off. Something that seemed . . . inhuman, though I couldn't put my finger on what it was. And seeing him use those powers only confirmed it for me.

"Trust me, you two . . . I'm a grounded person," said Cassandrix, and Kat could sense Cassandrix's heart racing almost as fast as her own. "I'll have trouble believing anything until I see it with my own eyes. And Lord Tenebris . . . he's no player. He's something far worse than that . . . far worse than you can even comprehend."

The four players sat in silence for nearly five full minutes, as Kat and Charlie tried to absorb everything that Crunch and Cassandrix had just said. Finally, Charlie spoke.

"So . . . as far as you know"—he spoke tentatively, and Kat sensed, for the first time in months, a tiny element of his old fear worming its way into his voice—"what exactly *is* Herobrine? And what exactly is the extent of what he can do?"

"That's th' scariest part . . . nobody has an answer t' either o' those riddles," Crunch replied solemnly.

"If I had to venture a guess," Cassandrix replied slowly, "Herobrine is most likely some sort of major coding glitch in Minecraft that managed to grow stronger and stronger the more the people at Mojang tried to fight it. And eventually, it got so strong that it was able to behave and act like some sort of mob."

"Aye, that be one theory," agreed Crunch, nodding his head. "Yet another be that Herobrine be th' agonized spirit o' th' dead brother o' Notch, th' creator o' Minecraft, that managed t' fuse itself wit' th' codin' o' Minecraft itself 'n' become some sort o' half code, half demon monster."

"Oh, please, let's try to stick to rationality here," spat Cassandrix at Crunch arrogantly. "Even if it were somehow possible for a dead person to become part of a game, Notch has gone on record to say that he doesn't really have a dead brother."

"That's jus' wha' he wants us t' think . . . I smell a conspiracy here, I do . . ."

"Anyway," continued Cassandrix, pretending that she couldn't hear Commander Crunch prattling on, "to answer your second question, Charlie . . . nobody really knows exactly what Herobrine is capable of. I think we can all agree that he was obviously born out of some sort of glitch—although we can only guess what that was—and the fact remains that he's already shown himself to have powers that are at least equal to those of an operator. If he can do that . . . well, as to the rest of his abilities, we can only speculate until the day when we get to see more of them firsthand."

"I gotta say, Cassandrix," cut in Commander Crunch in a taunting voice, "fer somebody who claims they ne'er believed in Herobrine till now, ye seem t' 'ave a decent amount o' knowledge about 'im."

"Well, I think you'll find a solid reason for that, Commander," Cassandrix replied coolly. "While I never saw fit to believe something with no evidence behind it at all, I always found it a pleasure to look on at those who did and have a good laugh to myself about it. And yes, I do in fact remember a thing or two of what those gullible saps said."

"Oh yeah?" cut in Kat. For some reason, something in Cassandrix's reply had plucked a nerve in her. "Well, if you're so high and mighty, how does it feel to know that this entire time, you were wrong and those 'gullible saps' were right?"

Cassandrix whipped around to face Kat, and opened her mouth to retort, then abruptly closed it. Kat was shocked; she had never seen Cassandrix rendered speechless before. There was a split moment of silence before finally, Charlie cut in.

"It's late," he grunted. "We've all been at sea for way longer than is good for us. It'll affect your mental state if you stay out there too long—"

"Hey! What're you tryin' to say?" Commander Crunch cut in, outraged.

"And we really need a good night's sleep," finished Charlie

without missing a beat. "Let's just go to bed now. We hit the road for Element City in the morning."

And with that, Charlie flopped down on his bed, turning his back to the others. Seeing no reason to argue, the other three players did the same thing, with Commander Crunch still grumbling softly to himself about Charlie's final comment. Kat hardly noticed, though. Her head was too full of thoughts from the stories she had just heard.

Kat had always fantasized about having operating powers. From the moment that she had heard about them, she had imagined herself wielding their incredible strength, using them to become the most unstoppable force in all of Elementia. And now here she was, preparing to fight against a being that not only had abilities that were apparently quite similar to operating powers, but were even stronger than that.

Long after the snores of the other three players had started up with various degrees of volume, Kat still lay awake in her bed, dreading just what exactly it was that she was preparing to face.

Are you kidding me?"

"Calm down, Khan!" shouted Arachnia, her firelit face tired and stressed. "The situation is bad enough, and getting angry won't help."

"Oh, just shut up!" spat Creeper Khan, his gritted teeth showing as he sunk his hand into a nearby tree in frustration. "Honestly, you have no idea how hard I'm trying to stop myself from blowing up this entire forest . . ."

"Arachnia, I don'd ged id," said Zomboy innocently, looking at her in confusion. "If dere were tree of you—and jusd two of dem—how come you did nod win?"

"Finally, that giant hunk of rotten flesh says something logical!" hissed Creeper Khan as he whipped back around to glare at Arachnia.

Arachnia took a deep breath, then replied, "I told you, they had the element of surprise on their side. I certainly wasn't expecting Leonidas to jump me like that. It's the same reason I was able to take down Kat and that other girl she was with by myself—they didn't see me coming."

"Well, even if you did manage to . . . ugh . . . lose to just two people, then why is it that Enderchick didn't warp Zomboy and me over to you guys?" Creeper Khan demanded. "We weren't doing anything, and if you knew that Stan was on that island, then we definitely weren't going to miss anything by leaving our posts. Why didn't Enderchick just grab us?"

"Ugh . . . right, that . . . ," spat Arachnia in disgust. She still couldn't believe the excuse Enderchick had given her. "Apparently, she was just *too tired* from warping three people at once, and couldn't bring herself to warp again until she rested."

"You cannot be serious!" bellowed Creeper Khan, a vein pulsing in his forehead. "You're telling me we lost the opportunity for the biggest paycheck we've ever gotten just because that little spoiled brat couldn't be bothered to move?"

"Yep," sighed Arachnia in disgust.

"Argh!" Creeper Khan gave a bellow of rage, and not too far away from him, an explosion came from nowhere and blasted all the leaves off the top of a tree, leaving the trunk engulfed in fire.

"Watch it! You'll kill us if you can't control yourself!" cried Arachnia, leaping to her feet before clutching the lump on her head, and forcing herself to sit back down on her tree stump while Zomboy lumbered over to the burning tree and punched the fire out.

"Whatever," shot back Creeper Khan, plopping himself onto the soggy ground with a wet smack, and beginning to punch the dirt in frustration. There was a moment of silence, with nothing but the ambient sounds of the dark, soggy swamp around them as Zomboy lumbered back over to the group and sat down next to Arachnia.

"You know, it's been way too long," grunted Creeper Khan impatiently after a minute. "Why isn't Enderchick back yet?"

"Well, that's a good point, actually," replied Arachnia, as she realized just how long Enderchick had been away. "She should be back. Her talk with Drake shouldn't be this long. Do you think that he might have done something to her once he found out what happened?"

"Doubt it," Creeper Khan said, with a dark snicker. "If there's one thing we know, it's that she'll always be able to warp if it's *her* sorry self on the line. Wouldn't you say, Marrow?"

Lord Marrow, who had been leaning up against a tree a distance from the campfire while looking down at the ground, glanced up to look at Creeper Khan. The player's skeletal face raised an eyebrow and took a tone of indifference for a moment before returning to its original position.

Creeper Khan gave a soft growl. To be honest, he was getting really sick of everybody on his team being so intolerable, what with Arachnia's condescension and Enderchick's ditziness, and the less said about Zomboy, the better. Lord Marrow was the only one who Creeper Khan had really been able to tolerate, and now even his perpetual stoic silence was wearing on him.

"You know, maybe I won't even wait," he spat. "Maybe I'll just use my Final Nova on all of you—"

"I told you not to joke about that!" Arachnia cried, suddenly looking terrified.

Creeper Khan's retort, however, was broken by the sound of teleportation, as Enderchick appeared next to the campfire in a puff of purple smoke.

"Finally!" grunted Creeper Khan in disgust as he whipped around to face her.

Arachnia sat up straight and asked, "What did Drake say, Enderchick?"

"Omigosh, just, like, give me literally two seconds to rest, people," whined Enderchick, sitting down on another tree stump and looking pouty. "Ya know, it's not, like, *easy* to warp from Element City to this stupid suh-*wamp* . . ."

"Cry me a river," cut in Arachnia, as Creeper Kahn sputtered in outrage, "build a bridge . . . and then go jump off it. You were the one who caused us to lose Stan, Enderchick. You're in no position to ask for favours."

"Well ex-*cuuuse* me, princess," huffed Enderchick. "You know, whatever, I'll tell you. Basically, Drake told us that he was, like, super mad at us for losing Stan. Like, I dunno, he said something, like, *'If you don't get Stan to me before he gets* to Element City, I will be forced to turn you over to Lord Tenebris.' I mean, he's like, so melodramatic . . ."

"Haha . . . melondramatic . . ." Zomboy chuckled, his mouth hanging open and a dopey expression on his face. "Haha . . . I like melons . . ."

Zomboy continued laughing while Enderchick absent-mindedly wiped a spot of mud off her leg. Creeper Khan gave a roar of frustration and glared at Enderchick and Zomboy, then yelled, "You two are nothing but a couple pieces of brainless, incompetent—"

"SHUUUUT UP!"

Arachnia's yell was so loud, so forceful, and so harsh that immediately, all three of her fellow mobhunters whipped around to face her, and were terrified by the wrathful expression on her face as she clutched her diamond sword. Even Lord Marrow glanced up from the ground, his eyes locked on to her.

"Do you people realize," whispered Arachnia with more power than a yell could ever convey, and her face devoid of anger but ripe with fear, "the position that we are in right now? Do you realize what will happen to us if we *don't* have Stan delivered to Drake on a silver platter within the next couple of days?"

The four other members of ELM just stared at her for a moment. They all knew the answer, but Arachnia said it anyway.

"We'll suffer. We'll suffer hard. I don't think that any of you truly comprehend the kind of forces that we're dealing with here. The Noctem Alliance is powerful, but they're also ruthless and merciless. I think that if you'd just put your ridiculous squabbling to the side for a minute, you'd realize that we've got one foot in the grave and another on thin ice right now."

There was yet another moment of silence, but now the truth of Arachnia's words sunk into the other mobhunters. They all remembered the things they had heard about the Noctem Alliance, all the horrible stories that had passed through their small outpost in the middle of the desert about what the Noctem Alliance was capable of. Never had it fully hit them that, should they fail, all that power would be directed on to them. They all knew now that the time had come to fully devote themselves to their work. Even Zomboy waited with bated breath for Arachnia's next order.

"OK," continued Arachnia, her breathing calm but her tone serious, "Enderchick, did you ask Drake how close they were to breaking into Element City, like I told you to?"

"Yes," Enderchick replied, no longer distracted but fully focussed. "He told me that they would be through the wall within a matter of days . . . that something special is headed for Element City, like, right now, and when it gets there, they'll finally be able to get in."

"OK then, team," replied Arachnia, her mind kicking into hunting mode as she glanced around at her four fellow members of ELM. "Here's the plan . . ."

"You can't be serious!" Stan exclaimed.

"As much as I hate to say it," replied Leonidas, his eyebrows knitted and his expression grim, "it's true, Stan."

"And . . . you're saying . . . ," continued Stan, as he tried to wrap his head around the ramifications of what Leonidas had just told him, "that . . . *that's* the guy who's leading the Noctem Alliance? The guy who can do all *that* stuff?"

Leonidas nodded, his expression dark. As much as he had hated to explain to Stan exactly who Lord Tenebris was, he knew it had to be done. Although Stan was most assuredly terrified out of his wits at the prospect of fighting the most powerful and evil being in Minecraft history, he still had to know as much as possible about what the Noctem leader was capable of. Suddenly, Leonidas realized that he was walking alone. He stopped, and looked behind him to find Stan stopped in his tracks, staring at the ground in foreboding between two particularly large swampland trees.

"Are ya all right, Stan?" Leonidas asked in concern, doubling back to where Stan was.

As he looked up to face Leonidas, Stan's face showed a mixture of confusion and fear. "Not really, no," he replied honestly. "So you're telling me that Lord Tenebris, or . . . how do you pronounce it . . . Hiro . . . Haro . . ."

"It's Herobrine, Stan," Leonidas corrected him, and he sounded it out. "Heh-roh-brine." Leonidas shook his head in disbelief. "Honestly . . . You're a Minecraft fan, you've been on the internet before, but ya still don't know who Herobrine is? How's that possible?"

"I don't know!" exclaimed Stan. "I mean, to be honest, I've just been playing on Elementia for as long as I've been in Minecraft . . . I've never really had to leave for anything, I learned how to play in the Adorian Village, and I've kind of been too busy since then to look around at a lot of other Minecraft-related stuff."

"Well, in that case, lemme make one thing clear to ya, Stan," replied Leonidas, and Stan looked him in the eye.

"All that stuff I just told ya about Herobrine, and what he can do . . . some of it might not be true. Everythin' that I think Herobrine can do is based off what people've spread around. Nobody knows for sure what he can and can't do, 'cause people keep on pullin' off hoaxes and pranks to make their friends think they've seen Herobrine and stuff like that. Matter of fact, the people who made Minecraft've said that Herobrine doesn't really exist. 'Cause of that, your guess is as good as mine what Lord Tenebris, the *real* Herobrine, is capable of."

"Wait . . . hold on," said Stan slowly. "You're saying that people fake sightings of Herobrine all the time? The same way that people fake, like, Loch Ness Monster sightings or Bigfoot sightings?"

"Exactly."

"Well . . . then . . . how do we know that Lord Tenebris is really Herobrine?" Stan asked, his spirit lifting slightly at this idea. "How do we know that the Noctem Alliance isn't just faking it to intimidate us?"

"'Cause I've been face to face with him, Stan," Leonidas replied darkly. "Once, months ago. Right after you and your army beat the King, me, Caesar and Minotaurus made our way to Spawnpoint Hill, and he appeared in front of us. And he was floatin' in midair, Stan. That's not just somethin' that any old player could do. He was either an operator, which ain't possible, or he was somethin' else.

"And trust me, Stan . . . it wasn't no special type of monster spawned in with mods or nothin'. When I first saw Lord Tenebris, I looked him straight in his dead, white eyes. but I could only hold eye contact for a second. I'm not entirely sure why, and to this day I can't put my finger on it, but there was somethin' in those eyes that was more sinister and evil than I can put into words, maybe because they definitely belonged to somethin' that wasn't human.

"To be totally honest with ya, Stan, I haven't seen Lord

Tenebris since that day. All my communication with him has been through Caesar, and 'cause of that I have no idea what he really is capable of. And maybe that's the scariest part. Besides, even now, months later, those eyes still haunt me . . ."

Leonidas realized how long he had been talking, and he looked up at Stan. The look on his face was concerned, anxious, and unnerved all at the same time. There was a moment of quiet, as neither of them knew what to say. Then, finally, Stan spoke.

"Well, I can tell you one thing, Leonidas. If the prospect of just seeing Lord Tenebris affected you that badly, then I can only imagine how hard it must've been for you to leave the Noctem Alliance and join us." Stan's voice was kind and sympathetic. "I'm glad that you're here with me, Leonidas, and I'm proud to call you my friend."

Leonidas looked up. When he looked into Stan's eyes, there was no fear. There was only simple joy and contentedness.

"Thanks," Leonidas replied with a smile.

Before Stan could reply, though, Leonidas suddenly became aware of a sound, and he held his hand up to silence Stan. A screeching noise vaguely reminiscent of a jet engine was coming from above their heads, and it was growing louder by the second.

"What is that?" Stan asked, looking skywards as Leonidas

glanced around, his eyes finally locking onto a small mine not too far from them. Without hesitation, Leonidas grabbed Stan's arm and yanked him down into the tunnel. The two glanced up through the canopy of leaves above their heads and into the pink glow of the sunset sky as the sound escalated into a deafening roar.

Then, without warning, a massive black form rocketed directly over their heads. The two players couldn't make out what it was through the thick foliage, but the deafening sound and strong tailwind that rustled the leaves forced them to duck their heads even deeper into the mine. They barely had time to comprehend what had happened when another giant black object flew overhead, bringing the same cacophony and strong wind stream with it.

Stan and Leonidas stood with their backs to the wall in the mine, their hearts racing, armed with sword and bow, trying to ready themselves for whatever it was that had just passed them. After a minute, however, nothing happened. The environment had returned to normal, and while Stan could still hear the jet sound, it was getting softer and softer.

"What were those things?" Stan breathed.

"No idea," replied Leonidas, "but I'm gonna find out."

And before Stan could stop him, Leonidas jumped up out of the mine and onto the soggy dirt blocks of the swamp ground. He aimed a few well-placed punches into those dirt blocks, and used them to create a stairway on the side of one of the tall trees they were next to. Leonidas sprinted up the dirt blocks and perched himself on top of the tree.

Above all the rest of the swampland forest, Leonidas could see the landscape stretching out for thousands of blocks. He scanned the darkening pink horizon, and there, far in the distance, he could make out two indistinguishable black forms, flying away. Leonidas glanced at the sun behind him, hardly noticing the gorgeous sunset, and realized that the creatures were headed southeast. As he realized this, Leonidas's heart skipped a beat.

"What did you see?" asked Stan apprehensively as he pulled himself out of the mine.

"I couldn't see what those things were, Stan," Leonidas replied, distraught. "But whatever they are, they're headed straight toward Element City."

"Ah, he lives!" snickered Jayden as G walked over to him. "How're you doing, man? And what've you been up to? You're hardly ever around any more."

"Well, there's a good reason for that," G sighed, sitting down on a seat next to Jayden in the only other available seat in the packed rec room. "Tess has been working me nonstop. To be totally honest, I'm exhausted."

"Wait, seriously?" asked Jayden, his mouth hanging open

in surprise. "You've been doing stuff with her this whole time? Even during training exercises?"

"She says that she needs me training with her more than I need combat training," G said, reaching into a nearby chest. "What've you guys been doing in combat training, anyway?"

"Well, to be honest, it's actually pretty boring. You should feel glad you're missing it." Jayden sighed. "It's pretty much a rundown of the same sort of advanced combat lessons we used to give in the Adorian Village . . . nothing too exciting."

"Sorry. Although I personally would be happy to take a break and be with you guys. I mean, Tess is nice to me and all, but she just has the constant need to keep training me. She never gives me a break, and I'm getting sick of it."

"Really," replied Jayden. "Do you think she might be into you or something?"

"I don't think so," replied G. The thought had crossed his mind, but he was pretty confident that that wasn't the case. "She might as well be, though. The constant work after training is done is really wearing me out, and I've just about had it with her."

Jayden opened his mouth, one step away from saying something, but he closed it before he could. Now that he finally had a chance to relax, Jayden was sure G wouldn't particularly care to hear what he wanted so badly to say. There'd be time for that later.

"Anyway, I just stopped by to grab my pickaxe," groaned G, pulling his iron tool out of the chest. He had his diamond pickaxe hidden on hand, but he was saving it for an occasion in which he really needed it. "I have to go see Tess again."

"Are you serious?" asked Jayden in disbelief.

"Yep," replied G glumly, standing up and walking away from his friend. "I'll see you later, OK?"

And with a stunned look on his face and an absent-minded waving hand, Jayden watched G walk out the door.

G looked up and saw General Tess, her pink face alert and attentive, standing at the same place in the marble hallway where she always was when they met up after hours.

"Good evening, MasterBronze," Tess greeted him, in the same way that she did every other night.

"Good evening, ma'am," G responded, as if programmed.

"Tonight, I have a very special job for you, soldier," Tess commanded, sounding rather important. "As I'm sure you know, in conquest of the lands surrounding Elementia, we were able to capture and occupy the Adorian Village. In doing so, we have taken several members of the village as captives, who will be used as ransom as soon as the glorious Lord Tenebris sees fit."

"I see, ma'am," replied G, trying as hard as he could to hide the fact that his heart was racing at the mention of these hostages.

"I feel that in the past few days, you, soldier, have proven yourself competent enough in my leadership exercises that I feel comfortable entrusting you with a task on your own."

"Thank you, ma'am," G said, his heart skipping a beat. What exactly did she mean by that?

"Therefore, MasterBronze, I am entrusting you with the checkup on the captives. You will go down into the left chamber of the ground floor, where you will find the Adorian Villagers. You will give them their weekly ration of food, ensure that no escape attempts are in progress, and report back to me."

"Will do, ma'am," said G. His response came out a bit happier than it ought to have been, but he was having trouble keeping himself from dancing with joy. Finally, at long last . . . he had a clear shot to free the prisoners. They were almost being gift-wrapped for him.

"Go ahead now, it shouldn't take you long," Tess commanded lazily, handing G a stack of bread before turning around and walking back down the hallway. "I'll tell the guard to give you clearance."

Wasting no time, G turned on his heel and made his way down the marble hallway, down a flight of stone-brick stairs, and into the central rotunda of the building, a bounce in his step the entire way. He followed the directions that Tess had given him, finally arriving in front of a player holding a diamond axe, dressed in full black leather armour and standing before an indentation in an obsidian wall alongside a lever and an iron door.

"Nobody's allowed in there," the guard grunted.

"My name is MasterBronze," G replied. "I was sent by General Tess to check on the prisoners."

With no hesitation, the guard pulled the lever, and the door scraped open. *Wow!* G thought to himself as he walked through the doorway. *This isn't nearly as difficult as I was expecting it to be!*

The inside of the room was dim. There were a few torches lighting the walls, but they kept the room just bright enough to keep mobs from spawning, and the little light they did cast seemed to be consumed by the blackness of the obsidian that coated the roof, floor and walls. Huddling over in the far left hand corner was a mass of players, looking malnourished and miserable.

One of the players turned his head around in a jerky manner, and glanced up at G in an equally twitchy way. All at once, G felt himself stop in his tracks.

G knew this player. His skin was identical to Stan's, though lighter overall. G guessed that this was a common skin, and so he looked into the player's eyes to be positive. It was true. G recognized this player from months ago—he would recognize the skin, eyes and twitchy mannerisms anywhere.

The strange thing was, though, G also knew this player was dead.

"Sirus?" G asked, as though he were addressing a ghost.

"Wha . . . how . . . how do you know my name?" the player asked, his face shifting from downcast to paranoid.

"Dude, look into my eyes . . . it's me, G. From the old Adorian Village," G answered with a smile.

Suddenly, comprehension flashed across Sirus's face for a split second, and then he broke out into a tremendous smile.

"Goldman! Oh boy, am I glad to see you, because, you know, it's so dark in here, and I've been stuck with these people for weeks. You know, I mean, no offence to you guys, but it's so nice to see somebody else, somebody I know, somebody who—"

And then, like the flip of a switch, Sirus ceased to be happy, and instead looked baffled.

"Who would never work for the Noctem Alliance in a million billion years, and so what gives, G? Why're you here? Did you have some sort of change of heart or what?"

"I'm here to rescue you guys," replied G hastily, more focussed on asking the dozens of other questions exploding in his mind as Sirus's face flipped back to ecstasy. "But I'll get to that in a minute. First of all, how are you still alive?"

"Whaddaya mean?" Sirus asked.

"I mean . . . I . . . you got killed!" cried G. "In the Battle for Elementia! Archie told me that he saw you get killed by one of King Kev's soldiers who was dressed up like a giant zucchini wearing a sombrero! How did you get back into Elementia if you died?"

"Huh . . . oh, yeah, that little thing," Sirus replied with a chuckle, shifting gears from confusion to laughter. "Well, it's kind of a funny story, 'cause you see, after I helped you guys disarm all those redstone contraptions before the battle started, I went into battle with you, and I managed to stay alive for a pretty long time, 'cause, you know, I can never stay in one place, so it's pretty hard to catch me, but then that thing happened where I took an arrow to the knee, and then the zucchini guy hit me with a potion and then killed me and stuff, and the next thing I know, I'm sitting right back on Spawnpoint Hill, and then I—"

"WHAT?" demanded G, so loudly that the other hostages, who had turned their heads in curiosity, jumped with surprise. "You managed to respawn? How is that possible? Elementia's a Hardcore PVP server. You can't respawn after you die!"

"Well, that's what I thought, too," continued Sirus, shrugging. "But it still happened, even though I have absolutely no idea what caused it."

G scratched his head, trying to think of what could possibly have caused this phenomenon. "Well, I guess it could've just been a glitch in the system or something. A lot of people did die in that battle, maybe the blacklist got overloaded or something . . ."

"Yeah, maybe," replied Sirus, still extremely jittery. "Anyway, after I respawned, I saw somebody duck into the woods and I figured that the hill probably wasn't safe, so I decided that I wanted to go out into the middle of the Ender Desert because I thought that could be fun, but then I got hungry and tried to eat part of a cactus, and it kind of caused me to hallucinate to the point where I imagined that I was at a wedding between a cantaloupe and a watermelon whose families disapproved of their union due to the parents' deeply rooted prejudices against fruits that were different from themselves, but then I woke up from the hallucination and found myself in the care of a player in a black uniform who was trying to teach me how to use seashells as toilet paper, and then I realized that the Ender Desert was a weird place and I wanted to go home, so I made my way to Element City, and may have gotten a bit lost on the way, but when I stopped in the Adorian Village for a snack break, the Noctem Alliance captured me and brought me here, and weren't you saying something about an escape plan?"

G, who had tuned out the insane redstone mechanic in the midst of his rambling, was still floored that Sirus was somehow alive. As he realized that Sirus had stopped talking, though, he realized that now was neither the time nor place to question it. He had a rescue to pull off.

"Yeah, I was. Take this," replied G, reaching into his inventory and pulling out his diamond pickaxe, relinquishing it to the deranged-looking yet brilliant player sitting across from him. "And here's your food for the week, too.

"Now I don't have much time," continued G as he removed the bread from his inventory and put it on the ground in front of Sirus. "If I'm in here too much longer, they'll start to suspect something. Here's the plan: Tess told me that they check on you guys once a day. So after three days, I want you to tunnel out of here. The pickaxe will be strong enough to break through the obsidian, and you guys can tunnel your way into the tundra and make your way back to Element City from there. Don't do it any earlier than three days from now, or they'll suspect me of helping you. Got it?"

"Sure do," replied Sirus, glancing down at the diamond pickaxe he was holding in his hand and feeling elated. "I'll be sure to get all these guys back to Element City safely, Gold-man, don't worry about nothin', you can count on me to—"

Suddenly, he was cut off by the iron door creaking open. Light flooded the obsidian room, and G heard the guard's voice call out, "Hey, is everything going OK in there?"

Without hesitation, G lunged forward and sunk his fist as hard as he could into Sirus's stomach. Sirus let out a tiny choking sound and shock flashed across his face, but he concealed the diamond pickaxe in his inventory all the same as he slammed to the floor, wheezing.

"And you'll get far worse than that if you ever mouth off to me again!" G bellowed harshly. Sirus's shocked eyes suddenly showed comprehension as he realized what G was doing.

"Do you understand, you maggot?"

"I do," croaked Sirus feebly, as he gave G an almost inconspicuous wink. G looked sympathetic for an instant, and mouthed the word "sorry" before turning his back on the prisoners, all of whom were looking at G with bemused expressions.

"Don't worry about it," G assured the guard, with a confident nod. "He won't be showing any more disrespect to a member of the Noctem Alliance any time soon. I've made sure of that."

The guard nodded, showing no signs of suspicion whatsoever as he pulled the lever down to close the iron door. As G walked down the hallway and back towards the rec room, he knew that he ought to be thrilled and relieved that their plan had gone off flawlessly, and the hostages would escape from Nocturia within the next few days. However, this was not at the forefront of his mind.

He couldn't wait to get back to Jayden and discuss the

fact that Sirus was still alive. That meant that somehow, something had gone wrong in the coding of Elementia, allowing Sirius to respawn after he'd been killed. And if it had happened once, G realized that it was possible that it could happen again. . . .

"**S**tan?"

"Hold up!" Stan cried out, holding up his hand and stopping dead in his tracks. Leonidas, who had been walking alongside Stan, stopped abruptly and turned in alarm. "Stan? Can you . . . hear me?"

"Yeah, I can," Stan replied, raising his hand to silence a perplexed Leonidas.

"Come to . . . SalAcademy. I have something . . . to tell you . . ."

"I'm on it," Stan replied, and with a pop of static, Sally's voice disappeared.

"What *was* that?" Leonidas inquired, sounding confused.

"That girl Sally just contacted me," Stan replied.

"Again?" Leonidas groaned. This had happened quite a few times before, and it always slowed their progress.

"Afraid so," replied Stan, and with that he sat down on the ground, taking a deep breath and preparing to disconnect from Elementia.

"Now wait just a sec, Stan!" Leonidas interjected, grabbing him by the shoulder and pulling him back to his feet. "Do ya *really* have to go see her right *now*? Do ya realize just how close we are to Element City? If we travelled all day, we'd be there by nightfall, get a good night's sleep, and we could spend the entire day tomorrow figuring out how to get past the Noctem forces outside the city walls."

"I know that, Leonidas, but I still really have to do this," Stan replied firmly. "I seriously do have important business to take care of. The fate of Elementia may depend on it!"

"I still don't understand why ya can't just tell me what this incredibly important *stuff* you have to do is," mumbled Leonidas bitterly.

"Trust me, if I told you, you'd think I'm crazy."

"I think you're crazy now," retorted Leonidas as Stan made his way to sit down again. "At the very least, though, could you join this other server in a more hidden spot? You realize I'm gonna have to defend the place you left while you're gone."

Stan nodded, and immediately, the two of them scouted the swampland around them until they came across a cave. They walked down into it and found a pool of molten lava, providing a nice, inconspicuous source of light at the bottom. Leonidas noticed a rectangular indentation in the wall, as if somebody had tried to dig through but hadn't gotten very far.

Stan sat down next to the pool of molten lava as Leonidas drew his bow. Leonidas looked on as Stan took a deep breath, and a moment later, he disappeared. Leonidas took his position looking up at the cave mouth. He was a little annoyed at Stan for forcing him to do this, but at the same time, he was intrigued by what this mystery task could possibly be.

Stan opened his eyes and once again gazed over the familiar sight of the midday sun peaked in the blue sky over the endless field of green grass. Intent on locating Sally, Stan turned his head to the right, only to find himself face to face with a Creeper.

"Augh!" bellowed Stan as he summoned a diamond axe into his hand with the power of his mind and sunk it as hard as he could into the creature standing beside him. As it fell over, Stan was shocked to see Sally's body fall to the ground with a smack, a tiny Creeper Head and a diamond sword bursting out of her inventory as she did so. Seconds later, there was a pop as Sally reappeared next to Stan, giving him an accusatory glare.

"What was that for?" she demanded. "I was just trying to have some fun!"

"I'm sorry, you scared me!"

"Ugh . . . I forgot who I was dealing with," spat Sally, walking over to her items and retrieving them from the ground. "The great Stan2012 . . . the guy who's gonna save Elementia from descending into chaos, and also freaks out the second a Creeper looks at him funny. Don't worry, noob, next time

I'll play a slightly more tame prank on you. Hmm . . . I know! How about I replace Element Castle's doorbell with a farting sound? You think you could handle that without freaking out?"

"Well, you're forgetting one thing," retorted Stan, flustered with embarrassment. "In order for that to work, you'd kind of have to be *in* Elementia, Sal."

"Ouch," she replied, her eyebrows raising. "To be honest, I didn't think you'd go there so easily. Oh, and speaking of which, thank you for killing me by sinking a diamond axe into my chest, Stan. That didn't give me any horrific flashbacks of the Battle for Elementia at all."

"Ooh," cringed Stan. He had almost forgotten that. "Sorry . . ."

"Eh, whatever, I don't really care. Just watch what you say to people, noob. Anyway, there are a few really important things we've gotta discuss," Sally said solemnly, and immediately, Stan wondered what could have made Sally suddenly so serious.

"First, though, let's do a little review. You know, just to be sure you retained everything from the last time we met up."

"Sounds like a plan to me," Stan replied.

"All right, noob . . . Take care of this for me." And Sally closed her eyes and stretched out her hand, instantly causing a wall made out of wood to appear.

Stan took a deep breath and stretched out his hand. He focussed hard on a feeling of warmth building up inside of him and then, with all his mind, he pictured a Ghast. All at once, a fireball shot out of Stan's hand, rocketing forward until it hit the wooden wall in a burst of flames. With a grin, Stan proceeded to launch a volley of fireballs at the wood until finally, it all burned away.

"OK, then . . . try this one!" cried Sally, and a solid stone wall appeared in place of the wooden one. Stan focussed all his power into his fist, imagining the explosive power contained within a lightning-charged Creeper as he did so. Stan launched a punch in the direction of the wall, and he felt a pulse of invisible energy leave his fist. An instant later, there was a powerful rupture in the centre of the wall, which formed a circular hole. Stan fired off a blitz of continuous punches at the wall until, finally, the last stone block had disappeared.

"Not bad at all," replied Sally with a smirk. "But now, here's the real challenge!" Sally stretched out her hand, and concentrated as hard as she possibly could on a patch of ground in front of Stan. Then, all at once, a swarm of about ten Blazes encircled Stan, taking deep metallic breaths and preparing to fire.

"Don't use a weapon, Stan," ordered Sally with a leering grin, "and get out of this one."

With only an instant to think, Stan realized what he had to do. He leaped into the air, narrowly dodging the storm of fireballs flying in his direction. The Blaze's projectiles all hit one another, yet they took no damage from the resulting fire bursts. The smoking mobs made of yellow rods rose up towards Stan, ready to pursue him, but Stan was prepared.

He took a deep breath, stretched out his hand, and after a moment, an arrow appeared from nowhere at the tip of his hand and flew directly into the skull of one of the blazes. With a laugh, Stan proceeded to fire a rapid chain of arrows as fast as a machine gun, which mowed down the entire row of mobs in a matter of seconds.

Sally clapped her hands together as a shower of Blaze Rods showered down onto her, and Stan landed gracefully on the ground a moment later. "Well done, noob," she said with a kind smile. "I've taught you well."

Stan gave a dark chuckle of reply. "Yeah, you have . . . although I hope it doesn't end up being useless. What's the status on getting me those powers in Elementia?"

"I'm glad you brought that up, actually," replied Sally, summoning herself a chair of leaf blocks to sit on, raising her feet on an ottoman made of a sponge block and crossing her legs at the knee. "We have to talk about that."

"Oh, boy," replied Stan, conjuring up a similar chair for himself out of wool blocks. "In my experience, 'we have to talk about this' means that I'm gonna walk away from this conversation unhappy."

"Well, unfortunately, you're right," Sally replied, and Stan gave a pre-emptive sigh of disappointment as Sally continued.

"I've been doing a lot of digging into Elementia's coding, trying to find a good access point to try to hack operating powers onto you. What I've found, though, is security has been increased big time. I'm not sure why, because I've been covering my tracks pretty well, so nobody can tell that I've been looking in there. And for some reason, most of the security seems to have been added to the player files—in other words, the place I have to hack into in order to give you operating powers."

"Well, that's just wonderful," sighed Stan in exasperation. "Why do you think that is?"

"I was about to ask you the same question, noob. I can't think of any reason they would beef up the firewalls and safeguards of the player files . . . unless, of course, you've told anybody about our plan?"

"I promise you, I haven't," replied Stan quickly, raising his hands into the air. "I'm not going to tell anybody about the plan, no matter what, not even Kat or Charlie when I finally get to see them again. I haven't even told Leonidas, and he's the only player besides you I've been able to talk to for weeks."

"Hmm," murmured Sally, a disapproving look on her face. "Stan, I know that I've brought this up before, but . . . that player you're travelling with has committed some pretty horrendous crimes. What makes you so convinced that he's really on your side?"

"Believe me, Sally," answered Stan with no hesitation, "I believe him. He nearly sacrificed himself to save an NPC villager. And he was raised by Oob's family. The Noctem Alliance lost him the second they attacked Oob's NPC village. He's a changed player now."

"OK, OK, I trust your judgment," sighed Sally, nodding. "Just . . . promise me you won't tell anybody . . . especially him."

"I promise," repeated Stan.

"OK, good. Unfortunately, though, noob, the increased security isn't the only bit of bad news."

"Ugh . . . what else is new?" spat Stan in disgust.

"You see," continued Sally, "when I was looking through the server's coding, I came across a few very interesting things. As it turns out, Elementia isn't like other Minecraft servers. It has a few unique tics to it that make it . . . different. And not in a good way."

"Example, please?" asked Stan, despite not really wanting to know.

"I was getting to that," growled Sally irritably. "One of the biggest things I noticed is that, even though I thought there were no mods on the Elementia server itself, just on a few of the players, there actually *is* one."

"Really?" Stan inquired, floored by this news. "But everybody tells me that, besides the whole you-can-only-die-once thing, Elementia is the same as every other Minecraft server!"

"Well, actually, noob, the mod I'm talking about ties into the . . . ahem . . . 'you-can-only-die-once thing,' as you so eloquently put it. The mod in Elementia is called the Modelock Mod. I'd be here forever if I explained to you everything that this mod is doing. To put it simply, the Modelock Mod makes it so that not only can operators die and get banned like everybody else, which is another something that isn't like other Minecraft servers—usually the operators are unkillable—but operators also can't change the game mode."

"Um, what do you mean exactly, when you say 'game mode'?" asked Stan, puzzled.

"Well, basically, game mode controls the settings for how difficulty in Minecraft servers works. Like, Elementia is a Hardcore PVP server, which means that you get banned if you die, you regenerate health really slowly, and the monsters are locked on the hardest setting. But in a normal server, an operator could change Elementia into a Regular PVP server, which lets players respawn when they die and makes the monsters easier to kill."

"So, are you saying that if King Kev hadn't installed that mod, and I got operating powers in Elementia, I could have made it so that people could respawn after they were killed here?" Stan asked, mortified.

"That's correct," replied Sally grimly. "Because of the Modelock Mod, the only person in Elementia able to change the server's game mode was King Kev, and only back when he still had operating powers. And because he died and got banned from his own server, now it's impossible for Elementia's game mode to ever be changed again."

"And . . . the only reason that King Kev isn't able to get back into Elementia . . . is because of that same mod?"

Sally nodded.

"Well, if that's the case, then King Kev is an idiot!" shouted Stan, leaping to his feet and punching his chair in frustration. "Why would he install a mod that could do that?"

"Well, I'll tell you at least one good reason," replied Sally glumly. "I looked up the Modelock Mod, and apparently it's one of the highest-quality mods ever made. It would take somebody way more talented than me to hack it now that it's set up. Once it's installed, it's not ever getting uninstalled. I don't think King Kev himself could undo it if he wanted to. Elementia's game mode is permanently locked onto Hardcore mode, and it's totally impossible for anybody to hack their way back in—all because of this one mod."

"Well," sighed Stan, "as much as I hate to say it, it's probably best that we don't even try to get rid of it. The last thing we need is for King Kev to make his way back into Elementia."

Sally nodded in agreement, but suddenly, her face looked even more distressed.

"Stan, to be honest, I really wish I could say that that was the worst news I have to tell you but . . . I can't."

Stan stared blankly at Sally. What else could she possibly have found out? She didn't wait for his response before continuing.

"When I was looking through all these files, there was one other thing that I noticed besides the new security and the Modelock Mod. And that was that the normal programs were . . . I'm not sure how else to put this . . . starting to fade."

"What are you talking about? What does that mean?"

"Well, to put it simply, the normal program files that run vanilla Minecraft—you know, the original code, with no mods, that allows regular Minecraft to run the way it does—they need power in order to run. Normally, when a Minecraft server is run, power is given equally to all the different parts that need it. But for some reason, in Elementia, power is being drained out of the programs that make the world run, and it's being sucked into something else."

"How is that possible?" demanded Stan. "And what does that do? Will it have effects on the server? Does it mean that the world of Elementia is going to start fading away or something?"

"To be totally honest, Stan . . . I have no idea. I've never heard of anything like this before, and your guess is as good as mine what the effects will be like in the world. But I can tell you one thing for sure: The Noctem Alliance is the cause of it. As I tried to find out what the power was being diverted to, I had to make my way around firewalls, and all of them were the same type used by the Noctem Alliance, telling me to go away or face the consequences."

"So . . . you're telling me that the Noctem Alliance is actually stealing energy . . . *from the server of Elementia itself*?" Stan managed to get out as he started to panic. "And you have no idea how, or why? Are you saying that the power they're stealing could be used to make their players more powerful? And, if they're taking power away from Elementia, then there's a chance that Elementia could be destroyed for good?"

Sally, who had begun to breathe heavily, nodded, took a deep breath, let it out, and looked Stan directly in the eye.

"Stan . . . as much as I hate to say it . . . it gets worse than that."

Stan's jaw dropped. "But . . . how?"

"The Noctem Alliance isn't just diverting power from Elementia. They're also taking power from other Minecraft servers, too, using the internet. I don't know how they're doing it, or why, but somehow, the Alliance is drawing in and stealing power from every other Minecraft server in the world, and putting it towards something."

Stan's mind couldn't comprehend what Sally was saying. She had said that there was a chance that, by drawing in power from Elementia, the server itself could be corrupted, and maybe even destroyed. So . . . if the Noctem Alliance was also drawing in power from other Minecraft servers using the internet . . . then . . . that meant . . .

"Stan, the situation is dire now," Sally told him. "You have to get back to Element City as quickly as you can. You have to lead your citizens to take down the Noctem Alliance. As soon as I figure out how to get around the Modelock Mod and get operating powers to you, you have to defeat Lord Tenebris immediately. We have no time to waste. Every second is precious. Stan, the fate of not just Elementia . . . but of the game of Minecraft itself . . . is in your hands."

"Bill! Yo, Bill!"

Bill, who had been surveying the depths of the tunnel with increasing anxiety, whipped his head around. His eyes locked onto Ben, standing at the mouth of the tunnel. Bill had to squint to block out sunlight from above, which was jarring after the dark of the cave he had been working in.

"What is it?" Bill hollered back up to Ben, struggling to make himself heard over the sounds of hundreds of labourers and the construction from deep within the bunker.

"I want to go see how Bob is doing, but I can't. I'm too busy up here!" Ben yelled. "Could you go do if for me, please?"

"Sure!" Bill responded, and he began to make his way back up the mines, running parallel to a rail track that led up into the street. To be honest, he had been totally wrapped up in leading the digging of the bunker, which still wasn't large enough to hold the entire population of the city if the Noctems launched an attack. He had nearly forgotten about Bob, who had been out of commission since earlier that morning, when Ivanhoe had tumbled down an uneven patch of rock and injured his leg.

With no Potions of Healing in the city to spare any more, Bob had been forced to use other foods to try to heal Ivanhoe as quickly as possible. Bill desperately hoped that Bob would be back on Ivanhoe soon—they were in need of all the help they could get. A group of labourers pushing a mine cart with a chest approached Bill, and he helped them push it over the last stretch of upward track until they finally made it out of the mine and back onto the street.

The labourers immediately emptied all the stone from their inventories into one of the scrap fires scattered around the street. Bill, figuring that he might as well help them finish, proceeded to help empty the chest in the mine cart into the fire as well. He only threw out the stone, leaving the coal and various ores that had been excavated in the chest. With the lack of supply lines from the outside, this mine was presently one of the only sources of materials for the people of Element City, and they weren't going to waste it. As soon as they had finished, the labourers gave Bill an appreciative nod of thanks, and brought the mine cart back down for another load as Bill proceeded to jog down the street.

Bill continued to walk until he reached an unassuming storefront a distance away from the entrance to the mine, where the ruckus of the excavation could barely be heard. The building was made of wood-plank blocks. It was clearly old and altogether plain and featureless, save a worn-out sign spelling out the word **APOTHECARY** above the door. Bill gave three sharp raps on the wooden door, and it opened. On the other side was a player dressed in an indigo robe emblazoned with golden stars, and a long white beard.

"Hello, Chief," the old player greeted him wearily, a smile spreading across his face.

"Hey, TrumpetBlaster. How's he doing?"

"Quite well, you'll be happy to know," TrumpetBlaster

replied. "I suspect that Ivanhoe will be ready to return to work by the day's end. He's already walking about by himself perfectly fine, and with a few more hours of healing he'll be able to carry Bob again."

"Excellent," Bill said, his heart lifting. "You're a genius, you know. Not just anybody could heal a pig up that fast using just stale bread and carrots. You have no idea how much we appreciate it."

TrumpetBlaster gave a wise chuckle. "Don't mention it, my dear boy. I'm always happy to assist any friends of the Apothecary. Thank him, if you're going to thank anyone. He taught me all I know. I only wish there were more in this city like me, who are able to appreciate the art of healing without the assistance of—"

"Bill? Is that you?" a shout from within the house cut in.

"Yeah, it is," Bill shouted in reply, giving the old player a look of apology, to which he gave an understanding smile.

"Bro . . . you need to see this."

Instantly, Bill was seized with dread; he hadn't heard Bob sound that scared in a long, long time. Ignoring TrumpetBlaster's raised eyebrows of confusion, Bill ran into the house. The inside was bare, containing only a few chests, and a staircase, next to which Ivanhoe was lying down. On the wall directly opposite the door was a bed, on which Bob was sitting, staring out the window, unmoving.

Bill sat down on the bed next to his brother, and followed his gaze out the window. What he saw made his heart stop.

They could see the entire city. Hundreds of houses and buildings stretched out for thousands of blocks, finally culminating at the Element City wall, which was raised high above the tallest buildings of the outer ring of the city. And far beyond the wall, outside the city and up in the sky, were two black forms, growing closer and closer by the second. As they drew nearer, the sky outside Element City darkened. As Bill focussed intently on them, he could make out two mobs as large as Ghasts, with skeletal black bodies and three skulls sitting atop of each of them.

Leonidas's head popped up out of the hole as fast as lightning, his hand instantly going to his bow. Before he could draw an arrow, though, Leonidas's gaze fell onto a chicken, wandering in and out of the trunks of the dense grove. Leonidas released his breath and let out a sigh, shaking his head. This wasn't the first time an animal had spooked him, and he had a feeling it wasn't going to be the last.

Ugh, I am gonna kill Stan when he gets back, Leonidas thought to himself bitterly, as he sunk back down into the stone basin of the cave in which he was sitting. *Why is he takin' so long? He knows that we've gotta get back to the city!*

What could he possibly be doin' that's more important than savin' Elementia?

Leonidas took a deep breath and sighed to himself. He supposed that he had signed himself up for this. After all that the Noctem Alliance had put Stan and his people through, Leonidas hardly felt that it was his place to be complaining, especially considering that Stan had forgiven him. It was still frustrating, though. Although Leonidas had faith in Stan and was sure that he had a plan, it was infuriating to be left in the dark.

With a sigh of acceptance, Leonidas glanced down into his inventory and checked his supplies. They were nearly out of food again. Perhaps he could go do some hunting before Stan got back. Leonidas drew his bow, glanced back up, and froze.

Four players were standing on the dirt above Leonidas, encircling him from all sides of the cave entrance. Turning his head slowly, Leonidas realized he recognized two of them. Kat had a stone sword clutched in her right hand and was giving Leonidas a steely glance, her wolf beside her, snarling. Charlie looked ferocious, as if he were barely keeping himself from diving into the mine and tearing Leonidas apart with the stone pickaxe clutched firmly in his right hand. The other two players Leonidas didn't recognize. One had an Elementia soldier uniform and a scruffy beard, while the other was wearing a dirty white robe and had gigantic red lips. Both were staring Leonidas down with equal contempt.

"Make one wrong move and we attack," growled Kat.

Stay calm, Leonidas, he told himself, taking deep breaths, glancing around nervously and suddenly becoming aware that his weapon was still clutched in his hand.

"Where is Stan?" the girl in white asked, an upper-class accent in her voice.

"He's gone for now," Leonidas answered calmly. "But I'm—"

"What do you mean?" Charlie barked, causing everyone to jump. "Where's Stan? What did you do to him?"

"Boy, if ye so much as laid one single finger on 'im," the bearded soldier growled, "I'll 'ave yer head!"

"That's not what I mean!" Leonidas replied, a note of panic creeping into his voice now as he scolded himself for his choice of words. "Stan's alive, he's just . . ."

"Are you torturing him somewhere?" the big-lipped player squealed, sounding abhorred.

"No!" Leonidas shouted desperately. "Stan's totally fine!"

"Then where is he? Show him to us!" demanded Charlie, a passionate rage emanating from him that shocked Leonidas. The last time he had fought Charlie, he had come across as a cowardly wimp.

"I . . . I can't!" Leonidas sputtered as he tried to explain himself. "He's just . . . he went to . . ."

"If you don't tell us *exactly* where Stan is *right now,* then we are going to kill you, Leonidas," Kat said, jabbing her sword in his direction.

"That's what I'm tryin' to tell you guys! Stan is . . . well, he left . . . he's not here, so . . ."

"Charge!" bellowed Commander Crunch, and in one motion, all four players and the wolf leaped down into the cave, weapons ready and flying directly towards Leonidas.

For a moment, Bill and Bob could only sit frozen, transfixed as the two giant, evil mobs flew closer to the city. With every passing second, they could see more details of the charred skeletal structure and empty eyes. And as the two mobs neared the outer wall, an alarming realization struck Bill.

"This is what they've been holding out for," he breathed, still staring out the window as his brother turned to look at him. "This is the Noctem Alliance's trump card. They've managed to create and tame a pair of Withers, and they're going to blast their way into the city by force."

Bill turned to face Bob. For a moment, the two of them stared at each other in silence as the reality of what was happening dawned on them. Then all at once, the aura of tension and panic in the tiny room of the shop broke.

"One of us needs to go down and help out the army," said Bob, his eyes wide with intensity.

"I'll do that," replied Bill, turning around to face TrumpetBlaster, who was standing in the doorway of the house with a concerned, confused look on his face.

"TrumpetBlaster," Bill ordered, "I need you to get Bob and Ivanhoe back to the bunker. Take as much medicine as you can with you. I have a feeling you're going to be needed down there."

"Understood," TrumpetBlaster replied. He darted over to his two chests and began filling his inventory with remedial medical supplies. Bill turned back to face his brother.

"I'll get all the workers down into the bunker, and tell Ben to round up the rest of the citizens," Bob said. "I can't move by myself right now, but I can still help organize from the bunker's entrance."

"You've got to do it fast, though," continued Bill, foreseeing a great danger and determined to prevent it immediately. "Once the Withers break through the wall, they'll probably start attacking the city next. The Noctems still don't know where the bunker is, but if the Withers see everybody rushing into it, then they'll know where we are. That means that you have to get everybody in the city down into the mine before the Withers get here. That should only be, like, a minute or so after they break through the wall."

Bob's jaw dropped. "But . . . but . . . there're no way that we can possibly get everybody in the city down into the bunker in time! And even if we could, it's not nearly big enough to hold everybody yet—"

"Then just get as many in there as you can!" cried Bill in desperation. "We can make runs back into the city later to get more people. For now, we just have to get as many people down into that mine as possible. Now stop wasting time and go!"

And without waiting for a response, Bill leaped up off the bed and sprinted out the door, leaving his brother, the pig, and the disgruntled pharmacist in the tiny shop behind him.

Bill looked around, and in a second his eyes locked on to what he was looking for—a stone-brick pillar, a support beam for the monorail track that ran above the rooftops of Element City. Bill sprinted down the street and before long, he reached the base of the pillar, and leaped up to grab the bottom rung of the attached wooden ladder. With a grunt, he pulled himself up on to the ladder in full, and proceeded to climb until he had reached the top of the pillar. Bill now stood on a flat brick surface, on top of which were two side-by-side train tracks, glowing red and gold with redstone power.

Reaching into his inventory, Bill set a tiny mine cart onto the tracks that, upon touching the rails, expanded into a full-size mine cart. Thankful that he always carried one of these around with him (one never knew when a crime might take place on the railroad), Bill leaped into the cart and drew out his fishing pole. He drove the wooden rod into the ground and gave an almighty push, setting the cart in motion.

The redstone-powered rails accelerated the mine cart at an astounding rate until Bill was rocketing full speed down the rail tracks in the direction of the outer wall of Element

City. There was nothing to do now but wait to arrive at his destination, so Bill watched in awe at the scene unfolding over the wall.

The two Withers were still approaching, getting closer to the top of the wall itself. Despite the fact that it was midday and the sun still shone overhead, the sky above the two Withers was eerie and dark, a deep purple fog blocking out the light. It was like the onset of some ancient evil. Then, when they were just outside the wall, the two Withers stopped. They simply hovered in midair, each of their heads looking down at the scene below them, as if they were scouting out the situation. Even from halfway across the city, with the rumbling *clickity-clack* of the rails singing beneath him, Bill could make out the cacophony of yelling soldiers in the wall, barely audible at such a distance but still clearly shocked, panicked and terrified.

Suddenly, a ghastly sound fell over Element City, as if some evil, metallic skeleton were taking a dying breath. The middle head of one of the two Withers began to glow, and two black projectiles shot from their mouths. They flew almost faster than Bill's eyes could track, and they ruptured with thunderous blasts on the wall, leaving two sizable holes.

The response was immediate. Bill could make out what appeared to be a flock of birds rising from the wall, but which he knew to be hundreds of arrows flying up towards the two Withers. The giant mobs were forced to double back to avoid the rain of attacks from the Elementia soldiers, and the workmen inside the walls repaired them in an instant, regenerating the walls as though its cells were growing back.

The moment of victory, however, was just that—a moment. The Withers began to glow again, this time not just the two middle heads but all six of the black skeletal heads. A rapid-fire, machine-gun spray of black bombs flew from the Withers' mouths, causing a destructive flashing over the walls more intense than the fireworks at a Fourth of July finale. The constant barrage of skulls tore into the wall, shrinking it faster than the soldiers within could put it back together.

The soldiers weren't going to go down without a fight, though. All throughout the barrage of explosive attacks from the Withers, the soldiers were firing back. Arrows thickened the air, and the constant sound of high-pitched fire charge attacks gave Bill goose bumps. At one point, Bill was amazed to see a block of TNT fly up into the sky and make contact with one of the Withers, sending it careening backwards.

However, throughout the attacks on the Withers, the monsters kept firing, and Bill realized that they were becoming surrounded in some sort of dark energy. Streams of purple smoke seemed to be rising out of the walls of Element City and wafting back up to the Withers, and, despite the fact that the monsters were clearly raking in a few hits from the counterattacks, they continued to fire on the wall.

It was then that Bob realized, with a terror-stricken start, what was happening. In their police academy training, he and his brothers had learned about the Wither, alongside all other hostile mobs in the game. What he was witnessing before him was proof of the Wither's most terrifying attribute, which made it arguably harder to kill than the infamous Ender Dragon. Every living mob that the Wither hit with its blasts was inflicted with the toxic Wither effect, the same type of deadly poison that a Wither Skeleton could give a player. However, unlike the Wither Skeletons, the Wither was healed by all the health that it stole from its victims.

The Withers had to be poisoning dozens of Elementia soldiers by the second. And as long as they kept doing that, the Withers would keep healing. There was no way they were ever going to die.

The attacks from the wall were starting to die down. The soldiers below were running out of arrows, or retreating to avoid the onslaught, or . . . Bill realized with a clench of his heart that they might all be dead. The two Withers continued to fire, the barrage of explosions never slowing down, until finally, the two monsters ceased their attack.

The outer wall of Element City, which had once stood so tall and proud, and defended the city from the attacks of the Noctem Alliance, now had a giant hole right in the centre. A huge expanse of the wall had been totally destroyed, leaving Element City, the only safe haven from the Noctem Alliance left on the server, completely vulnerable. From his elevated perch on the rail tracks, Bill could see hundreds of black-clad Noctem soldiers rushing across the ravaged landscape and into the streets of the city.

Bill reached into his inventory and drew an iron sword. Usually he only held it as an alternative to his fishing rod, but he was glad he had it now. He grabbed the hilt of the sword with both hands and jammed the tip of the blade into the stone ground below him. Sparks flew out from the iron blade, showering the rails and, slowly but surely, bringing the mine cart to a screeching halt.

Now that the wall had fallen, there was no point in going there any more, Bill thought gravely. He had told his men what to do when this inevitable day finally came. As he sat there in the mine cart, his men were falling back, preparing to fortify secondary defensive positions within the outer merchant district of the city. With any luck, they would be able to hold the Noctem Alliance at bay for a while, allowing the citizens time to retreat into the bunker.

When he and his brothers had made those plans, though, they hadn't accounted for Withers. . . .

In any case, Bill knew where he was most needed. He used the sword to give himself a solid push back in the direction he'd come from. It wasn't long before the mine cart was barrelling down the tracks yet again, carrying the steel-hearted police chief back to his two brothers to help get as many citizens into the mines as possible.

Bill turned around and glanced behind him at what the Withers were doing. They appeared to have set off in opposite directions, using their machine-gun-fire explosions to rip the now undefended wall to shreds. Bill was perplexed. That didn't make any sense . . . surely, the Noctem Alliance would want to keep the walls as intact as possible, right? He imagined they would want to keep the defensive measures around the city, so that the city wouldn't be defenceless when they won the war.

Suddenly, Bill realized the errors in his thinking. *If,* he told himself sternly. *If they win the war. Which they won't. Because we're going to beat them.*

Before long, Bill reached the stone pillar where he had first boarded the train. He hopped out of the moving cart and landed gracefully on the tracks. He slid down the ladder and landed on the ground, just as the redstone lamps around the city started to go on. The darkness of the Withers had spread over the city, and it was now dim as night. Bill sprinted down the street, and eventually reached the entrance to the mine.

It was pandemonium. Everywhere the eye could see, players were rushing around desperately, all clambering towards the entrance to the mine in a massive wave. Bill saw one player, with a red skin and a purple sash, trip as he made his way to the entrance, and the rush didn't slow down or even acknowledge him. He struggled to get up, constantly being forced back to the ground by the people trampling over him. It wasn't until Bill drew his sword and stepped into the midst of the crowd, creating a disruption in the flow, that the player was finally able to get up and continue his way into the bunker, giving Bill a look of thanks as he did so.

"Ben!" shouted Bill, locating his brother and running up to him. The black-haired police chief was leading a group of volunteers, assisting them in pulling up the rail tracks that led out of the mine, erasing any evidence that the bunker had ever been there. When he heard his name, he looked up and jogged over to meet his brother.

"Are they almost all in?" Bill yelled, struggling to be heard over the panic around him.

"Yeah, almost," Ben shouted back. "Bob's down in the mine, getting people organized. I say we close up the bunker door in a couple minutes. We can organize missions from inside the bunker to get the people who we had to lock out."

"Fine," Bill grunted, sadness gripping his heart as he thought of the hundreds of people who would be left exposed in the city.

"How's the wall holding up?"

"Not good, bro," Bill sighed. "The Withers tore through it entirely, and the Noctems are in the city now. The soldiers are going to their secondary positions, but they won't be able to hold them for long. The Noctems will reach Element Castle within the next ten minutes, I'd say."

A look of despair crossed Ben's face at the news, but then, all of a sudden, he looked mortified, like he had just realized something.

"Oh, no . . . ," he breathed. "Element Castle . . ."

"Yeah? What about it?" Bill yelled, the noise still deafening. "We can't worry about it now, I'm sure we'll be able to take it back eventually—"

"No, it's the Mechanist!" Ben shouted, looking his brother in the eye. "The rest of the staff of the castle came by a few minutes ago . . . but not him! He's still up there, and I have no idea why!"

Bill glanced up at Element Castle, with its proud stone spires silhouetted against the ominous black sky. If the Mechanist was still in there by the time the Noctems arrived . . .

"Go to the castle now, bro," ordered Bill, gripping his brother's shoulders. "I'll tell Bob what's going on."

Ben nodded and sprinted as fast as he could toward Element Castle as Bill turned around and ran down through the throng of players and into the bunker.

Leonidas's senses tingled, and he dive-rolled to the side as the big-lipped player, who Kat had called Cassandrix, swung her sword around the side of the tree he was hiding behind. As her stone blade wedged into the tree, Leonidas simply got to his feet and ran. Try as he might to explain what had happened to Stan, he had never been able to get more than two words out before another one of the four players had been on top of him, thirsty for his blood.

Leonidas doubled back yet again as the bearded soldier, apparently named Commander Crunch, leaped out and jabbed his sword directly at Leonidas's head.

"Stand 'n' fight, ye lily-livered swine!" the Commander bellowed, following up his initial strike with a series of swipes. Leonidas ducked and weaved through them all, just as he sensed another player coming up behind him. Thinking fast, Leonidas sprawled to the ground, dodging Charlie's pickaxe. The two fighters, who had both been aiming for Leonidas, locked their blades together, and he used their recovery period to draw an Ender Pearl from his inventory and pitch it up to the top of a nearby tree, warping there an instant later.

Leonidas took a deep breath, relishing the brief moment of peace. As good as he was at evading attacks, even he couldn't deal with the constant onslaught for too much longer. For the past five minutes, every turn he had made had seen one of the four players ready to bear into him with the full force of their weapons. It was a miracle that Leonidas hadn't been hit yet.

"Get down here right now, Leonidas!"

As he heard Charlie's voice screaming from below him, Leonidas glanced up from the leaf blocks he was lying on and looked down at the clearing, only to immediately duck to avoid the arrow flying at his shoulder. Leonidas popped back up, outraged. The four players were standing in the clearing, eyeing Leonidas with the utmost contempt, as Kat loaded another arrow into her bow.

"Get down here!" Cassandrix screeched up at him yet again.

"I'll come down only if y'all promise to stop tryin' to kill me!" Leonidas bellowed back. He was beyond enraged that these players, who were supposed to be the representatives of goodness and justice in Elementia, couldn't stop attacking him long enough for him to explain.

"If you don't come down right now, Leonidas," Kat growled, looking at him through the sights of her bow, "then I'll make you come down myself."

Leonidas gave a harsh laugh. "Oh, and how're ya gonna do that, eh, Kat? Ya gonna shoot me or somethin'?"

Kat put her hand up to her mouth, and let out a two-note whistle.

Leonidas heard a rustling in the tree behind him. He barely had time to turn around before Kat's wolf barrelled into him, head-butting him out of the tree and crashing them both to the soggy ground with a thud. Leonidas cringed, the wind knocked out of him. He was barely aware of Kat calling the wolf back to her side.

Slowly, Leonidas forced himself up onto his elbows and then his knees, only to realize that two stone swords, a stone pickaxe, and a bow were all aimed directly at him.

"Put yer hands in th' air, ye dirty rotten villain," Commander Crunch spat at him.

Slowly, trying to be as cooperative as possible despite the anger boiling in his stomach, Leonidas obliged.

"Tell us where Stan is right now," Kat continued, her voice monotone and her face steely as she continued to train her bow on him.

"I told ya," Leonidas replied desperately, "he ain't here . . . in Elementia, I mean . . . he left . . ."

"So Stan was killed?" Cassandrix demanded, her already pale face now nearly colourless.

"No, he ain't dead . . . I'm helpin' him now, I swear . . ."

"Cut the crap! Where is he?" Charlie bellowed, his face radiating with supreme hatred. *"Answer me!"* He dashed forwards, a noticeable limp in his step, with pickaxe drawn, and shoved it up under Leonidas's chin until they were nearly face to face. *"What did you do to my best friend?"*

"I . . . uh . . . he . . . ," Leonidas sputtered, panicking as he stared directly into Charlie's wrathful eyes. "I mean . . . he left . . . to go to . . . another . . ."

"That's it!" Charlie screamed, and he raised his pickaxe high over his head.

There were shouts behind him. "Charlie!" from Cassandrix. "Charlie, no!" from Kat. "Control yerself, lad!" from Commander Crunch. But it was too late. Charlie's pickaxe fell fast and hard towards Leonidas's skull. There was no time to react. Leonidas simply closed his eyes and winced, waiting for the blow to connect.

Then, with no warning, there was a powerful gust of wind in front of Leonidas, followed by a sharp clang of weapons colliding and the grunt of Charlie falling backwards to the ground. Amazed, yet perplexed, Leonidas opened his eyes. What he saw made his heart skip a beat.

Directly in front of Leonidas, between him and Charlie, was a cloud of purple smoke, the by-products of an Ender Pearl. As the smoke particles cleared away, the form of another player became visible. Leonidas would recognize the navy trousers and dark shoes, flowing black cape, and head covering anywhere. The Black Hood turned around and looked at Leonidas. He still couldn't make out the upper half of the face, but the player's pale mouth was curled up into a reassuring smile. Leonidas could nearly hear the words ringing in his head—*It's going to be all right*.

The Black Hood turned back around, diamond sword still raised in front of him in a block, to face the four players and the wolf before him. Rex looked curiously up at the strange player, while Cassandrix, Commander Crunch and especially Charlie, who was still lying on the ground, looked terrified at this mysterious stranger, who had appeared from nowhere to aid Leonidas.

Kat, on the other hand, stepped forwards, hardly daring to believe her eyes. She looked into the hidden face of the Black Hood, and suddenly recognized him.

"It's you," she whispered, staring in awe. "From the Mushroom Islands."

The Black Hood turned his head to look at her, and gave a subtle, yet very distinct, nod.

"Then . . . why are you protecting Leonidas?"

The Black Hood cocked his head to the side for a moment, and then turned to look down at Leonidas again. He proceeded to give a small smile, before again turning back to Kat. She looked at him, and suddenly, an overwhelming feeling came over her. Inexplicably, she knew what the Black Hood was trying to tell her.

"Are you . . . trying to tell me . . . ," Kat managed to get out, hardly believing what she was saying, "that . . . Leonidas is telling the truth? That he *is* helping Stan?"

As her three friends glanced at Kat as if she had gone insane, the Black Hood said nothing. Instead, he turned on his heel and proceeded to sprint towards the cave opening where Leonidas had been hiding. When he had reached the mouth of the cave, the Black Hood jumped into the air, and an instant later, was consumed by a cloud of purple smoke. When the smoke cleared, the Black Hood was nowhere to be seen.

All five players stared at the smoke, transfixed. They continued to stare until the purple smoke had dissipated completely, and even then they still found themselves unable to move as they tried to comprehend what had just happened.

Then, all of a sudden, the players heard footsteps echoing up out of the cave. They looked on expectantly, waiting to see the mysterious player emerge from the ground. And yet, the Black Hood was not the one who emerged.

Instead, Stan2012 emerged from the cave, staring down at the ground, his face heavy and troubled, as if he had found out that the weight of the entire world was resting squarely on his shoulders. As he set foot on the soggy ground again, Stan suddenly realized that he was being watched. He glanced up, and immediately did a double take, not willing to believe his eyes.

"Guys?" he let out, barely breathing.

"Stan?" Charlie whispered, afraid that if he spoke too loud, he might scare Stan away.

There was a moment of silence as Stan stared into the eyes of his friends, and they all stared back. Then, all at once and without warning, Kat rushed forward, tears streaming down her face with Rex hot on her heels, and embraced Stan, hugging him hard and long, as if she was never going to let go.

"Kat . . . I can't believe it . . . ," Stan managed to get out as he choked back his sobs of joy. "It's so . . . I mean, it's just . . ."

"I know, Stan," Kat managed to get out as she buried her face into Stan's shoulder. "I know."

Stan became aware of the sound of uneven footsteps, and he glanced up to see Charlie, clearly on a damaged foot, moving as fast as he could directly towards Stan. Immediately unaware of anything else, Stan let go of Kat and ran towards Charlie. The two best friends met in the centre of the clearing and threw their arms around each other, squeezing as hard as they could. Neither of them could say anything. There were no words. They just continued to hold each other in an embrace. Nobody spoke as these two players who had come so far since their first day in Elementia and grown closer than brothers were finally reunited.

"I missed you so much, man," Charlie sobbed, not even

trying to hide the fact that he was crying.

"Me, too," Stan choked out in return. "I'm . . . just . . . *so* glad you're OK . . . you . . . you have no idea."

The two players finally broke apart and were immediately pulled back together as Kat threw herself back into the circle, and the cycle started all over again. The three players, companions since the beginning, couldn't leave one another now that, after months of separation, they were finally together once more. Leonidas, Cassandrix and Commander Crunch could only look on with joyous tears in their eyes as Rex jumped up against the trio of players and began to lick Stan's hand.

The wolf's presence finally caused Stan to remember that the others were there, and he let go of his friends to face the others.

"Guys, I just . . . I can't believe . . ." Stan still seemed to be overjoyed, and at a total loss for words. "How . . . how did you manage to find me? Was it you, Leonidas? Did you find them?"

All at once, Charlie, Kat, Cassandrix and Commander Crunch all turned to stare at Leonidas. Even Kat, who had understood what the Black Hood had been trying to say, was completely floored by this. "Nah," Leonidas chuckled, looking back at Stan. "It was just a bit of dumb luck is all. Although I gotta say, it's lucky ya turned up when ya did."

"Aye, Leonidas," Commander Crunch suddenly burst out, his voice sounding deeply remorseful, "we be so sorry fer wha' we did." The other three players stared at Leonidas with equally mortified and repentant looks on their faces. "We should've listened t' ye . . . we didn' realize that . . ."

"Don't worry 'bout it," Leonidas replied with a smile. "Frankly, I don't really blame ya . . . after all the stuff I've put ya through in the past, I'd call ya stupid if ya trusted me up front. Tell ya what, let's make a deal. If y'all can find it in your hearts to forgive me for all the terrible things I did, then we can just let bygones be bygones."

Without hesitation, all the other players nodded and gave their assurances of agreement. All, that is, except Charlie. Try as he might, he couldn't find it in himself to say the words out loud, and couldn't help but feel an uncomfortable pit open in his stomach the more he looked at Leonidas, smiling and being initiated into their group.

Thankfully, he thought to himself as he forced a joyful look onto his face, *nobody noticed.* And as Charlie turned to Stan, his best friend in all of Minecraft, finally standing next to him once more after all this time, he found that he didn't need to force himself to smile in the least.

Bill stood attentive at the base of the stone staircase with an iron sword drawn. *What is taking Ben so long?* he thought in desperation. *What if he wasn't up there? Or what if somebody else was up there? A Noctem soldier? Or what if . . .*

Suddenly, footsteps echoed from the top of the stairs, and Bill caught a glimpse of a player coming down the stairs. As he grew closer, Bill realized with a start that it was Ben, hauling the unconscious Mechanist on his shoulder. Bill sprinted up the stairs to meet his brother, helping to lift the limp form of the Mechanist.

"Thanks," Ben grunted as they continued down the stairs.

"Don't mention it. What happened? Why is he unconscious? Did somebody attack you guys?"

"No," Ben grunted in disgust. "He was passed out on top of his papers, and a half-empty potion bottle was on the table next to him. He's been hitting the SloPo again."

"What?" Bill asked, shocked at this revelation. "I didn't know he used that stuff!"

"He told me about it once," Ben grunted as he readjusted the unconscious Mechanist on his shoulder. "Apparently he started when King Kev banished him to the desert. It made it easier for him to forget his guilt over helping the King with his redstone contraptions. He told me that he hadn't done it again since he had joined Stan's army."

"Well," Bill replied, "either he was lying or he started again."

"Clearly," Ben agreed. "I tried everything to wake him

up—water, food, hitting him, everything I had on me—and I couldn't find any milk to clear the potion effects, so I figured it was best to just bring him down the way he is."

"Well, we can worry about that later," Bill said as they reached the doorway to the castle courtyard. "OK, the entrance to the bunker isn't too far outside the courtyard. We should just be able to make a run for it without anything happening."

"Sounds good," Ben agreed. "Let's move!"

And with that, the two brothers sprinted out of the castle and into the open. Bill felt incredibly exposed as he dashed past the lava moat and across the wide-open courtyard, nothing above his head, and nothing to duck and cover behind should an attack come. By the time they had finally reached the castle gates and found an arch to hide them, Bill's heart was nearly beating out of his chest.

"There's the entrance!" Ben cried, pointing. Indeed, he was right. Just a block down the street, the gates of the mine opened into what appeared to be just a hill. They could barely make out Bob sitting at the mouth of the bunker, looking wildly around, presumably for them, his hand on a lever. Bill knew that, when Bob pulled the lever, as he would be forced to do if the Noctems appeared, the entire face of the hill would close up. The bunker door would blend into the hillside completely, creating a totally natural-looking stronghold that was invisible to anyone who didn't know where it was.

Bill and Ben, still carrying the Mechanist between them, made a mad dash down the cobblestone street towards the entrance to the bunker. Bob finally noticed them and gestured for them to move faster—it was only because of them that the bunker hadn't yet been sealed.

Just as the two police chiefs and the Mechanist were less than twenty blocks away from the mouth of the bunker, a giant, dark form rose from behind the hill. For an instant, the two brothers froze, locking eyes with the Wither. Bill grabbed his brother's shoulder and steered the three of them to the right.

"What're you doing?" screamed Ben as they sprinted forwards, the skull-like projectiles the Wither was shooting tearing up the street behind them.

"We can't go in there now!" bellowed Bill in reply. "The Wither will know where the entrance is! There, go into that house over there!"

They continued to sprint, and finally ducked their way into a two-storey mansion, made almost entirely from gold and lapis lazuli blocks. Bill and Ben collapsed onto the blue and gold wool-block carpet in the entrance. They were so exhausted from running to escape the Wither while simultaneously dragging the Mechanist between them that they could barely move. However, as soon as the explosions began to rock the house around them, both brothers found themselves racing with adrenaline.

"What do we do now?" asked Ben desperately, as the explosions continued from above. "The Wither will blast its way in here in the next minute. And if it sees us going into that bunker, then the entire city is dead. What do we do?"

Bill glanced around for a minute before his eyes locked on a window on the other side of the house. He took a deep breath, let it out and then turned to face his brother.

"Get the Mechanist to the bunker," he said pensively. "You'll know when to go. Don't worry about me, whatever you do."

Before Ben had a chance to ask what that meant, Bill leaped to his feet and sprinted at full speed towards the window before punching through it and disappearing outside.

Ben stared at the window, trying to comprehend what had just happened. What was it that his brother had just done? And *why*? A giant blast from above jarred all the questions from his mind. He ducked down and threw himself over the unconscious Mechanist, covering his head as a rain of rubble fell onto them. When the dust cleared, Ben glanced up, and his heart stopped.

The Wither was levitating directly over the mansion. It had blasted its way through the upper storey, and now it had a clear shot at Ben. As the three mouths of the Wither began to glow, Ben didn't even bother to try to run. Instead, he merely threw his body over the Mechanist, hoping that he could at least save him, and then maybe Bill could get him to safety in the mine. Ben stared the Wither's middle head directly in the face, determined to leave Elementia in a dignified way.

Then, without warning, the entire Wither jerked backwards and careened sideways, as if it had lost its balance. The three black projectiles shot off in random directions— two flew into the sky, while a third fell with a blast onto the street outside. Ben looked up in confusion, and as the Wither attempted to restabilize, he noticed a tiny white object lodged in the back of the Wither's main head, and a string leading off it and down onto the street.

Ben knew what this meant. This was the diversion. It was time to go.

He hoisted the Mechanist onto his shoulder and sprinted as hard as he ever had sprinted in his life out the door and towards the entrance to the bunker. The Wither didn't even notice him. It was too focussed on trying to shake off Bill, who had latched a fishing line onto it and was now yanking and pulling, doing all he could to unbalance the evil beast. The Wither fired off a volley of blasts at Bill, but they were all uneven and untargeted, so he was able to jump out of their way.

Ben barrelled headfirst into the bunker, and the Mechanist

flew off his shoulder and into the arms of two soldiers waiting on standby. Ben stood by Bob, still standing with his hand on the lever and ready to pull it. The two of them watched the battle on the street, eyes wide, breath bated and hearts racing.

Slowly but surely, the Wither was regaining its focus. Despite the fact that Bill was still disorienting it, its shots were getting closer and closer to him, and Ben knew that it was only a matter of time before Bill would be hit. He glanced around wildly at Bob, who showed an equal look of horrified confusion, and then at a soldier standing next to him.

"You have to do something to help him!" Ben bellowed at the soldier.

"What can we do, sir?" the soldier asked desperately. "If we do anything, we'll reveal the location of the bunker. In fact, if Bill even lets the Wither turn around, it'll see the location of the bunker. Sir, I'm sorry, but we need to close the blast doors now."

Ben's response was cut off by the anguished cry from outside.

He watched but didn't comprehend, as Bill flew through the air, wisps of black smoke trailing off him, and landed with a thud onto the cobblestone pavement below, his fishing pole still gripped tightly in his hand. With monumental effort, Bill raised his head and caught the tear-stained, anguished eyes of his brothers. "PULL THE LEVER!" Bill yelled at the top of his voice as the three black projectiles flew down from the sky above him and hit him in a tremendous explosion.

Ben could only stand there, unmoving, and watch the scene unfold, while Bob pulled down almost robotically on the lever, as if he were a machine that had been voice activated by Bill's final yell. The redstone machinery in the bunker door roared to life, and the hilltop above them seemed to slide down towards the ground. All the soldiers backed away from the bunker door as the pistons did their work.

Ben and Bob didn't move. Their eyes stayed locked in sheer disbelief on the body of their red-haired brother, items scattered in a ring around him on the cobblestone street, and charred fishing pole still clutched tightly in his hand, until the bunker door finally shut, closing them into the mines.

TO BE CONTINUED. . .

It's the Republic's darkest hour. The Noctem Alliance, under the command of the ruthless Lord Tenebris, has finally conquered the entire server of Elementia. The citizens of Element City are forced to hide underground as Withers patrol the skies, creating an everlasting night.

Although President Stan has reunited with his friends, the relentless Elite Legion of Mobhunters is still in hot pursuit.

Lord Tenebris is drawing more and more power from the server and his actions threaten to create a devastating glitch that could destroy Minecraft forever.

Time is running out. Will President Stan be able to defeat the evil demon before it's too late?

Find out in:

THE ELEMENTIA CHRONICLES

BOOK THREE: PART TWO
HEROBRINE'S MESSAGE

IT ALL ENDS HERE

There was silence in the Capitol rotunda, save the sound of hundreds of pairs of feet marching. Row by row, the black-clad troops filed into lines. Jayden and G glanced around the room nervously at the dozens of dark figures positioned in the upper balcony, all of whom had loaded bows aiming down into the giant mass of soldiers.

G took a deep breath and let it out. He knew what was going on. Four days had passed since he had left Sirus alone in that obsidian chamber with a diamond pickaxe in his hand, and now Tess had ordered that all soldiers meet in the rotunda for an emergency.

Sure enough, Tess emerged on the highest, most ornate and most pronounced balcony of the rotunda, made from chiselled quartz blocks. There was no hint of joy on her face. There was only a scowl as she looked down on all the soldiers. Gazing back up at her and cowering under her intimidating leer, they were all silent. Finally, Tess spoke.

"Last night," Tess announced, "our hostages from the Adorian Village escaped captivity."

A collective gasp rolled across the soldiers as they realized what that meant.

"To escape, the hostages tunnelled through a five-block-thick wall of solid obsidian," continued Tess. "This is a feat that would take at least two full days to complete if done by anything other than a diamond pickaxe. And seeing as no guards saw any sign of an escape in progress during their checkups, this can only mean that somebody in this room managed to sneak a diamond pickaxe to the hostages."

A collective burst of panic rose off the crowd, and though nobody dared to speak, the tension in the room could be cut with a sword.

"I know that someone among us is the traitor," Tess said slowly as her eyes swept over the soldiers below her. "If you step forwards and reveal yourself to me now, then you shall simply be executed by firing squad, quickly and painlessly. However, if you don't, then I shall be forced to begin interrogations, and when I discover who it is, you will be tortured without mercy before you become food for the Zombie villagers. If anybody would like to speak out, you may do so now."

G, who was struggling to keep his own heart from exploding with panic, heard Jayden beside him take a deep breath, let it out, and then raise his hand.

"I confess," Jayden said, a slight warble in his voice. "I did it."

G's mind went blank, refusing to comprehend what was happening. He turned to stare at Jayden in utter shock, totally blindsided and utterly bewildered by what his best friend had just said.

"Is that so?" asked Tess, a hint of surprise in her voice as all the soldiers around Jayden backed away from him in abhorrence. G followed suit, convinced that he had gone totally insane. "How did you do it, Drayden? And what was your motivation?"

"My name is *Jayden*!" he exclaimed, pulling off his black leather cap, throwing it to the ground, and stomping on it. "I am a member of the governing council of Element City, and a friend of President Stan2012. I have been living under-cover among you for these past weeks, working to free the hostages you have taken from us. Now, my work here is done." A manic smile crossed Jayden's face as he pumped his fist into the air and, with patriotic fervour, he bellowed, "LONG LIVE THE REPUBLIC! LONG LIVE PRESIDENT STAN!"

G's mind was still reeling from what was going on. He was hardly able to comprehend that Jayden had just revealed himself for no good reason, and that soldiers were drawing their bows and taking aim at him. Suddenly, a lightbulb clicked on in G's head. There was at least one good thing that could come from this turn of insanity. G leaped forwards and into the ring, letting the overwhelming despair that was boiling inside him burst from his mouth.

"How could you do this?" G shouted, tears streaming down his face as he let all the white shock he was feeling burst through his voice. "You were my friend! I trusted you! How could you work for that evil president?"

Jayden glanced back at G, and caught his eye. For an instant, he looked miserable, as if all he wanted was to be able to say "sorry." However, the look soon vanished, to be replaced by nothing but zeal.

"I'd never lower myself to the level of calling myself the friend of a Noctem!" Jayden spat in disgust.

There were so many things that G longed to say but knew he couldn't. He was forced to simply stand still, quiet and motionless. It was all the same, though. Words could not describe the agony that wrenched his heart as two soldiers pinned Jayden to the ground, and a third raised a bow to his head. G looked away, preparing for the arrow to fly.

"Hold your fire!" Tess's voice rang out from the balcony above.

G looked up, hardly daring to believe his ears. The collective group of soldiers, including those who were restraining Jayden, seemed to follow suit as their eyes locked on Tess. She was staring back and forth between Jayden and G, an intrigued look on her face. G's heart skipped a beat. Did she suspect something?

"Executioner, stop," Tess said again, holding up her hand. "I have a better idea. All troops, move out. Leave this rotunda. Guard and MasterBronze, stay put."

G was petrified as the troops began to move out around him, giving him uncomfortable glances as they flooded through the doors. The executioner put his bow away and drew a glowing diamond sword, jabbing it up against Jayden's back and grunting, "Hands in the air, dirtbag." Jayden complied, and his eyes darted to the side and met G's. He could tell they were both thinking the same thing.

Tess knows, G thought in a panic. *She's got to know. Why else would she have singled me out? All the recruits probably realize that Jayden and I have been talking this entire time. And why did Jayden reveal himself anyway? She might not have ever guessed it was me. He didn't need to sacrifice himself!*

The sounds of footsteps on the stone-brick floor echoed throughout the cavernous rotunda as Tess made her way to the centre G and the executioner snapped to full attention as Jayden scowled at her.

"General Tess," the guard asked in disbelief, "why did you tell me not to execute this spy?"

"Trust me," Tess replied, a devious grin creeping across her face, "I know what I'm doing. Guard, you are dismissed now."

The guard stared at Tess with a total lack of comprehension, and then turned around and made his way to the door, grumbling the whole way. Jayden watched as he went, hands still raised, and Tess drew a glowing diamond sword from her own inventory, pointing it at Jayden.

"MasterBronze," Tess said slowly, turning to face G, "I understand that you are friends with this traitor. Is this correct?"

"I thought I was," G grunted, trying to sound hurt and betrayed, and not let his true dread be too obvious. "He always seemed like such a nice guy, I can't believe that he's been working for President Stan this entire time."

"Well, I hope that you can bring yourself to believe it," Tess chuckled, "because you're going to be the one who kills him."

G heard, but he didn't understand. "I'm . . . sorry . . . ?" he finally croaked.

"For the past few weeks, I have been training you as my apprentice, MasterBronze," Tess continued matter-of-factly. "I must say that, so far, I am quite impressed by your progress in combat and skills training. However, if you are truly going to become a great leader of the Noctem Alliance, you must learn to make sacrifices for the sake of our cause . . . even if it means stabbing your best friend in the back. And besides, if your loyalties are in the right place, then you should be able to get over it quickly."

G stared blankly at Tess, still not understanding what he was being asked. Then, out of the corner of his eye, G saw Jayden staring at him with wide, fearful eyes, and finally snapped back to his senses.

"Um, well . . . ," G sputtered, trying to think fast. "I mean . . . General Tess, ma'am . . . can I at least kill him in private? It's . . . going to be difficult enough without you watching."

Tess sighed and rolled her eyes. "Whatever. We'll go to the holding chamber. Move it, you worthless piece of trash!"

Tess poked the diamond sword into Jayden's back and he began to walk forwards, hands still raised above him. G followed Tess down the hallway. He realized that they were headed towards the room where Sirus and the others had been imprisoned. G glared with contempt at the back of the general who was walking in front of him, and his hand started to crawl towards his pickaxe before he stopped himself. As easy and satisfying as it would have been to strike Tess down right then and there, he knew that he couldn't do that. They were the only ones in the room, and Jayden was unarmed, so the rest of the Alliance would know that he had done it. And regardless of what happened, he still had to cure Mella and Stull, something that would be much easier if the Noctem Alliance trusted him.

It wasn't long before they reached the obsidian room. At Tess's command, G pressed the button to open the iron door. Once it had swung all the way around, Tess gave Jayden a kick in the back, sending him tumbling. He face-planted on the floor of the now vacant obsidian chamber. G glared at Tess with burning hatred but forced himself to curb his anger as she turned to face him.

"I'm coming back shortly," Tess decreed sternly. "And I will expect you to bring me his weapon."

And with that, she stepped back into the hallway and pressed the stone button again, swinging the iron door shut.

"What were you thinking?" bellowed G, spinning around to face Jayden the second the door closed.

"Don't yell at me!" Jayden retorted, crossing his arms over his chest. "Do you have any idea what I just did for you?"

"You almost left me without a best friend?" spat G. "You made Tess expect me to kill you? You put me into an incredibly difficult position? Take your pick, they're all true!"

"Oh, open your eyes, man!" cried Jayden. "It was only a matter of time before Tess realized that *you* let those prisoners go. Since I took the fall for you, you can stay in Nocturia for as long as you want! You can free the villagers, you can find out so much information, do so much damage to the Alliance. For the first time since we started fighting this war, Element City has eyes on the inside of the Noctem Alliance, and that's not something worth giving up, even if it means I have to die. Actually, the fact that Tess ordered you to kill me makes all of this so much better!"

"How do you figure that?" exclaimed G incredulously.

"Because now she's going to have total faith in you!" Jayden said, sounding as if this should be incredibly obvious. "She's already rearing you up to be her little lackey. If you do this, then she's going to trust you with anything and think that you're totally devoted to the Noctem Alliance, and to her."

"Oh, my apologies. You're right, Jayden!" G replied, a mock cheerful tone in his voice. "I mean, gee whiz, why didn't we do this in the first place? Oh, yeah, that's right! Because in order for this plan to work, it still required *me killing you!*"

ABOUT THE AUTHOR

Sean Fay Wolfe was sixteen years old when he finished writing *Quest for Justice*, the first book of the Elementia Chronicles trilogy, and seventeen when he finished *The New Order*. He is an avid Minecraft player and loves creating action-adventure tales in its endlessly creative virtual world. Sean is an Eagle Scout in the Boy Scouts of America, a four-time all-state musician, a second-degree black belt in Shidokan karate, and has created many popular online games in the Scratch programming environment. He goes to school in Rhode Island, where he is deeply involved with his school's drama club. Sean lives with his mother, father, grandmother, two brothers, three cats and a little white dog named Lucky.

THE ELEMENTIA CHRONICLES

COMING SOON: